Hearts of the Children

William D. Mecham

Olympus Story House

Table of Contents

*And he shall turn the heart of the fathers to the
children, and the heart of the children to their fathers,
lest I come and smite the earth with a curse.*

—Malachi 4:6 (KJV)

1

Jerry's first sensation was of being cold. It brought to mind being on camping trips with the scouts, when the temperatures suddenly dipped overnight. In his mind, he knew when he managed to struggle out of his sleeping bag; he could light the camp fire and be warm within a few minutes. Opening his eyes, he expected to see the fabric of a tent above him. Instead, he saw tree limbs and leaves, creating a mosaic pattern against the dim light of early morning. This did not alarm him, since he had slept "under the stars" many times. What puzzled him was the feeling of not only cold, but dampness as well. Messages received from various parts of his body were telling him he was lying in cold dampness with a whisper of breeze passing across his body. For the first time, he moved—to let his hands explore—and he was shocked by what they found. He was lying on leaf-covered ground, and he was naked. Totally disoriented, he let his body shiver, then curl into a fetal position in an attempt to conserve his warmth, such as it was. Letting his mind backtrack, trying to recall his last remembered actions, he searched to find some logical explanation for his present condition. Only lying in position for a few seconds, he decided he needed to obtain warmth somehow. Struggling to stand, he found his joints stiff with cold, but he surveyed his immediate surroundings. There was nothing he could use to cover himself. If it were not for the dew, he reasoned, he could pile the accumulated leaves atop his body to keep the wind off and insulate himself from the cold, but as they were, he would only be colder. He had to find a way to get warm, until hopefully, the sun brought warmth to the land.

Creeping through the undergrowth in the growing light, his movements were starting to generate some warmth, though hardly enough to make him comfortable. Spying a thicket which promised to keep the breeze off him, he crawled into the foliage by way of a dim game trail. Since this trail indicated the thicket was used by animals, he could be disturbing some creature's sleep. Suddenly, he heard the crash of brush on the other side of the thicket. Instantly stopping all motion, he paused for a slow count of ten. Despite his chilled body, the sweat of fear popped out on his forehead. Screwing up courage, Jerry continued into the undergrowth until he was in a slight hollow at the center. An ideal resting place for animals, it allowed only a minimum of light to enter its interior. The grass was matted down where the animal had lain, and Jerry could still feel warmth left by what must have been a deer. Quickly lying down, he took advantage of the residual heat, curling up and letting his muscles ease up. He was not as warm as he wished to be, but he had shelter from the breeze; there was no dampness from the dew here; and he tried not to think of being infested with fleas or ticks. His body began to relax. As his mind slowly slipped out of its emergency mode, and familiar thoughts came to him, Jerry started, and his eyes came wide open. He remembered being in Professor Blanchard's lab. It had all been about time travel. Now, not only was he stranded in the wilderness with no clothes or means of providing for himself, but he was somewhere and "some-when" unknown to him, for sure. By planning and experimenting, he should be somewhere in the Massachusetts Colony in the early 1690s. If the calibration of the portal was truly accurate, he shouldn't be far from Salem Village during the late summer of the year 1691, but it sure felt like summer was long gone. How was he going to find "where and when" he was, with no clothes? His studies of this period in history told him the colonists were pretty touchy about showing the body off in public. They wouldn't be kindly disposed toward his traipsing through the center of town like Lady Godiva, without even a horse. Jerry remembered going to a lot of effort to find an outfit more fitting for this time and place. He was now wistful of how warm it would be, and he hoped it would be somewhere in the vicinity, or back in the professor's lab rather than lost somewhere in time.

Deciding he couldn't do anything until it warmed up a little, he settled back and tried to get his body into the tightest ball he could. If he could sleep, the time would go faster. Then, during the warmth of day, he could go exploring and hopefully find his clothes packet. Relaxing his mind, he prepared it for sleep. A crashing of brush brought Jerry rudely awake. It took a split second to realize something was crashing into his thicket. At first, he thought some animal was trying to enter the brush, and then he saw the dead branch which had been thrown into the brush, apparently meant to spook any game hiding in the foliage.

"Hello, out there! Don't shoot! I'm coming out," Jerry called, hoping the hunter would not be careless.

Crawling through the entrance, he tried to shield as much of his naked body as he could. Standing about twenty yards away and partially hidden by another clump of brush, Jerry saw a tall young man of about his own age. His hair was combed back and held by what Jerry remembered was called an "eel skin." He had knee-length breeches, stockings, and a jacket over an open-necked shirt. In his hands, held in a ready position, was a musket, and his face wore a puzzled expression. Jerry had considered what his story would be if he made contact with anyone of this time period. Reckoning the community would be close-knit and its citizens possibly having relatives throughout the Massachusetts Colony, he would use his own name, because it was of English ancestry, but he would be from the Virginia Colony or further south. This would account for his strange accent and his ignorance of local events and customs. Now, in these new circumstances, he needed more answers to explain himself.

"Good day to you, sir. I am Jerrold Tanner from Virginia. You catch me at a disadvantage."

The young man stepped closer, pausing when he stood ten feet away from Jerry. He recovered quickly and spoke with a hint of an English accent but closer to the dialect to later be associated with people from New England.

"A good day to you, sir, but I see you are in distress. My name is Matthew Lloyd of Middleton. May I offer you my jacket and possibly my game bag for your lower limbs?"

Matthew removed his coat, removed a bundle from a bag hanging from his shoulder, and handed them to Jerry. Jerry unrolled the game bag and wrapped it around his waist like a towel, then pulled on the jacket—the warmth was delicious. Though they now knew each other's name, there was still the matter of why a grown man would go around naked in the woods.

"I was attacked and captured yesterday by a group of Seneca warriors."

"Seneca you say? Never heard of them this far east. The only tribes around here are the Pawtucket, Narraganset, and Wampanoags."

Jerry realized his research had not been that thorough, and now he was on shaky ground.

"It could have been one of those tribes. I am not familiar with your local tribes. They took all my belongings, including my clothes. I loosened my bonds and slipped away, then ran all afternoon and evening to get away. Finally, fatigued, I collapsed in this thicket, hoping they would not track me here. I am truly grateful for your assistance."

Trying to talk like he imagined the colonists did in those days, being careful of contractions, slang, and new words, Jerry hoped his debut was successful.

"I have cold venison and bread that I can share with you. As soon as I finish my hunt, I will take you to my home and allow you to rest and regain your strength. Please go back into your hiding place. I will return for you as soon as I am able."

Matthew gave Jerry a pouch which contained his lunch. Jerry watched Matthew move away into the forest. Judging the position of the sun, it was about eight in the morning. With so many other things on his mind in the lab, eating had been the least of his worries. He now realized he was very hungry. Crawling back into the undergrowth and settling down in his borrowed clothes, he opened the pouch. Inside were a half loaf of coarse, whole wheat bread, a half dozen slices of meat, and a small flask of water. He could have eaten all of the food with little effort, but limited himself to half, because Matthew was sharing the food, not giving it. The meat was bland, with a gamy taste to Jerry's corn-fed-beef palate. The bread tasted much like his mother's homemade bread, and the water had the mineral taste of untreated water, perhaps from an artesian well. Unaccustomed as he was to this type of food, it went down well and gave him a pleasantly satiated feeling. Jerry's thoughts turned to his rescuer.

Matthew Lloyd was close to his own age, but his manner was that of someone much older. He was fair haired and strong-limbed, probably working at a job very physically demanding. It occurred to Jerry that Matthew, by his hunting, was doing the equivalent of going to the meat market, and he probably had a garden on his land where he grew wheat, other grains, and vegetables. Jerry heard a gunshot not too distant. Matthew and most others probably purchased very little at the local store, although they might have their corn and wheat ground into meal and flour by the local miller.

Realizing he must be prepared to do without some things, from the smell of Matthew's jacket, he figured his usual long, hot showers would be one of them. He also would be required to do many things manually he was used to having ready at hand, such as carrying water, cutting firewood, and heating water.

"Hello, Master Tanner? Are you there?"

Jerry crawled out of the thicket and saw Matthew standing in the same location where he had first seen him. Hitching the game bag up on his hips, Jerry walked over to the hunter.

"I normally take the better cuts of venison and put them in my game bag, but since you have it and since we need additional meat, we will carry the entire deer back home. Come, I will find a suitable branch to make into a game pole, and we will go back to where I left the deer."

With that comment, Matthew struck off at a brisk pace, leaving it up to Jerry to keep up, forgetting that Jerry was barefoot. Along the way, he found a branch some ten feet in length and two inches in diameter. He took a small hatchet from his belt and cut all leaves and smaller side branches from the future game pole. When they came to the deer, Jerry could see that Matthew had already dressed the deer, tossing the entrails into the bushes. Tying the feet of the deer, front and back, together, they slid the pole between both front feet and then both hind feet. Jerry handed Matthew the food bag, and the young man sat with his back against a tree and slowly ate the remainder of the food. When he was finished eating, Matthew looked at Jerry.

"What is your trade, Master Tanner?"

Jerry relied on his plan and answered, "At present, I am a student of mathematics, and you, sir?"

"That is a good question, sir. My father, who was the village wheelwright, taught me to follow in his footsteps, but I work the land as much as I do the forge. I own acreage and harvested a bounty of vegetables and wheat last fall. I care for my widowed mother, two younger sisters, and two younger brothers."

Jerry congratulated Matthew on a good harvest and gave his condolences.

"How far is Middleton from Salem?"

"Do you know Salem, sir?"

"No, sir. I planned to visit a distant relative there."

"I know a good many people in Salem Village, which lies eight miles south east from Middleton. I know a few in Salem Town which is still further south and east. Perhaps I know your relation."

"Perhaps. His name is Jeremiah Meacham."

"I know both Jeremiah the elder and the younger. Both of them are good brothers of the church. Old Jeremiah is in his seventies, a revered man. Young Jeremiah, alas, has recently become a widower, leaving the raising of his brood to his eldest daughter, Hope. His first-born—yet another Jeremiah—went to Boston last year and signed on a whaling ship. Naught has been heard of him. That leaves Hope to care for the other seven, though I hear Jeremiah is beginning to court one of John Browne's daughters, Deborah I believe. Master Browne is the miller of Salem…forgive me, Master Tanner. I sit here and go on like an old gossip after Sunday meeting. How are you related to Old Jeremiah?"

"My mother's father is brother-in-law to one of the sisters of Old Jeremiah. Like I said, a distant relative. Taking a sabbatical from school, I felt it would be interesting to see some of the northern colonies."

"You came all the way from Virginia by yourself?" Jerry was caught off guard.

"Uh…no. I sailed to New York from Virginia, then accompanied a group traveling to Boston. From there, I struck out on my own, thinking I could find Salem easily enough."

"Why didn't you take a sailboat from Boston to Salem, or follow the coastline on horseback?"

Caught again!

"I wanted to see what the interior of the colony looked like. I am used to riding for one or two days into the Virginia countryside without need of an armed escort."

Matthew turned from offense to defense.

"Normally, so can we. I have been considering what you said about the Indians who accosted you. It may have been Seneca. There have been reports of the French, who have attacked Falmouth, north of here, sending Indian raiding parties into English territory. It may now be Massachusetts's turn. Did you lose anything of great value?"

Back on the spot.

"Uh…my clothes, the ones I wore, plus those in my bags, a volume of mathematical theory, a small pistol—packed away in my bags—a letter of introduction from my grandfather, and fifteen pounds, some in my luggage and the rest in my small clothes (Jerry, remembering the old term for underwear, instead of saying 'underwear'). That was all I carried with me, other than a few toilet articles for washing and shaving."

"That is too bad, Master Tanner. I can clothe you, though maybe not in the finery you are used to, and replace the toilet articles and even the pistol, but I can't replace the letter, book, or money. We have very little cash money in the colony, and fifteen pounds is no small amount. Sometimes, we see a few old "Pinetree" shillings—Massachusetts own coinage—but most transactions are by barter. It is time we started toward my home."

The two young men stood and, each grabbing an opposing end of the game pole, swung it to their shoulders, suspending the deer between them, and walked in the direction Matthew indicated.

Walking for about twenty minutes, Jerry finally began seeing signs of civilization. There were stone fences, erected as much for having a place for the stones as for needing a boundary. The fields seemed not to be in use.

"How long has it been since you harvested?"

"It was last fall… September."

Jerry was puzzled.

"When do you plant again?"

"As soon as the danger of frost is past. Probably another month."

Realizing he had made an error in assuming it was late summer or early fall, Jerry now guessed it was early spring. But what year? Matthew must be wondering about his questions.

"I guess I take a winter crop for granted. In Virginia, we have cold weather, but in some parts, it rarely freezes."

"It sounds like a fair land, with plenty of warm sun I would wager. It must be to allow you to go around with so few clothes on and darken your skin, as you have."

He'd forgotten about his suntan from long days at the beach. It definitely would seem odd to someone from New England, who saw very little skin, except tanned faces and hands, and then only in the summer. For Jerry to have a deep tan in the spring was surely out of place.

"Carolina and Georgia are even warmer than Virginia, and we often go about the plantations with just short pants and sandals."

This explanation seemed to satisfy Matthew, and they continued on their way.

Knowing that homes of this time period were made of various materials, such as brick and clapboard, in the cities, Jerry expected homes this far into the wilderness to be log cabins, so he was not prepared for his first site of a genuine seventeenth-century house. Though not large, it was well built of clapboard and had been white washed in the past year. There was virtually no landscaping around it, but window boxes were evidence they cultivated flowers or herbs during the growing season. A white picket fence surrounded the house on three sides, which seemed out of place to Jerry since the nearest neighbor was probably a quarter of a mile away.

"This is my mother's home. Mine is not far."

As they passed the house, Jerry could not take his eyes off it, trying to etch its image into his memory, longing for the camera, hidden in his clothes packet.

"Soon, you will be warm and fully clothed. Later, I will introduce you to my mother, and she will invite us to supper, but in the morning, there is work to be done. We must finish preserving the deer by curing. Some will keep a couple days in the cool cellar, but the rest needs to be pickled or dried."

Matthew's home was not as impressive as his mother's, but only because it wasn't completed. Apparently, the home had been built within the last year and had yet to be whitewashed. Lumber was stacked in the rear, probably for an addition to the basic structure. Matthew went to an outdoor table at the back of the house where they left the deer, then entered the dwelling by a rear door.

"It is a humble dwelling, but I have many ideas. I plan to add two more rooms on the rear, both bedrooms. Right now, I sleep in here, but when I take a wife, we will have a room and one for the children."

"Do you plan on marrying soon?"

Matthew seemed embarrassed at the question.

"As soon as I complete the rooms and make my request to the father for courting rights."

"Congratulations, Master Lloyd."

Jerry didn't want to pry, so he let the subject die of its own will. An awkward lapse in conversation stretched for a long minute.

"Well, sir, let me find you something to wear. My father died last year, and my mother passed most of his clothes to me, since we were of a size, as you are."

Digging in a trunk, Matthew produced breeches, shirt, stockings, jacket, and shoes. The shoes were too small, but the rest fit reasonably well. Having no buttons, the shirt pulled over the head and tied at the throat. Pulling on the breeches, they were found to be a snug fit, by design, and a wide belt held them up, with no belt loops. Jerry found the stockings were made of wool, like the shirt, and they both itched.

"My apologies, for having no small clothes. We wear them little here. As for the shoes, I have some tanned deer hide I can cut into a pair of leather slippers the Indians call moccasins. It will take a day or two for the lacing, but you can wear an old pair of mine, and they will at least protect your stockings."

Feeling warm at last, Jerry cared little for what he wore, though he longed for a bath or shower. He expressed his desires to his host.

"It is only Tuesday, sir. The bath tub is only brought out on Saturdays at my mother's house, and I have none yet. If you really want one, there is a stream a short distance from the back door, but the water is fearfully cold this time of year. How often do you bathe in Virginia?"

"In the warmer seasons, we bathe two or more times a week, but the reason I require one now is to wash off the sweat from my run and the smell of that animal nest where I slept. I might try the stream before I go to bed tonight. I have bathed in cold water before."

Before they left the house, Matthew offered Jerry an eel skin to tie his hair back. Jerry wore his hair long, against his parent's wishes, and now was glad he did. With the eel skin tied, he longed for a mirror and his camera.

Knocking on the front door of his mother's home, Matthew waited for an answer. A stocky boy of about fourteen opened the door and invited them into the front room. What would have probably been a friendly meeting between brothers, with the accompanying teasing and joking, was stifled when the boy saw Jerry. He was curious, but his rearing demanded politeness. Soon, a woman of some forty-odd years came into the room. Surprisingly tall, she was also large boned and healthy, apparently thriving in the wilderness. Her hair was under a cover, but Jerry could see it was medium brown with flecks of gray. Her cheeks were rosy, because she had been cooking at the hearth.

"Mother, this is Master Jerrold Tanner from Virginia. He was attacked by Indians yesterday. They took all of his belongings, leaving him in distress in the forest. I have offered him hospitality at my home and some of Father's clothing to wear until he is able to recover.

"Are you injured, Master Tanner?"

"Fortunately not, Mistress Lloyd, but I owe a great deal to your son. Without him, I may have perished in the wilderness. I am in his debt."

"What brings you to our area, sir?"

"A sabbatical from school and an excursion to visit a distant relative. My destination was Salem, but I left the main track and was fallen upon by savages. I fear they had plans to end my life. Fortunately, I escaped."

"I am thankful that you did. You are welcome to join us for supper, which I should return to preparing. It should be just a short time. Matthew, see that Master Tanner is comfortable."

Supper was a memorable meal for Jerry. Though comparatively bland, it was plentiful and different. A roast was cooked on a spit over the fire; a Dutch oven had been buried in the coals to cook a mix of potatoes and parsnips; a pan of biscuits had been baked in an oven compartment over the fire; and tea, served without sugar. After the meal was eaten, everyone wanted to hear about Virginia. Jerry felt bad about so many fabrications. He had to dredge up everything he had ever heard about the southern states, then wonder if what he was relating to them had happened yet in their time.

Jerry met not only Matthew's brother, Jonathan (the fourteen-year-old), but also another brother, Daniel (who was seven), and two younger sisters—Rebecca, sixteen, and Rhoda (who was nine). Rebecca kept smiling at Jerry. He thought she was just being friendly but soon realized a major difference between sixteen-year-olds of his time and the sixteen-hundreds. In his time, sixteen was the generally accepted age for girls to start dating, but in this time, sixteen was considered the normal age for a young woman to marry. Her attentiveness had not escaped her mother, so Rebecca was reminded of her aftersupper chores. Now Jerry figured he could relax, because Rhoda was only nine.

Back at Matthew's home, Jerry decided he had to brave the cold water tonight because he knew it would be colder in the morning.

Taking a tanned deer hide with the hair still attached, he walked to the stream. It was still daylight, though the sun had passed below the horizon, so Jerry looked around before undressing, more out of habit than expecting to be seen. Undergrowth covered a good portion of the banks, so he passed through some bushes to get to the water. Steeling himself for the cold, Jerry plunged into the stream, knowing it was better than trying to do it a little at a time. Coming to the surface, he sucked in his breath with shock.

He kept his body below the surface, so the air would not cool him more, and scrubbed his body with his hands, paying extra attention to his armpits and groin. He wanted to wash his hair but had brought no soap. He wondered what Matthew used to keep his hair from getting greasy. After two minutes or so, he decided he had had enough. Wading to the shallow water at the banks, Jerry came out of the water. Just as he reached ankle depth, he heard a sound directly in front of him. Stopped in mid-stride, a bucket in her hand, stood Rebecca. She stared wide-eyed and open-mouthed at Jerry, who was also in a state of arrested movement. They remained statues for about fifteen seconds before Rebecca, crimson-faced, averted her gaze and turned, poised for flight. Jerry hurriedly left the water and dashed into the bushes, calling to Rebecca.

"I'm sorry, Rebecca. I didn't know this was where you fetched your water. I hope I have not offended you."

"It is I who should be sorry. I usually make more noise, but my mind was occupied. Please do not mention this to my brother."

"Have no fear, I will mention this to no one, believe me. Good night, Rebecca."

"Good night… Jerrold."

Walking back to the house, Jerry did a quick analysis of his first day as a time traveler. It was really a mixed bag. On the upside, he had landed in Massachusetts, not far from his destination; he was at least within the right decade, since the ages of his relatives were confirmed by Matthew. On the downside, he had no money; he had a dangerous lack of knowledge about this time period; and he had been caught naked—twice.

"I regret putting you on the floor, Master Tanner, but I have no bed. I am accustomed to sleeping there, but my mother gave me an extra quilt to put under you."

"Think nothing of it. I have slept on the floor many times, and after my sleeping arrangements last night, this will seem like heaven. Could we be less formal? Would it be allowable if I called you Matthew, or Matt and you referred to me as Jerrold or Jerry?"

"I would enjoy being less formal. Here, in Middleton, we are not so formal as in the larger towns, but we are always respectful to our elders and to strangers. If you prefer it, we will go on a first-name basis, but I am not called Matt and have never heard anyone referred to as Jerry."

"We will just make it Matthew and Jerrold then. I am truly grateful for all your assistance, Matthew. I will try to help you as much as I can, though I have no great skills in building and farming." After the fire was banked for the night, and each man had performed their ablutions and devotions, the candle was extinguished. This plunged the house into darkness, except for the glow from the embers of the fire. Jerry undressed and snuggled between the many layers of quilts and deer hides he had amassed for bedding. Tomorrow would be another day of new experiences and priceless insights into the seventeenth-century way of life. It still seemed a dream. He had spent so many hours imagining how his ancestors had lived. Now he was actually near to them and may still be able to meet them. How had it all started? What had started him on the road to the late seventeenth century?

"In the course of the semester, we have studied the many nationalities which make up the population of the United States. Your semester research paper will consist of a report on your individual national origins. The instructions are on the printed page on the back table. Please take one as you leave the class! This will involve a great deal of digging, since I want you to include not only the countries your family came from but also a description of traditions native to those countries which may still be observed by your immediate family. The paper length will be a minimum of..."

Jerry groaned inwardly, as he reminded himself to pick up his copy of the assignment, to put into his notebook. Why couldn't the professor just give them a book to report on, or a research paper about some historical figure? This was something he was used to doing. Cliff's notes were always readily accessible, and he enjoyed working out of encyclopedias. Laziness was not the issue here. It was more a matter of time—time to do the research, along with all of his other homework.

He regretted taking such a heavy semester load, because he still worked almost thirty hours a week at the store. Loading and unloading furniture and appliances was physically demanding, which he didn't mind, but he sometimes envied the students with night clerk jobs where they could do their homework while they earned money.

He was lucky, however, to be able to work such an agreeable schedule. Working four or five hours per night on week nights, and ten hours on Saturday gave him time to do homework after work and on Sunday after church. It also allowed him to take advantage of the wider selection of classes available to daytime students. Trying to complete his lower division classes as quickly as he could, Jerry was determined to earn his degree in mathematics as soon as possible. Because he was a serious student, he never seemed to find the time to date, so his experience with the opposite sex was sorely lacking. It was not a disappointment to Jerry, however. He was driven to complete his education and then when he was established, there would be plenty of time to cure his social retardation.

Rushing home after his last class, Jerry changed clothes and went to the kitchen to grab a quick bite before heading for the store. His mother was preparing dinner in the kitchen, as he walked in to investigate the refrigerator.

"Hi, sweetie, how was school today?"

"Hello, Mom. School was fine. What's for dinner?"

"Don't get into the sliced chicken or Jell-O, but help yourself to the rest of the chicken and the tossed salad."

"Can I have some of these carrot and celery sticks, too? I barely had time to grab a carton of milk and a sandwich today."

"Sure, honey, have anything you can find. Are things getting tough at school?"

"A full load and a job are about to kill me. It seems like I'm always either in class or at the store. My social life is nonexistent."

"Be careful, or you'll get sick. Remember…you were the one determined to earn your degree before you turned twenty-one. Just because you had your high school diploma at seventeen doesn't mean you can take college by storm. Just relax a little. Enjoy your years at college. You'll soon be out in the world, establishing a career, and you'll be too busy to have much leisure time…"

Jerry had heard this little speech many times before, but to interrupt or argue would get him nowhere. So he just stood there, occasionally nodding his head, and waiting for the end, or a good place to change the subject. When it came, he jumped, "Yeeesss, Mother. Uh, Mom, I know our ancestors came mostly from England, but do we know where and when, and are we carrying on any traditions which originated in England?"

"Whoa! Let's take those questions one at a time! All the 'wheres' and 'whens' are in our genealogy, but I'll have to think about the traditions. Sometimes you do things as a matter of habit and never think about where they originated."

"I've heard about genealogy all my life, but I never thought much about it."

"Well, I'm sure you learned some things about it in Sunday School. I understand the information we have, but your father is really the one to ask. He can probably tell you many things without even opening our *Book of Remembrance*. Ask him when you get home from work tonight."

After work that evening, Jerry knocked on the door to his father's study.

"Come in."

Entering the small room, Jerry moved toward his father as the elder Tanner turned in his chair.

"Hi, son. How are things going in school and at work?"

"I'm holding my own, barely, at school, but work is going fine. They always have enough work to keep me busy, and I'm staying in shape."

"Good for you, son, I was hoping you'd slow down a bit, but at least one of us is getting exercise. I'm beginning to feel I'm permanently attached to chairs—this one and the one at the office. What brings you out of your books? I rarely see you out of your room."

"I hate to tell you this, Dad, but it's about one of my classes. In my history class, our semester paper is on our ancestry. Mom says you could help me find the information I need, or at least point me in the right direction."

"I wondered when you'd become interested in genealogy. You came to the right person. I've compiled all the information I could get from both mine and your mother's side of the family. It's quite a bit of information. I think you can find what you need for your paper."

"I'm afraid you'll have to show me what I'm looking at."

"Just a minute. Sit down in that chair."

Getting up, Jerry's father went to his filing cabinet and, stooping, opened the bottom drawer. He took a large book from the file and closed the drawer again. Coming back to his desk, Stewart Tanner placed the book on the desktop so that both men could look at it. The book was about nine inches high, fourteen wide, and four inches thick, with a hinged binding on the left of the cover. The cover was of leather, or an imitation-leather material. Scrolled designs spread across the face of the cover, and in the center was the title *Book of Remembrance* written in calligraphy.

"This book contains our family history, as far as I've been able to research. It is arranged in pedigree charts and family group sheets. There are copies of journals, written by some of our ancestors, in the bottom file drawer. A pedigree chart is shaped like a tree. In fact, that is probably why people call it a 'family tree.' In a pedigree chart, the tree is on its side, with ancestors making up the "branches" (or "roots") of the tree (again, maybe that is why people refer to genealogy research as a search for their roots). On the pedigree chart, only direct lineage is covered—child to parent. No mention is made of each child's brothers and sisters.

The family group sheet has information on parents and all their known children. Each family unit should have a group sheet, but if you checked our book, you would find some missing. These are ancestors I have not found the information on yet. Why don't you leaf through the book and see if you can understand the gist. I'm available if you have any trouble or specific questions."

Jerry gathered up the large tome and took it to his room. It was after midnight before he closed the cover, his mind crowded with family names—Tanner, Meacham, Fox, Brown, Trask, Hacker, West, Boyce…and many more. Dreams kept him from sleeping well that night—dreams of names and dates marching in neat rows until, at irregular intervals, they would explode in a flurry of nonsensical digits and letters.

Next morning, he groggily pulled himself from bed and let the hot shower beat his body into wakefulness. Too soon came his first class, in which he heard little of what the instructor was saying. He was awake but preoccupied; his mind still on the large volume of data sitting on his desk at home. Between classes, rather than hurrying to the library to get a short period of studying in, he went home and leafed through the genealogy book again. Never giving much thought to how families came to be, he saw before him how one family unit could fan out across time and space to populate the land. Families large and small.

He read of children, who lived very short lives or none at all. They were listed as "stillborn" or "died young." Most likely, they left behind grieving mothers, anguishing because they lacked the power to restore life—or wishing to trade places, so that the tiny ones could taste life, no matter how harsh. By comparing dates, Jerry could almost see the events take place in his mind. Some of the families, riding the crest of the westward tide, recorded each successive birthplace a little farther west; young mothers, with death dates coinciding with the birthdates of their youngest child, who may have joined their mothers within a few days or weeks. Some had "place of death" listed simply as Nebraska or Wyoming; their burial place, along the westward trail, an eternal secret, known only to the Almighty.

Jerry felt insignificant: a coddled, complacent drone, never having tasted true adversity. Since childhood, he had heard stories of the Pioneers and their settling of the western lands, but they had been just that—stories. He had watched movies and read books, but they had been fiction to him—distant and having no connection with him.

Suddenly, pride in his forebears swelled, and he said a silent prayer, thanking the Lord for allowing him to come from such hardy stock.

Going to his father's study, Jerry took a couple of the journals from the file drawer, looking at the titles to decide which he'd choose to read first. He settled on a manuscript with the name "Helen Louise Meacham Taylor" neatly printed across the title page. He knew this was his mother's maternal grandmother, whom his mother had been named for. Living from 1857 to 1949, she was the first generation of her family born in their new home in the Rocky Mountains.

In a life spanning nine decades, she had accomplished many things. Of English ancestry, she and her family moved about the west until, in her teens, she married a man nearly twenty years her senior; bore him twenty children—fourteen lived past infancy; divorced him when he was eighty years old; married a widower and lived with him more than twenty years before passing on. All the names, dates, and places had been in the *Book of Remembrance*, but here was the flesh on the bones of her life.

Jerry read of hardships—not just from mere pioneer life on the frontier, but insecurities, sickness, depression (economic as well as emotional), anger, and hope—and lack of it…despair. As she chronicled everyday living, Jerry could not fathom living in such conditions, but she was not lamenting her lot, just recording matter-of-fact insights to her existence. She had lived through one of the greatest eras of United States history, with all the advances in technology and civilization, and she had written of life at the grass roots level, not just the record of popular and political events found in any college history text. She had been a stalwart woman, and wise, to leave her thoughts for her children and her children's children.

Quite a story, Jerry thought, as he put the history back in the file. This great woman had died a couple of years after his own mother had been born. He had heard her mentioned in family conversations, but he never really knew her, as he felt he did now. Rummaging in the file, he came across a notebook. It contained a list of the families for which his father lacked a family group sheet. There were also notes concerning dead-ends in research. Jerry looked through the tablet, and he could see where each missing group sheet fit into the lineage. Among a number of entries, there seemed to be a large gap in the group sheets for the Meacham family starting in the mid-1600s, and there was little to go on except the pedigree chart, which also had holes. If he could only discover some information needed to complete one of the family groups, he could be assisting his father. Deciding to concentrate on the Meacham line, he ignored the other entries.

But Jerry had no illusions. He knew it would be next to impossible to add anything to the records of his father, who had a knack for genealogical research. If his dad wasn't able to find the information by haunting the various genealogical libraries, even the large one in Salt Lake City, Utah, what chance did Jerry have? Throughout his life, Jerry had been able to overcome seeming insurmountable obstacles to reach goals he had set for himself. This time, he hoped it would be the same.

Fascinated by the idea his predecessors had lived, and possibly participated, during events he previously had considered dry and boring. Jerry noted the birthplace and date of Jeremiah Meacham— Salem, Essex County, Massachusetts, in the 1600s. How did they manage without the conveniences Jerry took for granted each day: lights, electricity, hot water, refrigeration, and fast-food? He had read *The Crucible* by Arthur Miller in high school, and his college level US History class had briefly touched on the Salem witchcraft trials of the 1690s. At the time, he found it hard to believe people were so gullible and superstitious as they were illustrated. Here was an intriguing place to start.

Trying to imagine life during that period of time, his mind became flooded with a collage of mental images—memories of the numerous movies and stories which were set around the same era. These images included: somber-faced men, tall and strict in their dark brown clothes and "pilgrim hats"—flat brims and a flat, tapered crown; short, dowdy women in their long sleeved dresses and even longer hemlines, afraid to smile because others may think them lightminded; children, sitting perfectly straight and quiet during school or church, as though catatonic; people walking about a small village, giving others a curt nod and nothing more, as they passed on the street, and everything perfectly quiet, as though someone had just died. Existence in such an atmosphere seemed almost unbearable to Jerry. Did one of his ancestors really live this way?

Records showed Jeremiah's birth—and his father's birth and death—but nothing told Jerry what linked Jeremiah's lineage to later generations. He had only the entry in a volume of Daughters of the American Revolution records revealing his mother's direct ancestor, Samuel Meacham, was the great-grandson of Jeremiah Meacham of Salem. What he needed to find was a record of which son and grandson completed the line. So Jerry began to dig, and over the next few weeks, his college coursework suffered.

It was not that he didn't attend his classes; he did, but his attention was on ancestry, not analogs, and pedigree instead of perigee. Spending his study time in the school library's meager genealogy section was unfulfilling. He longed for a full-scale ancestral library. He felt limited, confined, and frustrated! In the end, he just caved in and quit looking. Going through the motions, he wrote his history term paper on Helen Meacham Taylor. He felt special about her and managed to put some of this pride into the paper. Then he went on with his life, with an empty spot in his heart.

Two weeks later, he received the self-addressed card he had left with his history teacher, Professor Jarvis, for the purpose of finding out his grade without waiting for the official grades to come out. A postscript was added to the card asking him to stop by the teacher's office to discuss his term paper. When he visited Professor Jarvis, he was ushered into his inner office and offered a seat.

"I thoroughly enjoyed your paper, Jerry, but have to admit it smacked of fiction."

"No, sir! The facts are documented in my great-grandmother's own handwriting and passed down to her descendants."

"She must have been an author of fiction herself to come up with such a story."

"Professor, are you trying to make me angry by demeaning my family? The paper I wrote was gleaned from several diaries she had written over the span of her life. She was a matter-of-fact woman, according to my mother, and she would think it frivolous to fabricate a story, when she felt it more important to record the daily events in her life."

"Okay! I'm not trying to insult you, Jerry. It's just yours was the only paper which had any substance to it. All the others were just names and dates, with a few claims to royal bloodlines. It made pretty boring reading until I came to yours. Where did you get such a fascinating record?"

It wasn't easy telling Professor Jarvis about Jerry's family beliefs concerning genealogy, without some of his religious beliefs creeping in, since they are so closely intertwined. A couple of times, tangents took them completely away from ancestry, and Jerry wished he were more familiar with the missionary tracts. Finally, the professor called a halt, not so much because he thought Jerry was trying to convert him, but because he had to teach his next class. He invited Jerry to visit him again.

Over the next week, Jerry spent a number of hours with "Hal," as Professor Jarvis preferred to be called. In the course of their conversations, Jerry brought out his frustrations concerning his search for the missing names in his lineage. From there, he and Hal began fantasizing about the lifestyle of Americans in the late seventeenth century. Jerry had always been an avid science fiction buff and brought up the idea of time travel. Hal reminisced about the movies and television series he had watched in his youth, which had dealt with time travel. But "reality" set in, and they laughed at how far afield from the matter at hand they had strayed.

Hal was not the only person with whom Jerry had expressed his disappointment. Both of his parents listened to his comments. His father was the most sympathetic, due to his own futile attempts to track down his families' ancestry. He listened quietly as Jerry proposed a possible trip to Salt Lake City at the conclusion of the current semester. Later, after Jerry had returned to his studies, his father and mother talked over the idea. With relatives in the intermountain area, they felt sure Jerry could keep expenses to a minimum. While spending as much time as possible at the genealogical library, he would stay with family who lived within commuting distance. The next morning, before he left for classes, Jerry's mother told him about their decision. She would call her sister to make the arrangements. The prospect of possibly making some progress in his research buoyed Jerry's spirits high enough for him to manage the rest of the semester.

Salt Lake City was not a new town to Jerry. He had visited it many times with his parents. The city and its suburbs filled the entire Great Salt Lake Valley. It appeared very different than it had in July of 1847 when the first Mormon Pioneer wagons had passed down Emigration Canyon, with one of the wagons carrying their ailing leader, Brigham Young. How desolate it was then! Yet, within a few days of entering the valley, the persecuted Saints had already begun planting their crops, with hopes they could be harvested before the first frosts of winter. In the next half century, the settlers endured innumerable hardships: famine, disease, and hostilities from both the Red and the White man, government interference in their spiritual and temporal lives. Salt Lake became known as the "Cross-roads of the West" since it was the only large city between the Mississippi River and the Pacific Ocean. People traveling west, could go south towards Los Angeles, or continue west to San Francisco. Today, it still occupied a popular center for tourism, offering a hub from which many scenic wonders could be enjoyed within a day's travel; and in the nearby Wasatch Mountains were some of the most popular ski resorts in the US.

But Jerry had not come to the Salt Lake Valley to be a tourist. He was eager to continue his research into his family tree. Arriving at the airport in the midmorning, he was greeted by his cousin, Steve. Despite Steve's protests, Jerry insisted he be dropped off at the Family

History Library (which was owned and operated by the Church of Jesus Christ of Latter-Day Saints). Cousin Steve took Jerry's luggage to his aunt Meryl's, who was busy fixing a special dinner for her visitor, and she was not altogether happy with her nephew's attitude on this trip.

During the next week, Jerry prowled the aisles of the library, poring over volume after volume; making his eyes ache from perusing hundreds of feet of microfilm; and using the library's new computer data bank on archived research. His frustration was nearly palpable. He had failed to add anything concrete to his father's research, though he did have a number of possible lineages he could connect to, if the missing records could be located and verified. He finally had to give up, and returned home, so he could continue his job and prepare for the next semester. His grades had come in the mail, and he had done okay, in most of his classes, though the grades were slightly lower in some than he had originally hoped, due to his preoccupation with his history assignment. All in all, his GPA was not severely hurt because his cumulative was high to begin with.

Jerry finished his summer by working as many hours at the furniture store as he could, to swell his bank account to the point he could pay for his tuition and books for the fall semester, without asking for help from his parents. He stayed in contact with Hal Jarvis, and they discussed his trip to the library in Salt Lake. When Jerry received his schedule, he showed it to Hal. Hal noted his class in physics was being taught by Professor Blanchard.

"You know, Jerry, Dr. Blanchard is even more interested in time travel than you are, and he is seriously trying to perfect a method to do so."

Hal noted the look Jerry gave him.

"Don't think Bill Blanchard is a crazy scientist, or nutcase! He is a serious, dogged researcher, and the author of a number of books concerning the mathematics he feels deals with such things as spatial anomalies and time travel. He won't talk about it, but I believe he has built some sort of apparatus he plans on experimenting with. Maybe you can get close enough with him to discuss your interests. I can introduce you to him, as he and I go way back!"

"Uh, Hal, we were fooling around with all our talk of time travel, just daydreaming!"

"I know we were. I didn't even think of Bill Blanchard until I saw your new schedule. He and I used to spend hours over beers, postulating theories about traveling in time. I don't have the math he does, but I have a vivid imagination. We got pretty wild sometimes. He used to have fun poking holes in all the movies and TV series about time travel."

"We'll see what happens after I get a couple sessions in his class under my belt, okay?"

"Sure, but don't sell him short!"

chapter

4

Jerry started his fall schedule, and it was nearly as heavy a load as his spring semester had been. In addition to physics, he had two math classes and had chosen ancient civilizations and creative writing. His physics class also included a lab period. Hal had introduced Jerry to Dr. Blanchard, and he was impressed with the professor. They had not broached the subject of time travel because Jerry felt it was too soon to bombard the teacher with his interest. His first class with Bill Blanchard was fun, as the professor enjoyed acting the part of a mad scientist for the first hour or so, then let the class know he was putting them on. This method of breaking the ice was a great way to start a class, and it piqued the interest of nearly everyone, which he supposed was the general idea. To the unmotivated, physics can be pretty dry. So Jerry looked forward to the class each time and would sometimes engage the professor in conversation after the class.

About three weeks into the semester, Jerry was caught off guard one day, after class, when the professor asked him if he believed in time travel.

"Um, uh, I don't know! I have my imagination and have day-dreamed about it, like a lot of people!"

"Jerry, Hal figured you would never come right out and ask me about it, so I thought I would get the ball rolling. He gave me an idea of what you are up against, with your family history and all that stuff. I've never thought about that sort of thing but have thought a lot about being able to actually witness some of the great moments in history. I say 'witness' because I have a firm belief anyone who could travel in time could make drastic, if not disastrous, changes to history with very little effort. Consider what would happen if someone saved a life, or took a life, while traveling through time. It would have far-reaching effects, like the overused analogy of the rock thrown into a pond, creating the ripple effect. There have been hundreds of stories and plenty of movies about time travel, where the so-called paradox of time travel is examined. The old TV series *Star Trek* dealt with it a number of times. The *Terminator* movies were all about it. The whole idea of *The Time Tunnel* and *Quantum Leap* were all about making things better by altering events. I have nightmares thinking about the damage which could be caused by meddling fools. I want to perfect time travel, but in such a way that we are just witnesses." Dr Blanchard paused for a breath and any reply from Jerry.

"But, Professor, what if someone with prior knowledge of an event, such as JFK's assassination, or the kidnapping or murder of some child, and they had the power to prevent the event from happening? Could you just witness it? There are so many people who meet tragic ends, and if I could stop it, I would. Would it be so wrong?"

"Now you know why I have nightmares! When I think about traveling around in time, especially the past, I sometimes dwell on events we know happened. Take the murder of that little girl, JonBenet Ramsey, in Colorado. No one seems to know what happened to cause her death and who did it. A lot of people would like to know, but if we were able to witness it, could we also prevent it from happening? Let's hypothesize for a moment: Let's say the murder was prevented and the perpetrator was convicted of attempted murder. Just for argument's sake, the murderer was originally destined to discover the cure for cancer, but if they were in prison, they couldn't do it. See the far-reaching effects of altering history? I see where so many lives may have been saved if Adolf Hitler was killed when he was a child, but then someone else could have come into power, who was much more atrocious! It's maddening to contemplate all the pros and cons of such actions. There are times I just want to give up because it could give someone power to play God!"

"I think I understand your position and your torment. I never really thought things out that far. I guess it wouldn't be a good thing after all to go back and find out what I need to know."

"No! Don't you see? You have the perfect motive for being a benign observer, doing time travel to gather data on something which would not alter history. You would be a true observer and with no agenda to alter history. I think I could feel secure sending someone like you back in time."

"Uh, Professor, we are talking hypothetically, aren't we? I mean you don't have anything perfected, right?"

The professor got a crafty look on his face.

"Well, let's say, for starters, you should call me Bill! Our working relationship just got a lot closer. Okay! Let me admit I have been somewhat successful in a few minor experiments, using lab animals and inanimate objects. My actual methods are beyond anything you have studied yet mathematically. I've been keeping the notes on a lot of my experiments out of my normal journals, which are open to the department heads. I'm not ready for them to start dictating to me as to what I can do and possibly turn the project over to the oversight committee from the military. You realize this would be a great coup for the military, and they would not hesitate to take over entirely, if I were to declare success with my time travel experiments. So this is very "hush-hush!" Not even Hal knows as much as I have just told you! I think he feels I'm just a harmless crackpot, spending grant money for some frivolous wild goose chase."

Jerry was wide-eyed and had been holding his breath but had to rebut the last statement.

"Oh, Hal has a much higher opinion of you than that! But wait a minute! You mean you can really do time travel? You have it perfected?"

"I wouldn't say 'perfected,' but I guess you could say I have done some time travel, or should I say I have permitted other things to travel through time. I made a lab stool blink out of our time and reappear five minutes later in the same spot. I also had it change locations, across the room, and reappear an hour later, more or less. I had a lab rat, in his cage, which I tried the same thing with, but the rat reappeared without its cage. The cage showed up a couple minutes later. So I theorized living matter travels at a different rate than inanimate objects. I have been trying to determine what the difference in rate turns out to be, and then I may be able to compensate for it, such as sending the cage on ahead and having the rat reappear inside the cage. I have not been successful so far, but I haven't killed off any rats either. The cage came through a bit mangled a couple times, so I need to find out what that is all about. Eventually, though, I will need an animal able to communicate the sensations and experiences of travel through time and space. That pretty well dictates the need for a human being. I hope you will volunteer for that job, but I have to practice with rats a lot more before I can use you, my boy, in good conscience. I noted you had signed up for a physics lab. Do you want to assist me in my experiments? Of course, this will be at times other than when normal labs are held."

"Uh, I have a part-time job some evenings, so I'll have to work around my work schedule, if that's all right. I'd like to help you, Professor, um, I, uh, mean Bill!"

"That will be fine. I've worked alone all this time, so I can just plan the experiments I need your help with around your work schedule. But you must keep this in strictest confidence, you understand?"

"Yes. I understand!"

So thus began Jerry Tanner's adventures in time travel. Actually, it was tedium, bordering on monotony in the beginning. The hours he spent in the lab late at night and on weekend evenings, doing the lifting, running, and recording the results of Bill Blanchard's painstaking and pedantic rigmarole for moving objects through time and space. By unofficial count, Jerry estimated he and Bill had moved various objects, not including the rats around the lab in and out of time some five hundred times. The rats were done likewise about the same number of times. The amount of electrical energy Professor Blanchard's apparatus used had to be stupendous, but no one seemed to take note as far as they could tell. They managed to synchronize the reappearance of the rat and the cage at nearly identical times, though it meant the rat had to be outside the cage for the requisite amount of time prior to the transfer in order for the cage to reappear at the proper time to cage the rat when it reappeared.

All of their initial exercises were to send things into the future to rematerialize somewhere and "somewhen" in the lab. They soon realized they should be perfecting their ability to send objects into the past. This began with one of Bill's textbooks being sent to Jerry's bedroom. The first time was just after Jerry got to the lab. They sent it to the coordinates they'd set up for Jerry's room, and he immediately went home and retrieved the book, which he knew hadn't been there when he'd left for the physics lab. From that point on, he just assumed anything appearing in his room was sent from the future, and they began putting notes in the book, or object, telling Jerry when it had been sent and allowing him to bring the object back the next day. Another theory which had been drummed into people's heads was the one about an object occupying the same space at two points in time, so just to be safe, they were careful about placing the object Jerry was returning—in proximity to the same object before it had been sent back in time. It was all very confusing, and they had to keep detailed notes and also to carefully mark each object, so they could differentiate it from its time-traveling "doppelgänger." Because of the impossibility of knowing why things were showing up at various places and times in the past, it was agreed upon, and guidelines set up, early in the semester where they'd witness the appearance of many weird things in and around their homes and the lab, which would not make sense until later in the semester when they had actually sent the object.

In anticipation of the main event, Jerry had been moved around the lab, forwards and backwards a number of times, in the same evening. He had even been sent home from the lab and then walked back to the lab, to be tested by Bill Blanchard, to see if there were any adverse physical affects. As they expected, his clothes did not travel with him. He left the portal fully clothed but ended up on the far side of the lab, naked, and his clothes ended up in a wad a few seconds later. The time he was sent home, he had to put on fresh clothes to return to the lab since he was not sure when and where his clothes would appear. The culmination of this round of experiments was for Jerry to be sent home, naked, a week into the past, redress, return to the lab in that time, then be sent to the lab in the future a few minutes after he had originally left. It was a bit confusing for Jerry, but he adjusted, and there seemed to be no physical harm done. Professor Blanchard spoke with Jerry at length about what sensations he experienced while moving through time and space. Jerry wasn't sure how to explain it, but he wasn't aware of being in-between times and places. He just seemed to be one place and suddenly somewhere else. The only sensation he was really aware of was a slight disorientation or lightheadedness. This type of experiment allowed them to calibrate the apparatus, though it was only in the very low end of the incremental dial, so jumps of greater time differences could only be calculated in rough orders of magnitudes.

Professor Blanchard kept testing his theory about sending inanimate objects in tandem with living tissue. He'd previously experimented with sending capsules ingested by rats through the portal. They appeared intact. He eventually implanted a small metal capsule under the skin of Jerry's arm. When he was sent home, he immediately checked his arm. The capsule was there! So Bill's theory was provisionally proven—an inanimate object inside living tissue traveled at the same rate. This was made a part of each experiment. They were careful what objects Jerry took with him, especially in his mouth, as they were concerned with choking him, if there were any spatial distortion. They tried inserting small objects into his anal cavity, but it proved to be too painful.

Finally, they began working on the problem of retrieval. It wasn't going to do them any good to send anyone back in time, or into the future, if they couldn't return to their own time and place. Bill Blanchard first experimented with "markers" implanted inside the rats to allow him to pinpoint when and where they were. This helped a great deal in his calibration efforts. He found, as he went further and further into the past and future, the markers inside his lab rats would sometimes disappear. He had to theorize said rat had died either from natural causes or because it appeared in a dangerous situation, either inside a solid object or where a predator or vehicle killed it. Bill found, if the marker was intact and could be detected, he could use it as a beacon and retrieve the subject, be it inanimate or living. His success rate for retrieval was usually affected by where and when he sent the subject. He recovered a couple rats, one of which looked like it was just taken out of the deep freeze; the other, like it had been in an oven. This led them to contemplate and plan very carefully in the event Jerry became eligible for travel any distance—spatially, temporally, or both. To ensure Jerry didn't end up inside a hill, topographical maps of the target area of Massachusetts were studied. They also planned to send him into a time of year which wouldn't put him in a frozen lake or stream. They decided to gamble he wouldn't end up inside a tree.

Next, they performed a series of small "jumps" (always into the past.), allowing the professor to further fine-tune his "time machine." Jerry was under strict instructions to interact with no one due to Bill's fear of altering time. They practiced moving him about their general area of the country, moving him back and forth in the past. The marker, or beacon they were using, was placed under Jerry's skin in a couple different places. For the short jumps, it was very small, but the professor had developed a larger version he considered needful for the final jump in time and space. It was decided it would be placed on the inside of Jerry's thigh, where normal contact with other objects would not damage it. They agreed Jerry wouldn't attempt to run and jump into the saddle of a horse. It was a joke since Jerry couldn't do it even without the beacon! The experiments continued into the winter and early spring of his junior year in college. He turned nineteen in March. And due to the time required to keep his job at the furniture store and his ever-mounting interest in time travel research, Jerry dropped one of his classes. He did this early enough to prevent being penalized. Of course, his parents had no knowledge of this, and it wouldn't impact him greatly since he planned on taking the course during the summer semester if it was offered then.

chapter

5

In late April, a major milestone was reached when Bill and Jerry decided to attempt a significant "jump." The plan was to move Jerry back one hundred years to the desert of Southern Nevada. They'd planned on his appearance to be in an uninhabited area where his arrival, in the nude, would not shock anyone, but close enough to civilization to afford him a chance to survive if the jump back to the present was not successful. They assembled a packet of clothing which would not arouse interest if he were required to seek help. They borrowed some old paper money from the university archives, which they could return at the end of a successful jump. The money, they encapsulated, and he carried it in his mouth. The clothing, they would send on ahead at the rate they assumed would precede his arrival by a short margin. The coordinates were locked, so he would be near the packet. The target time was spring of the year 1897. They had no way of checking the date upon arrival without Jerry seeking information from the inhabitants, and they were reluctant to do so unless the chance of conflict was at a minimum. The plan was for Jerry to activate the beacon as soon as he got his bearings and could describe what he saw. In the clothing packet was a small digital camera. All was ready, and they decided to do it on a Wednesday evening after Jerry got off work. Since time at the lab was subjective, Jerrywould only be gone for a short time.

First, the packet was sent through the portal, and Jerry stripped down to his birthday suit. Neither Jerry nor Bill were being nonchalant about the risks they were taking. They'd been over every aspect of the process numerous times. The process was the same as any other time, the difference was the scope of the attempt. This would be a dress rehearsal of sorts for the ultimate attempt to answer Jerry's family lineage questions and to validate Bill Blanchard's theories about time travel. With the professor watching the clock on the apparatus, Jerry stepped into the time machine and signaled he was ready. At what Bill estimated was the correct instant, he energized his creation. Jerry's image wavered and blinked out, as he had done dozens of times before, but this attempt was of much greater importance. Dr. Blanchard watched the meters and dials on his invention, wanting to know precisely what his lab assistant was experiencing. He was understandably anxious since not only was this a living being but also their relationship as close friends had developed. He was used to the lonely, apprehensive feeling from the previous times he'd sent this young, adventurous man into an uncertain fate!

Feeling minor disorientation and with a compulsion to spit out what he had in his mouth, Jerry went to his knees in the rocky sand of the desert landscape he suddenly found himself standing within. Immediately, he spotted the packet of clothing about ten yards distance. Getting his bearings, he attempted to find some geological formation he could photograph for later research to pinpoint his landing site. Shakily, he walked to the packet. Digging out the camera, Jerry took several pictures in all directions. Estimating the time of day as midmorning, he noticed the day was already warming up and would be quite warm by noon. Seeing no immediate signs of civilization, he searched the horizon for a lookout point to see further afield. There was a small rise of land a couple hundred yards to what he figured was the south. Pulling out the sandals from the packet and donning them, he explored his immediate surroundings. Since, as planned, he would not be here for a long time, he did not dress. He was not concerned with sunburn since he already had a tan, though more than an hour of exposure could burn his delicate parts, not accustomed to sunning. He struck off for the hillock.

Climbing the incline, he surveyed the horizon in all directions. Off to the north, he spotted what he concluded was a small amount of smoke or dust. It didn't appear to be a dust storm. Estimating the distance at over ten miles, he had no desire to walk that far, especially since it would be in the heat of the day. If he headed there, it would be early afternoon by the time he arrived, and it was not critically important for him to make contact with people. Taking a couple more pictures, he then returned to his arrival spot. It amazed him he didn't "feel" like he was standing in a place one hundred years in the past, thinking it would be interesting to be there at night and have the knowledge and equipment to note the positions of the constellations. He had read about being able to calculate the date from this data. Oh, well, so much for dreaming about that.

Picking up the plasticized roll of money, he put it in the packet, along with the camera and his sandals. The packet had its own beacon, so he activated it and then stood back. It took about five minutes for the packet to blink out of existence. For some reason, he felt like he had failed by not validating the date but felt it would've been more difficult given the distance and uncertainty of the smoke column on the horizon. It could have very well been a small band of Indians, and he had brought no weapons. So taking a last look around and with a sigh, Jerry manipulated the beacon on his inner thigh and waited to be taken home.

Jerry found himself in the relatively dim lab after so recently being in full sunlight. Again, he was slightly disoriented but did not lose his balance. He saw the relief on the face of Professor Blanchard and felt much the same way. He was not afraid of his ability to survive should he be stranded in another time, but how would it all be explained to his parents and all his friends. And how would Professor Blanchard explain the loss of a lab assistant on a government-funded project, which the overseers had no idea he was anywhere near capable of doing such things. He saw the clothes packet at his feet and almost immediately stooped to retrieve the camera.

Downloading the pictures into a computer, he started a program which would convert the digital images into data to be compared with topographical information of the general area they had targeted. If they were too far off the mark, the program would display an error, but if they were within the scope of the target, it would pinpoint his location. While he was waiting for the results of the comparison, he got dressed and joined Bill Blanchard at his desk. He could see the strain on the professor's face and reassured him everything went fine, and he was back safe and sound. Bill told him they should think about having Jerry draw up a will in case something "did" happen. Jerry smiled and told him he doubted anyone would believe it anyway.

The computer beeped, and Jerry ran to check the readout. He was all smiles when he looked at the professor. The map indicated he had been about fifteen miles south of the town of Pahrump, Nevada. Almost exactly on the Nevada state line. They had been in the right state but had planned on being a little further east. This would lead to a slight "tweak" to the machine. Doing research, they surmised the smoke was from the small town of Pahrump, which had been settled in the late 1800s. The absence of any highways in the pictures lent credence to the fact it was sometime in the past, before paved roads came to the area. Both researchers were frustrated because the date could not be more accurately pinpointed, but it was not bad! They were true pioneers in the field of time travel, and they were learning as they proceeded.

In what little spare time Jerry could find, he delved into the history of Massachusetts, in general, and the area of Salem specifically. He found out there were two places named Salem—Salem Village and Salem Town. The original settlement called Naumkeag (a local Native American name) was established around 1626, but renamed Salem a few years later and had grown up around what became Salem Bay.

Salem became a major seaport in early New England. As the town grew and surrounding land was developed by farmers, an unexpected friction between the urban and rural populations sprung up. Due to the two groups being at odds, Salem Village came into existence. It had a village center, but the boundaries were quite extensive compared to the town. Because the Puritan religion had a strong influence, Salem Village wanted their own meeting house and minister, so their voice and needs would not take a back seat to the townspeople. The animosity between the two groups led some historians to believe it was the root cause for the hysteria and persecutions of 1691–1693. During the 1700s, Salem Village changed its name to Danvers, possibly to escape the stigma of the historic witchcraft trials.

Jerry and Bill Blanchard spent many hours discussing how, if he found the information he needed, he was going to cache the documents required to validate the names and dates. Because of the passage of time and the changes which take place in any area, a hiding place would have to be found which would be secure for the three hundred odd intervening years. Hillsides were risky due to the chance the earth would be moved to accommodate some changes in land use. Most homes would not survive the interval, although some existed in Jerry's time. The ones which survived required extensive restoration. The longest surviving home in Salem was the so-called House of the Seven Gables, named thusly because it had inspired the novel of the same name by Nathaniel Hawthorne. The house, which had been built by the Turner family and later acquired by the Ingersoll family, was more properly known as the Turner-Ingersoll Mansion. It would be a likely place to deposit the documents, though Jerry and Bill doubted the inhabitants, in either time period, would be happy to see strangers excavating on their property. The house underwent numerous additions and modifications over the first two centuries of its existence. If a hiding place was decided on, the documents would have to be protected against all dangers of deterioration—be it water, heat, insects, etc. Despite the temptation to add ziplock bags to the clothing packet, archivists would not take ancient documents protected by plastic too seriously. In the seventeenth century, things were preserved by such things as oilcloth and sealed with wax and pitch. It took an extra bit of research for Jerry to decide on the best methods of archiving documents in a manner consistent with historical methods, or at least would not be questioned, when uncovered. In the end, it was valuable research!

It became apparent they shouldn't delay the trip Jerry and Bill had worked toward for so long. The numerous experiments they'd performed had given Professor Blanchard so much data, and he was grateful for Jerry's assistance. He could publish his theories and lab notes with enough data to back them up, without fear of rebuttal, except from the doubters. They decided to make the jump on a Sunday afternoon in early June. Jerry had gone to church with his parents, then told them he had work to do on a lab project. He felt apprehension about this possibly being the last time he saw his parents, so he made sure he hugged each of them, told them he loved them, and thanked them for all they did for him. They each had a strange look on their faces, but he told them he would be back later in the evening, hoping he was telling the truth. He knew he may be raising suspicions but felt he had to part with them that way. He had previously written a long letter to them, explaining what he was doing and why in attempting time travel. This letter was in the desk of Bill Blanchard, to be given to his parents if, for some reason, he didn't return from his journey.

When he got to the lab, Bill already had the clothing packet assembled and had added a few items such as the digital camera, some energy bars, and a small first aid kit, and despite their decision to not put the documents in ziplock bags, he had put in two gallon-sized bags to be used for "whatever!" They could find no currency for that time period, neither paper or coin, so he would have to live off the land so to speak. He could perform manual labor, if need be, but he was educated far beyond the average person of the 1690s would be.

He could work as a schoolmaster if he needed a vocation. So all was in preparation for a "go!" Jerry felt impressed to take a moment and say a prayer. Though Bill was not a religious man, he stood silently as the young man communicated with his Deity. When Jerry raised his bowed head, he immediately began disrobing. Bill had estimated the spatial coordinates and locked them into the time machine. He had spent more time with the temporal adjustments and felt satisfied they were correct. This was not a time to be "in the ballpark!" He wanted to be "right around home base." Shaking hands with Jerry, he then took him into a hug to show him the affection he had developed for the young man. Jerry stood by as Bill put the clothes packet into the portal and energized his invention. As the countdown for Jerry's turn began, the two men could not look each other in the eye due to the emotion of the moment. Finally, as Jerry entered the portal, he looked at the professor, and each grinned and winked at the other. Jerry saw Bill energize the machine.

6

As he lay on the floor of Matthew Lloyd's humble home, Jerry brought his thoughts up to his present time and place, remembering all. He knew the professor had been successful in his endeavors to send Jerry to within a few miles of Salem and was surely within a year of his target date. Bill Blanchard had done almost all he said he would! Now it was up to Jerry to do what he had come for, and then he would see if Bill could perform the final miracle—return him to his own time and home! What should Jerry's next move be? If possible, he should return to his area of arrival and try to find the clothes packet. The items in the packet could be very useful if he could keep Matthew from seeing anything but the clothing. What would someone else think if they found it first? What would they think of the strange objects within the clothing? Its discovery by anyone but Jerry could have far-reaching effects. He needed to come up with a plausible excuse for returning to his arrival point, but may need Matthew's help in finding the place once more. He was sure Matthew would expect his own agenda to take precedence in the morning, and the longer Jerry delayed looking for the packet, the better the chances someone else would find it.

If the clothing could be found, they would be advantageous, especially the boots he had decided to include. But if he couldn't make use of the items, it would be better no one else found them. The moccasins Matthew loaned him were okay, but they would not last long if he used them constantly. The boots, being work boots, were not the type footwear worn in the vicinity, but they could be explained to be a design native to Virginia. Luckily, his clothing was pretty nondescript. He chose not to bring underwear due to the elastic waistband and fine stitching of both the top and bottom pieces. No zippers, no denim, and no molded buttons. It was difficult finding shirts which were laced or tied at the throat, and trousers using no metal rivets or catches. So Jerry decided he had to put forth his request to return to the area where he'd been found, even if it meant Matthew would accompany him.

Seeming like he had just fallen asleep moments before, he was being roused by Matthew to begin another day. After getting up and dressing, Jerry had assumed they would eat a light breakfast at Matthew's home but was told they would go to his mother's for breakfast. The home was pleasantly warm, and the smell of cooking was strong. Breakfast consisted of hot tea and "porridge," which was a boiled dish of oats or wheat. He was surprised to find they used a type of maple syrup for sweetening the dish. Upon inquiry, Jerry found out the early settlers of the area had learned from the natives how to tap the local maple trees for its sap. This was done in the early spring. Then the sap was boiled down, concentrating the sweetness. It was not plentiful but was the local sweetener, since sugar was essentially unavailable and honey nearly as scarce.

The meal was a lively activity, as the family discussed the agenda for the day. Rebecca blushed readily whenever she caught Jerry's eye, but she still smiled, and Jerry tried not to encourage her as her mother was always watchful. Jerry decided now would be the time to put forth his request to return to his landing site. He expressed his wish to go back to the area and have a look in the vicinity to see if any of his belongings had been left behind. Matthew said he had many tasks and would not have the time. Matthew's mother quickly had reasons Rebecca could not accompany Jerry, which he readily understood. Daniel was too young, so it fell to Jonathan, who was fourteen, to go with Jerry. Jonathan was eager since it would get him away from the normal labors around the house. Jerry was surprised to see Jonathan had a rifle of his own. Jerry was loaned a pistol, which was already loaded, much to his relief. After hearing Matthew describe the area where he had found Jerry, Jonathan stepped right out to begin the journey, promising to be back as early as possible. They had taken a small bundle of bread and meat with them in case they were gone for the midday meal. If opportunity presented itself, they would also hunt more game.

It took less time returning to Jerry's arrival point due to the fact they were not carrying a full-sized deer. Jerry found his animal bedding-down site and began trying to remember his line of travel after he had arrived. Keeping his eyes on the lookout for his bundle, he was sure he would see it before Jonathan. He was wrong. Eyes, accustomed to searching out game and constantly on the lookout for danger, were sharp! The bundle was discovered by the boy and had been picked up before Jerry could reach for it. Only deep-seated training in respect for others prevented Jonathan from immediately opening the package. Jerry tried not to seem anxious to open the bundle, but he asked Jonathan to give him a moment or two to examine the clothing. The short time he had allowed him to separate the clothes from the other items. The food packets were shiny foil, so he hid those upon his person and then took the first aid kit and camera and hid them inside the clothing. He put the plastic bags inside the boots and stuffed the remaining small clothes articles in after them. Since he did not bring underwear, the small clothes items consisted mostly of handkerchiefs and stockings. Rejoining Jonathan, they began their return to Middleton. It had surprised him when they had found the packet so soon, so they had ample time to hunt. Jonathan shot two rabbits and a small deer. He had a game bag for the rabbits, and they cut another branch for carrying the deer.

Jonathan was almost swaggering, as they came into sight of his home. He had always been in Matthew's company and had never received the recognition he felt he should. Now, though, he was the lone shooter and was returning from a successful hunt. Jerry, in praising his prowess to his mother, made a fast-friend of Jonathan. After helping to hang the deer near the rear door to their home, he took his leave and walked toward Matthew's small house. On the way, he took the opportunity to step out of sight of all who may be around. Taking a few pictures toward the Lloyd home, using his zoom lens, he then repackaged what he was going to keep near, caching the first aid kit and food bars inside the plastic bags in a hole he dug in the ground beneath some bushes. By the time he arrived at Matthew's home, he was anxious to help his rescuer in his work.

It was very instructional to Jerry to assist Matthew in his labors. There was still venison to prepare for curing. They cut the meat into long strips, then salted it down. It was then hung in a small shed built to smoke meat. The source of smoke was outside of the shed, but the ducting built into the system allowed the smoke produced to be drawn from bottom to top inside the smokehouse. Jerry could think of a dozen ways to improve his methods but kept quiet because they may be things which were not being done yet in this time. He felt stifled by his promise to the professor to not meddle with history. With the two of them working, the preparations for the meat curing were completed, and the curing process begun. It would take a day or two to properly cure the venison. This was an ongoing process, and the same thing was being done at Matthew's mother's home. It seemed redundant to Jerry until he realized how much space was required to actually cure the meat, making it necessary to have a smokehouse at both homes. Matthew told Jerry he planned on building a larger smokehouse in the future. The addition to the house took a higher priority, however. Matthew hoped to have a wife before the harvest next fall, and he wanted to have at least one bedroom completed.

By evening, the venison was all in the smokehouse. The two young men started laying out the lumber required to frame the first room of the addition to Matthew's house. Jerry had enough experience in framing; he made a number of recommendations to his companion which resulted in a much stronger framework, and Matthew was impressed with his houseguest's assistance. When they finally quit work and went to the family home for supper, Matthew and Jerry were somewhat preoccupied with their building plans. Matthew's mother had to remind them there were others present. Again, Rebecca kept a close eye on Jerry, and her mother watched her in return. The normal socializing was cut short when Matthew told his mother they wanted to get to bed early, so as to get an early start in continuing their building efforts. Rebecca was disappointed when Jerry was not at the stream that evening. Jerry had considered going but decided he should find an alternate bathing area and would seek one out the next day.

For two days, Matthew and Jerry labored on the house, completely framing two bedrooms and started the outer sheathing, using the strips of clapboard, the preferred building method native to the area. Jerry saw the wisdom of insulation but had no materials to do so. The inner walls were attached to the framework, just as the outer clapboard had been, and the airspace between was the only insulation medium used to keep the warmth in and the cold out. Jerry kept trying to think of some material native to the area, which could possibly be used, but did not have enough information to discover a solution. On the second evening, Matthew announced he and Jerry would travel to Salem to buy supplies and see a few people. The family knew who he was wanting to see, and he took some gentle teasing about it. When they returned to Matthew's home, Jerry asked about the family he was referring to, and Matthew reluctantly admitted it was a young woman, and she was a relative of Jerry's. Her name was Hope Meacham. She was seventeen and the eldest daughter of the younger Jeremiah Meacham. So when they traveled to Salem, not only would Matthew be visiting the young woman he was romantically interested in, but he would introduce Jerry to his distant relatives as well. Jerry figured this called for another bath.

Before going to the stream again, Jerry asked Matthew about what they used for soap. Matthew produced a crockery jar of homemade soap. It had no perfumes like Jerry was used to but hopefully would cut the grease in his hair. Jerry hadn't had an opportunity to find another bathing spot but decided his encounter with Rebecca had been coincidental. As he approached the stream, he heard voices, which turned out to be Rebecca, and her younger sister, Rhoda. They both had buckets in each hand and were just leaving the stream's bank. When Jerry came face-to-face with the two young women, he felt apprehensive. Rebecca wanted to stop and talk with Jerry but couldn't think of an excuse to do so, without allowing Rhoda to be present.

"Hello, Rebecca. Hello, Rhoda."

"Hello, Jerrold," Rebecca said breathlessly.

"Hello, Master Jerrold," came the high-pitched voice of Rhoda. Her greeting ended in a giggle. She knew of Rebecca's interest in Jerry, and in her adolescent way, she too was interested in this newcomer. He was exciting to listen to, and he was quite handsome.

It was obvious what each was there for. The girls had their buckets, and Jerry had his container of soap and a towel, so that was not an avenue of conversation. While both Jerry and Rebecca were at a loss for words, Rhoda had no such restriction!

"Oh, how can you stand bathing in that cold stream? We get to bathe in the warm bathtub. Why don't you wait until Saturday and you can bathe with us?"

Rebecca let out a squeal of surprise!

"Rhoda? How can you say something like that? He's a man, and we're women?"

"I don't mean at the same time! I just mean on Saturday."

"I understand what you mean, Rhoda. I appreciate the thought, but I need to be presentable to meet my relatives tomorrow. Are you finished fetching water for the evening?" Jerry looked at Rebecca meaningfully as he spoke.

"Yes, Jerrold, we have enough to meet our needs until tomorrow. Will we see you for morning meal?"

"It depends on how early your brother wants to leave for Salem.It is a far walk."

"Oh, he will ride the horses, of course!" Rebecca giggled.

"What horses? I see no horses."

"We keep them further away from the house. We use them mainly for plowing, but when we go to Salem, we either ride them or hitch them to the wagon. We only walk around here!"

"Oh, well, your brother did not mention we would ride. I guess he assumed I would know. Maybe we will see you in the morning before we leave then!"

"Yes, perhaps you will. Good night, Jerrold!"

"Good night, Rebecca. Good night, Rhoda."

"Good night, Master Jerrold."

Watching the girls walk away with their burdens, Jerry thought he should have offered to carry the buckets for them, but he couldn't carry all four and which one should he choose to carry for—the younger or the one who was flirting with him. He finally shrugged and turned back toward the stream. Removing his clothes, he once again decided to plunge into the water. It had been a warm day but had cooled quickly once the sun was below the horizon. The water was just as frigid as he remembered, so he wasted no time in scooping up some of the homemade soap and quickly washing his hair and body. Sluicing off the soap residue, he quickly attained the shore and briskly rubbed himself dry with the towel. He began dressing and had just got his breeches pulled up and his shirt over his head when he looked up and saw Rebecca standing about twenty feet away.

"How long have you been here?"

"Long enough to get my first good look at a man. You are dark on a lot of your skin?"

"Yes. In Virginia, where it is much warmer, we do not always wear as many clothes as they do here when we are off at the seashore or away from civilization. We do not let the women see us, however, as that would be impolite!"

"I am ashamed, Jerrold, that I have spied upon you in your bath! I told mother I had dropped my bonnet and had to retrieve it. I have sworn Rhoda to secrecy, but I fear she may still confess my wicked intentions. I just had to take a chance to see you without my entire family around. I did not intend to spy on your nakedness. I wanted to talk with you and not have my mother watching me so closely! Will you forgive me my wicked ways, Jerrold?"

"I am embarrassed I have shown myself to you twice. I forgive you and beg your forgiveness in return!"

"I forgive you, Jerrold," Rebecca replied breathlessly.

Finished with donning his clothes, Jerry slipped the moccasins back on his feet and approached Rebecca. She stood timidly and lowered her eyes. Jerry lifted her chin with his hand and looked into her eyes. They were truly beautiful eyes, and they exuded total innocence. He saw tears form at the corners and flow toward the center, where they threatened to spill down her crimson cheeks. Jerry gently wiped at her tears with his index finger.

"Do not cry, Miss Rebecca. You are totally innocent of all but curiosity. You are at an age where you are seeking out the mysteries of life. Would I frighten you or would it be too bold if I were to attempt to kiss your lips?"

"Nooo," she said tremulously.

Bending down, Jerry lightly touched his lips to Rebecca's slightly parted lips, applying a slight pressure. Her face turned even more scarlet, and he could hear her breathing quicken.

"I will not hurt you, Rebecca. Please do not fear me."

"I do not fear you, sir. You make me quake and shiver when I am around you, but you are a kind man. I feel safe with you, but I fear myself. I am shameless and want to be held, as I used to see my father hold my mother in the years before he died. I fear I will be damned for my thoughts, but I cannot help myself!"

"Patience, Rebecca. You are just dealing with the feelings within your body which tells you, you are of marriageable age. I trust your mother was married already when she had attained your years."

"Yes, she was, but there are not so many marriage-minded men here as there were in my mother's town. I fear I shall be a spinster and die without knowing what marriage is like."

"Again, I preach patience. There is ample time for you to find a husband. I am sure your mother has contemplated your betrothal and may have a possible suitor, even now."

"Nay! She would have told me so, I am certain."

"Have no fear of spinsterhood, Miss Rebecca. I doubt many bachelors have looked on you, who were not taken with you. Let your mother do her duty, and you will have many a suitor, I trust!"

"But what of you, sir? Do you not find me appealing? Or is your troth already pledged?"

"Nay. I am not betrothed. I have nothing to offer a bride yet, and my future is uncertain at this time. In a year or two, I will have the means to offer a home, but I will not speak of this to you, for I may never return to Massachusetts, though I am flattered you find me of husbandly material, and I am naturally attracted to you."

"I feel you are just being kind to me, sir. I am young but would labor to be a good wife if given the chance. Fie on me! I speak too boldly, and you think me unvirtuous! I must return home, Jerrold, or my mother will suspect I have played false with her. Here is my hat, so I must be on my way. I think I shall have troubled sleep this night, remembering your kiss and our talk. Good night once more, Jerrold."

"Good night, Miss Rebecca. I pray you sleep the sleep of innocence as you should. On the morrow!"

"On the morrow."

The young woman moved off at a brisk walk, attempting to make up time so her extended absence may not be noted. For his part, Jerry picked up his things and walked slowly back to his accommodations, his mind awhirl at the ease with which history could be screwed up. Here he was, minding his own business, and if he was not careful, he may get himself into a position where he could be forced to take a wife in this time! Then what would happen, especially if he were to consummate that marriage? How would he explain to his parents about the daughter-in-law and possibly grandchild they would never see? He reminded himself of his mission, and that it did not include making any changes to history!

chapter

7

The next morning came just as early as each preceding morning, and he was even more groggy due to his much-interrupted slumber. He was actually hoping Matthew would decide not to go to his mother's for breakfast but no such luck! When they arrived, he dreaded seeing Rebecca. She was there, however, and he could not avoid her. Surprisingly, she acted normal and only smiled a little. He thought how she was either a better actress than he expected or she had resigned herself to accept whatever came. If her mother noted the change in her mien, she did not reveal it. Matthew and his mother had a brief conversation in private, and Jerry was worried about the topic. By the time the men were ready to leave, Jonathan and Daniel had collected two horses and had them saddled. Before mounting, Jerry made sure his secreted camera was secure, so it would not be lost. He was glad the camera was a small digital model, so it was not bulky, and he made sure the built-in flash was disabled, so if he had the chance to take pictures, the flash would not bring him attention.

Taking leave of his mother, Matthew set a comfortable pace along the trail to the southeast. Inquiring of his companion, Jerry asked how long it would take to get to Salem. He was told they were heading for the dividing line between Salem Village and Salem Town, where a collection of businesses had sprung up, providing services to both communities. They would be there around noontime. Their destination was the home of Jeremiah Meacham, the younger. He provided for his father, who was in his late seventies. It was not rare for a man to live to his age, but it was not common either.

Old Jeremiah, as he was known, had fathered ten children with his first wife and five with his second wife. Jeremiah, the younger, had been born in 1644, the youngest boy of Old Jeremiah's first wife. Old Jeremiah was now a widower. Jeremiah, the younger had been married in 1664 and his wife had borne him twelve children before dying in 1690. He was courting a young woman of twenty, named Deborah Browne. She was the daughter of the miller, who ground the grain for the community. She had been betrothed to a merchant who was lost at sea on his way to England. She had waited for three years, after losing him, before accepting the proposal of the younger Jeremiah, who was also a merchant, but who sent others to do his traveling.

Jeremiah, the younger, had lost four of his children to illness, and his oldest, a daughter, was Hope. She acted as a mother to her seven younger siblings. Hope was seventeen and looking forward to her father's remarrying, so she could be partially relieved of the responsibility of raising her brothers and sisters. She had plans for her own family, hopeful of being courted by a young man who lived outside of Salem. A tall, independent man named Matthew Lloyd. Matthew had already approached her father to inquire whether his courtship of Hope would meet Jeremiah's approval. The young Jeremiah had asked the even younger Mr. Lloyd if he would delay the actual betrothal until after his own marriage could take place and his new bride was installed in his home, so she could relieve Hope of the care of his children. Of course, Matthew could only agree. This gave him the time needed to complete his own preparations for marriage.

The ride to Salem was an adventure for Jerry. He was filled with awe at his opportunity to view the farms and homes of seventeenth century America. He wanted so much to have his camera available to him to record things which had only been preserved in the paintings and drawings of the time and in the modern perceptions recorded by cinematographers of his time. Without the ability to openly use his camera, Jerry tried to etch the various scenes he encountered into his memory. He gradually became aware things were dirtier than he had expected. The smells, especially of the people, were stronger than he had imagined. His own experience made him realize personal hygiene was not a top priority, and deodorant would not be around for hundreds of years. In addition to washing, dental hygiene was lacking, and he saw a number of women whom he thought attractive until they opened their mouths. Then he saw neglected and decaying teeth. In the short time he had been present in this century, he was aware of his own lack of oral hygiene. Never really considering these things before, it was total "culture shock" for Jerry. He felt like the tourist he really was and had to remind himself to remain nonchalant about things.

Before they reached their destination, Jerry was feeling the pain of being in a saddle for longer than he was accustomed. He figured he may have to delve into the first aid kit sooner than expected! But being a resilient young man, he endured the discomfort. Finally, however, he was told their journey was almost at an end, as they approached a more densely populated area. Noting the contrasting structures, some weathered and others painted, he also noted the diverse methods used to advertise the various commercial enterprises. Matthew directed Jerry's attention to one such business.

"That used to be my father's wheelwright shop. I have leased the building to a blacksmith, but I sometimes spend a day or two laboring at my father's trade to make a little extra and to keep my skills sharp."

"Why don't you move into Salem and work at it full time?" asked Jerry.

Matthew looked at Jerry, then drew up closer, so his conversation could not be overheard.

"I have no knowledge of customs in Virginia, but in this area, ownership of land and businesses is a man's world. Women are not capable of running a business, and ownership of land is reserved for men. The reason I stay near my mother is because I am considered the owner of my father's land, where my mother resides. She cannot own it by local custom, so I work the land. If she were to remarry, the land may remain mine, or it could go to her new husband. I would not have my mother and siblings dispossessed. Should my mother want, I could move them into the town, and the land could be sold or tenanted. If my mother had no older sons, the land would be taken by the courts. The courts are bound to sell it and give the proceeds for her upkeep, but there is no guarantee the price would be fair. If I continue working it until Jonathan attains his majority at eighteen, then it could be transferred to him and on down the line until my youngest brother inherited, unless, again, my mother remarried. Is it the same in Virginia, Jerrold?"

Jerry attempted a plausible response. "It is not quite so strict in Virginia. The deciding factor is what the written will of the master of the plantation says. He may leave it to a male heir or relative, but it could be in trust to his wife if the heir is young. In effect, the wife, or older daughter, if such is the case, has nominal charge, but only with the understanding the young heir would take charge upon reaching majority. Remarrying would only mean the new husband would have charge of the wife, but the land still goes to the legal heir. In the absence of a will, the land would be probated by the courts. Ultimately, the wife becomes the ward of the courts, and any proceeds from the land would be used for her support and also for any children. I have never been directly involved in any of these matters, so I am mostly ignorant of the legalities. I know of no scandals, nor of any dispossessed widows."

"I plan on keeping my mother in her house until Jonathan can take over for me, but depending on what my future wife and I decide, I may continue farming or once more ply my trade here or elsewhere."

"It sounds like a good plan, Master Lloyd!" Jerry said, smiling.

"Thank you, sir! Now, let us continue to the Meacham home, so you can meet your relatives at last!"

Matthew was expected due to previous correspondence, so the entire family was present. Everyone knew Matthew, so Jerry became the center of attention, especially when the reason for Jerry's visit was announced by Matthew. When the patriarch of the family was told, he directed his questions to Jerry.

"Young Master Tanner, would you tell me how you are related? I know of no kin in Virginia."

"I bring you the greetings of your young sister, Joanne, who is married to my great uncle, William. He is not a Tanner, as is my mother's uncle. His name is Woolrich."

"Ah, yes, Joanne! She was but a young lass when I last saw her at our home in Crewkerne. That was in England, young man, in Somersetshire! How fares my sister, sir?"

"She suffers from the rigors of age, Master Meacham. Though she is younger than you, I believe, sir, she does not possess your vigor and is all but bedridden. I hesitate to say, but I fear she will not see another year."

Jerry inwardly cringed because most of what he was telling everyone was pure fabrication. If an authentic visitor from Virginia were present, he would be exposed as a fraud instantaneously! He knew old Jeremiah had a sister named Joanne, but he had no idea where she was or if still alive at this time. She was five years younger than Jeremiah, and women seemed to have a shorter lifespan. He knew old Jeremiah passed away in 1696, so he still had over three years left of life. Jerry was also amazed he had been able to pick up the manner of speaking. He still had to be careful about contractions and more modern jargon. He was thankful he had read so many stories from the "Romance Period" where the language was so stilted and formal. Any lapse could be blamed on colloquialisms and the difference in dialects between New England and the Virginia colony. "Well, Master Tanner, I fear I am not able to travel to visit my ailing sister, but if you would kindly deliver a letter from me, I would be indebted to you."

"It would be an honor, sir!"

A short time later, the family went into the midday meal, which had been delayed until their guests arrived. In addition to Matthew and Jerry, Hope had an additional guest, who arrived at almost the exact moment they were sitting down to eat. The newcomer was introduced to the two young men.

"Mistress Bonner, may I present Master Matthew Lloyd of Middleton and Salem. Master Lloyd is a wheelwright and farms in Middleton. May I also present our newest guest, Master Jerrold Tanner of the Virginia Colony. He is a relative, come to visit us, and has been staying with Master Lloyd. Gentlemen, may I present Mistress Constance Bonner. She is originally from near Boston but has resided in Salem for the past year. Her husband, unfortunately, passed last fall from an illness."

Matthew and Jerry bowed to Constance and made their condolences on the passing of her husband. Constance knew of Matthew and was not so interested in him, since Hope was all but betrothed to him. Though she had no compunction against stealing Matthew from Hope, she had few friends in Salem and could not afford to lose any. Constance was a black-haired beauty, who was shorter than Hope, but had a more voluptuous form than the slim Hope. She was born into a poor family and, in her struggle to survive, learned at a young age the benefits of using her looks to gain a better place in life. She did not flaunt herself but plotted and waited for the right man to come along. Finally, she met Ebenezer Bonner, a middle-aged man looking for companionship. She had merely exhibited herself as a likely candidate and let him court her. She had married him in Boston and then traveled with him to Salem. She did not like the small town, but this is where her husband had his holdings, which were considerable. His social position allowed her access to the upper crust of Salem society, backwards as it may seem to her. She was in the inner circle of the Turners, Hawthornes, Conans, Endicotts, and now the Meachams. When her husband died, she thought she was set, but the local courts would not allow her full title to her late husband's holdings. She lived on an allowance provided by the court, and she remained in residence in her husband's home. She was expected to remarry, at which time, her second husband would gain title to all Ebenezer's property.

Now that her six-month period of mourning was over, all eligible males in and around Salem would vie for her hand, a succulent and tender morsel, which came attached to more than any of those men now possessed. Constance, however, found most of her suitors oafish and loathsome. Now she has put off her widow's weeds, the competition for her hand was a major topic of speculation, with none of the principals wanting to be perceived as behind in the running. The major fears for Constance were, first, to be saddled with a domineering husband, which Ebenezer was not, and secondly, the courts allowed her two years to remarry. If, for some reason she had not, then the properties would be sold and the proceeds used for Constance's maintenance. Constance did not trust the courts to make a decision in her best interests, nor hold out for the best price. She would rather have a new husband she could control. Matthew had come to mind, but now she was looking at Jerry, wondering how strong-willed he was. Could he be manipulated or cowed? She intended to draw this man out.

Constance was not the only woman taking notice of Jerry, and this did not include Matthew's sister, Rebecca! Hope, who had set her cap for Matthew, was suddenly faced with an alternative to her prospective suitor. Jerrold was the same age as Matthew; he was roughly the same height; but Jerrold had finer features and appeared to be fit. However, being cautious, she did not reveal her sudden interest in Jerrold. He was just visiting after all! He could already have a wife or be betrothed to someone in Virginia. She was not being mercenary, but if she were going to marry and she were given the choice, she would pick the best man. She had the same range of possible suitors as Constance, but she was not as attractive to enterprising young men. She had the beauty, being taller and slimmer than Constance, with lighter coloring, but she had no property to entice a husband. A dowry, to be sure, but nothing like her friend Constance would bring to the marriage. She loved her family, but she had been restricted due to her family responsibilities, having traveled less than thirty miles from Salem, so the chance to go someplace else was appealing.

"May I be so bold, Master Tanner, as to inquire if you are married or betrothed, perhaps?"

"Nay, Mistress Bonner, I fear I am not fortunate to be in either position. As fair as the young women are in Virginia, I beg your pardon if I vow how Salem can boast competition."

"Fie on you, Master Tanner, for possessing such a silver tongue. You may turn some poor woman's head with such frippery!"

"Upon my word, I am sure Master Lloyd will agree Salem can boast fine examples of rare beauty!"

"I do, indeed, sir! Two such examples grace this home this very moment!"

All four young people were blushing after this exchange. Both Jeremiah's had sat by, listening to the repartee.

"My word, you are a bold bunch! Let us have no more of this outrageous flirtation. Save it for courtship when the time comes," said the younger Jeremiah, barely able to keep from laughing out loud.

"I think we should concentrate on the victuals, for fear this meal will be inedible if not consumed quickly. I will pronounce grace."

The meal was consumed in almost total silence, as each person garnered their own thoughts. While Constance thought about the conquest of Jerry, he thought of Hope and her quiet beauty. Hope was thinking of both Jerrold and Matthew, weighing the merits of each. Young Jeremiah was thinking how he should have considered Mistress Bonner before he betrothed himself to Deborah Browne, allowing there was only two years difference in their ages, but Constance had much more to offer, property-wise. The dowry of a miller's daughter could not compare to the largess of the Bonner holdings. Still, he allowed how he began courting Deborah prior to Ebenezer's death. Deborah was such a kind, gentle soul and would be much better as a mother to his younger children. Despite her youth, beauty, and wealth, Constance was likely too strong-willed to make a pleasant wife at this time in his life. He was forty-eight his last birthday, so he was not anxious to take such a spirited woman in hand as his wife. It was just as well he had chosen Deborah!

With lunch concluded, the children went about their chores or play as was appropriate. The two older men retired to their respective rooms, one to compose a missive to his sickly sister, the other to review invoices. The four young people went into the parlor to continue visiting. The parlor had several settees and chairs. It would have easily accommodated a dozen or more persons. Hope and Matthew sat on one settee, and Constance requested Jerry to join her on an adjacent settee. Conversation among all four was flagging because each couple had their own agenda. Matthew was anxious to tell Hope about the progress he and Jerry had made on his house. She wanted to hear but tried to follow the conversation of the other couple. For their part, Constance was busy trying to draw Jerry out to determine if she could get a ring through his nose. Jerry was being polite but did not give any indication whether he could be controlled or not. She asked Jerry if he would ever consider staying in Salem rather than returning to Virginia. He told her he could not consider it yet since he had obligations, such as his schooling to complete. He told her it would be a year or two before he could contemplate such a move. Constance was not happy with his response because she considered getting him to propose to her, with the understanding he would return prior to the court deadline to marry her. With a public betrothal, she should be able to get the court to relent and stop pressuring her to accept the proposal of a local oaf.

Constance had recently been approached by the new minister of Salem Town, the Reverend Witherspoon. He was recently called to serve the congregation of the meetinghouse in the town since there had been a division between the town and the village. He had a son, aged twenty-two, and the reverend had extolled the virtues of his son to Mistress Bonner. But Constance had seen the man around town, and she thought him to be an obnoxious boor, caught up in his physical prowess, and lacking the head for business Constance would consider an asset. She had excluded him from nuptial prospects. Considering, in her opinion, the eligible males in and around Salem, the pickings were very slim indeed. So with the arrival of Jerrold, Constance suddenly had a new, viable candidate.

Somewhat similar thoughts were in the mind of the young Miss Meacham. Jerrold represented the escape she had dreamed of since the death of her mother had stifled her freedom. Matthew was sure and steady, and she considered herself all but betrothed to him. He would be a good provider, but she considered him mundane compared to this exciting newcomer. She would do nothing to endanger her relationship with Matthew unless she could be assured of Jerrold's certain interest. She had no illusions, however, of the game Constance was playing. She knew of the scarcity of eligible men in the area, and she suspected Constance would not hesitate to take Matthew from her if the need arose. She could play games, too, but was not in the same class as Constance, who was a master at "parlor games." She wanted to talk with Jerrold but saw no safe way to do so, without offending Matthew.

Jerry had his own dilemma. He was interested in Rebecca, though she was younger, and at the moment, he saw the twin dangers of these two women. He sensed interest from Hope, whom he was also interested in, but Constance was bombarding him with all sorts of innuendoes. Given his unfamiliarity with the mores of the period, he was keenly aware he may say something which to himself would seem innocuous but, in this time, may amount to a proposal of marriage. He had to weigh each word carefully, lest his off-handed remark be misconstrued by Constance, Hope, or Matthew. He thought Constance was a strikingly beautiful woman, but her demeanor was much more forward than he cared for. He understood her desire to find a husband who could rescue her from the local customs, but he was in no position to assist her in any way. He thought Hope was even more attractive, especially since her manner was not as bold. He saw the devotion Matthew showed to Hope and he didn't want to interfere, but he still felt an attraction to her which he did not feel toward Constance. It was academic in any case, as he could only gather his information, deposit it in a safe haven, and then return to his own time. Any dalliance could adversely affect history. Damn the hormones!

With a conscious effort, Jerry withdrew his interest in both young women. He remained cordial, and was attentive, but he no longer entertained any hope of developing a relationship. He could "not" have a relationship. His time here was severely limited, and he had to focus on the task he had planned.

"Mistress Meacham, would you have any family history—writings of your father's family, such as birthdates and places of birth?"

"My father has some sort of records from his father and has added to it. I believe it is in the bookcase over there." Indicating a floor-to-ceiling, built-in bookcase.

Arising from the settee, Hope moved to the bookcase and drew down a binder which she handed to Jerry. Opening the binder on the table in front of his settee, Jerry saw he was going to have difficulty reading the spidery script which filled the pages. He likewise knew he could not let them see his own handwriting. Jerry thought how nice it would be to have a copy machine or the privacy to bring out his camera. Perusing the pages of the binder, Jerry knew he could not remember all the dates and names, but he took advantage of the information he could digest. He looked at the list of children born to Jeremiah, the younger, and his first wife, Margaret Stillwell. On the list were all twelve children, with birthdates and birthplaces. All were born in Salem. The children who had died were also listed, though below, so it could be confusing. He noted one of the males was listed as Samuel. He suddenly realized he had jumped too soon! He should be visiting the area about forty years later when he could actually look for the missing lineage. He felt the color drain out of his face.

"Are you not well, Master Jerrold?" remarked Constance, with concern. Matthew and Hope looked at him.

"I just had a sudden weakness come upon me, but I feel better now."

"Perhaps the journey has been hard on you, my friend. Or is it the closeness of such a delightful companion?"

"It could be either, but I doubt it was the journey as it was not so arduous!"

Jerry knew he had been forward but hoped Constance would not take it to heart. He looked at the dark-haired young woman and saw she was aware of what had been said and was looking at him speculatively.

"Hope, my dearest friend, I am grateful for your hospitality and the attention of two handsome gentlemen, but I must return to my home. Master Jerrold, may I impose upon you to escort me home? I promise I will not keep you long, and you can return to chaperone these two."

"And whom will chaperone you, Mistress Bonner?" asked Hope, with a slightly piqued attitude.

"I am but a widow, just out of my weeds. Why would I require a chaperone?"

"Why, indeed? It would be better if you still wore your weeds, my dear friend."

"Master Jerrold is a gentleman, I am positive, and I have naught to fear from such as he."

Matthew decided to step into the conversation.

"Perhaps we could all see Mistress Bonner home, then Jerrold will always be a chaperone for us. This would be best for all concerned, I wager."

"Yes, of course!" Constance said curtly!

"Come, Constance, let us prepare for going out!"

When the ladies had left the parlor, Jerry looked at Matthew with a look of gratitude on his face.

"Thank you, Matthew. Although I find Constance appealing, I was not looking forward to being alone in her company, especially in public. If the competition for her properties is as fierce as it appears, I feel I would be immediately embroiled in the maelstrom. It is much safer to be seen in public in a group."

"Yes, I thought as much, and it is better for Hope and myself also. If you had gone, we would have had to enlist the company of one or more of her siblings, just for appearance's sake. You may not know this, but we have been invited to be Master Jeremiah's guest this night. They have quarters in the rear, which are made up for us. Hope's father is a fine gentleman and is anxious for me to begin courting his daughter. If all goes well, I will be able to announce our betrothal within a month. The wedding of our host and the miller's daughter is to take place a fortnight from now in the new meeting house. It will be performed by our new minister, the Reverend Witherspoon. I do not care for the man myself, but he is our minister, and I must put on a friendly countenance, for he will perform my wedding also. It is not common knowledge, but the reverend wishes his son to be in the competition for Mistress Bonner. We will likely see father and son this evening. There is to be a dinner party here, and a number of the social elite are invited."

"But, Matthew, I have nothing suitable to wear to such an event!"

"I know, so I took the liberty of bringing my father's best suit of clothes in my baggage. I wasn't sure the dinner was still on when we left home, but Hope has assured me it is, so we must hurry the women along, so as to afford them both the opportunity to do their primping and preening and allow us to do likewise." Matthew smiled mischievously at Jerry.

It was but a moment before the young women returned to the parlor. They had donned shawls and bonnets and were in an earnest conversation until they came into the young men's presence.

It seemed they were in the middle of an argument and had hung back from entering so as to bring the discussion nearly to a close. Upon entering, both women gave the men a glance and ceased speaking. It was obvious to the men the women were mildly agitated, possibly with each other! Hope went to Matthew and took his arm. Constance looked at Jerry, then went to him and followed Hope's lead.

chapter

8

The walk to the home of Constance Bonner was only a few blocks, and the two couples spent the time in making small talk. The women were animated in their repartee, and the men just gave them their undivided attention. At the front gate of the Bonner home, Matthew and Hope paused, while Jerry walked Constance to the doorway, which was opened by a servant, allowing Constance to bid Jerry a quick farewell, telling him she would see him that evening. Jerry rejoined the other couple and they returned to Hope's home. Upon arrival, Hope let the men see her to the foot of the stairway, and they then proceeded to the rear of the house, where Matthew, knowing his way around, led them to their quarters for the night. They found their baggage already in the room.

"What do you suppose the women were quarreling about?" asked Jerry of his companion.

"Hope told me it was about you! It seems Constance wants to embroil you in her affairs, though she has just met you. Hope is upset because she doesn't want to get a cousin, however distant, involved in the local drama. She tried to tell Constance you wouldn't be around for long and had your own life in Virginia. Constance, being Constance, considers her wants to take priority over others. She is a strong-willed woman, and I do not envy her next husband. I trust it will not be you, Master Jerrold!"

"Nay! For a certainty, it will not be I! She is beautiful, but I fear her…may I be so bold as to say…cunning. She would rule the roost, and her husband would be her lackey or else!"

"Too true! I hear rumors she had Ebenezer Bonner at her beck and call, even at his age! So, Jerrold, what will you wear for footwear? I doubt the town shoemaker could fit you on such short notice. Perhaps one of the men in this household would have something to fit. Let us go inquire!"

One of the older brothers did have shoes suitable for Jerrold, though they were not a perfect fit. Because of this, Jerry knew his feet would suffer before the evening was over. Using a basin and cloth, Jerry and Matthew washed their bodies as well as they could, then donned their clothes. Jerry realized he was used to seeing the machine sewn seams of his time, so was impressed with the hand sewn workmanship of the suit Matthew had brought for him. It fit reasonably well, but he felt odd wearing finery from the seventeenth century. When they finished dressing, Matthew took Jerry to a larger room which he supposed would be a ballroom or a large dining room. It was configured for the latter, and the table arrangement would seat about thirty people. Out of habit, Jerry asked if he could assist in any way and was looked at oddly. Matthew clued him in to the local etiquette.

"I suppose you have no domestic servants in Virginia, sir? I know it is not the case, so why do you proffer your assistance? At my home, we all work together, but in a household such as this, the domestics do all household tasks. Of course, Hope assists in the kitchen, so as to learn the skill required to feed her family if she were to marry a man such as myself. I doubt, however, if any of the highborn women of Salem have ever lifted a pan or spoon, and would be unable to wash or sew for their family. I am grateful Hope was raised by a mother and father who do not let their children be idle."

"Yes, I was raised to work around the house with my parents and siblings. We, personally, have no servants, but there are those of the aristocracy who do, and I find that type of privileged children to be willful and selfish. When do the other guests begin to arrive?"

"I imagine some of the cronies of the two Jeremiahs are here, even now, partaking of spirits from the wine cellar! Do you fancy a glass?"

"Thank you, no, sir! I promised my parents to abstain from strong spirits, and I have no head for such things. I fear I would make a fool of myself if I should imbibe!"

"Well, then, shall we go to the parlor, to await the guests our own age?"

Following Matthew to the parlor, Jerry saw there were already a half dozen people in the room. Hope was the hostess, and as such, she was making the rounds of the various small groups. Matthew led Jerry to one group and introduced him to the members. One of the men Jerry met was introduced as Roger Witherspoon. Jerry took note of the man's condescending manner and the breadth of his chest and shoulders. This was the reverend's son, of course, and he saw immediately why Matthew was not a proponent of his courtship of Constance Bonner. Some of the others were young men who may or may not have designs on Constance since the matter was not discussed. Jerry did see, when Constance swept into the room, the interest shown in many of the eyes of the men. Not all were calculating. Some were slightly concealed worship of her beauty. These, of course, were the younger men, who knew they had no chance with her, as they supposed, and considered her unapproachable.

When Constance worked her way across the room, stopping at various groups to greet the members, she came to Jerry and engaged him in conversation. Jerry saw keen interest suddenly come to Roger Witherspoon. Knowing this immediately placed Jerry in the camp of the competitors, he was on his guard. Constance had not acknowledged Roger yet, so he came to them, greeting Constance and ignoring Jerry at the same time. Feeling like he should leave the two alone, he still felt obliged to stay as a support to Constance. After a minute, Constance made a point of taking Jerry's arm and telling Roger she had to greet some of the newest arrivals. She walked away from Roger, who looked miffed.

"Thank you, Master Jerrold, for not leaving me with that boor! He has such a high opinion of himself and would have me swoon for him. I would consider it a boon if you remained close to me, so as to discourage being accosted by other distasteful scoundrels."

"But, Mistress Bonner, if I were to monopolize you, others may think I have a leg up toward courting you, which cannot be the case, as you know. I would not have you accosted, however, so if you find yourself in the presence of a gentleman you consider worthy, please indicate it, so I may withdraw."

"I shall! May I call you Jerrold? I feel I may be familiar with you, as you are dear Hope's cousin, and she is such a sweet friend. I should warn you though, I have found very few men who I would consider worthy of courting me, present company excepted, and Matthew, of course!"

"Ah, Mistress Bonner, you honor me, and you turn my head with your praise. Matthew is a good man, but alas, he is all but betrothed. If not for my cousin, I would lend my support if my friend were to attempt to compete!"

"Fie, sir! All this talk about competition! But for truth, there are not so many as would make me a good husband. I fear the court's time limit will find me still a grieving widow, and they will turn me out of my home, selling it and my late husband's other properties from under me!"

"I can understand your consternation, as to being pressed for time in matters which should be taken slowly. Choosing a mate is not a task one should undertake pell-mell."

"So true! I see you understand my plight perfectly!"

As the two stood conversing, Hope announced they should proceed to the dining room. Jerry stayed with Constance, noticing Hope was keeping an eye on them. Matthew escorted Hope, and as they entered the dining room, each was directed to an assigned seat. Jerry was relieved to find he was not seated beside Constance but sat on Hope's left side, with Matthew on her right. The seat to Jerry's left was soon filled by a tall, nearly gaunt gentleman who could be none other than the Reverend Witherspoon. Introducing themselves, Jerry could sense why Matthew was not fond of this man. Making small talk, Jerry mentioned he had met the reverend's son. This gave the man the opening he needed to begin his testimonial of his son's virtues. Jerry wondered why since he was only here a short time. It was as though the reverend was his son's campaign manager, and he was either running for some office or thought Jerry might be able to put in a good word with someone else, presumably Constance!

Assuming the seating arrangements had been assigned by Hope, Jerry noted her friend had been seated far from Roger Witherspoon, but also from Jerry. She was seated between two young men in their early to midtwenties. They were already vying for the attention of the young widow, and Jerry could see Constance was enjoying playing them against each other. About half of the dinner guests were young people, and, of course, the immediate family, though the preteen members were being given dinner in the kitchen. The remainder of the diners were acquaintances of the two Jeremiahs. Most were men, but half a dozen were older women, presumably wives. Noticing a striking brunette down the table, he realized whom she must be as she was sitting on the right side of the younger Jeremiah. This would be Mistress Deborah Browne, his fiancée. In awe of her young beauty, Jerry reminded himself he may be one of her direct descendants on his mother's side, depending on which child of the younger Jeremiah he descended from. Was his (many greats) grandmother Margaret Stillwell or Deborah Browne? He once more chastised himself for a fool in that he chose to jump to this time when it really should have been some forty years later. He could still record what he could find in this time, which could help corroborate what he already knew. He felt he had to jump once more, but that would take additional planning.

Dining in the seventeenth century was an interesting experience. Jerry took his lead in table manners from his fellow diners. Noting the older women were hearty eaters, he saw the younger women barely touched their plates, concentrating on the social aspects of being in such a group. He supposed the light appetites of the young women could be one of two things—concern for keeping their figure or presuming they could always catch a snack later, gave their undivided attention to the table talk. The meal itself was mostly meat (wild game such as venison, wild turkeys, and wild pig), cooked on spits or roasted in ovens, with various side dishes which appeared to be root foods, such as parsnips, turnips, and carrots. Of course, no pasta was present, and he saw no potatoes. Breads were served, and since this was a seaport, shellfish abounded, as was fish, in chowder form. Beverages were wines, ales, and ciders. Jerry drank very little, as he needed to keep his wits about himself. Sampling most of the dishes, Jerry filled himself without eating too much of any one thing. It was quite a meal, and it lasted for nearly two hours, as people ate and talked, then ate more and talked more. It was a social event to be sure. As the meal wound down and the diners were becoming sated, young Jeremiah arose and made the announcement of his wedding, toasting his bride-to-be. Many already knew, but he was making it an official proclamation. Mistress Browne smiled widely, though her future husband was much older. This was a normal occurrence, so no one seemed concerned.

Fortunately for Jerry, Reverend Witherspoon concentrated on conversing with the person to his left. Only a few times did he engage Jerry in conversation, and each time, he came across as pompous. In his mind, Reverend Witherspoon thought himself the spiritual conscience of the community and felt it his duty to ensure the exaltation of all citizens of Salem. He noted the person to the reverend's left showed relief whenever the minister turned in Jerry's direction.

When the two Jeremiahs got up from the table, the other diners slowly followed suit and trailed the men out of the dining room and into the parlor. There were not seats enough for everyone, but most seemed content to stand around in small groups. It was at this point the Reverend Witherspoon and his son announced their departure, making a production of doing so. Jeremiah had escorted his fiancée to a prominent seat, allowing the guests to pay their respects and congratulate the prospective bride. Conversation was taking place all around the parlor in many small groups. Being a large room, it was not crowded, and the acoustics were very good. Glancing at Constance, as she fended off the advances of her two dinner companions, she looked to him to perform his rescue act once more. Hoping he would not cause a stir, he escorted her to a seat next to Hope, who had Matthew on her right hand. This left Jerry with the chair to his left vacant. He wondered who would choose to sit beside him, but Constance engaged him in conversation.

"Jerrold, do you dance in Virginia? The Calvinists do not allow dancing, and I miss it. In Boston, my late husband, may he rest in peace, would take me dancing, but he would have my poor feet simply throbbing, as he seemed to dance on them more than the floor."

"Yes, we do dance, uh, Constance, if I may be so bold?"

"Yes, of course. We must become fast friends while you are in our city!"

Sensing someone sitting next to him, he turned and saw it was his younger cousin, Lydia. He greeted her and, being his gregarious self, engaged her in conversation as though she were an adult. He was unaware of the thrill this gave her. Being nearly fourteen, Lydia had resigned herself to sitting beside some older man or spinster, but now, sitting next to a handsome young man, albeit a cousin, made her feel like something wanted to burst within herself. She felt giddy, and at the same time shy, unable to speak. Attempting to draw her out, Jerry began asking her questions about herself and her life. He eventually realized the impact he was having on Lydia and felt tender toward this young cousin, wanting to make her feel grown-up. He did not want to ignore Constance, on his other side, but she was earnestly engaged in conversation with Hope and Matthew.

At a propitious point in his conversation with Lydia, Jerry excused himself and approached young Jeremiah to wish the betrothed couple well. He was introduced to Mistress Browne, and as they talked, Jerry had to again fabricate responses to questions about life in Virginia. Considering the law of averages, Jerry thought it only a matter of time before he was asked a question by someone who knew it to be a falsehood. He dreaded the prospect! Luckily, Deborah Browne was not that person, so he regaled her with some of the same information he had already given to others, wondering if this was how urban legends perhaps began! All the time he was talking to Jeremiah and his intended, Jerry noted Lydia could not take her eyes from him. In the vernacular of his day, Jerry thought "it was cute!" forgetting fourteen was not too young to be betrothed in colonial times. Being oblivious, he nonetheless did not encourage his young cousin. All too soon, the dinner party came to an end, and the guests were wished well as they took leave of their hosts and hostesses. Constance left in the company of her two ardent supporters of the evening.

Hope's father escorted his fiancé home, and her grandfather quickly retired to his room. The other family members had preceded the adults to their bedchambers. Being late, Matthew and Jerry saw Hope and Lydia to the foot of the stairway to the upper rooms, then the young men went to their room in the rear of the home. Once in the room, the two men talked for a few moments about the evening as they dressed for bed. The room contained what Jerry estimated was equivalent to a double-sized bed from his time, but it seemed shorter. The mattress was thin but soft, so he sunk into it and sleep overtook him quickly.

In the morning, both young men roused themselves from their bed and dressed in their traveling attire. On their way to the kitchen, they were met by Hope and Lydia. Jerry asked for permission to copy some names and dates from the book he had been reading the day before. Thinking he might get a chance to use his camera, it was not to be, for Lydia volunteered to take him to the parlor and provided him with pen and paper. As he waited for her to leave, he pretended to be making his choice of what he wanted to transcribe. Instead of leaving, Lydia asked if she could act as scribe, which he quickly accepted, so as to keep her from seeing his twentieth century penmanship. Inwardly pleased to be in his company, Lydia happily wrote down everything Jerry dictated to her. During this, they talked, and in so doing, Jerry finally found out it was late March of 1692. At last, he knew "when" he was! Soon, he had all the information he felt he needed, so he asked Lydia if he could get something to eat. With almost a giggle, his young cousin ushered him into the kitchen where they met Matthew and Hope. The girls had eaten earlier, but each seemed to enjoy watching the young men make a meal of what was available in the kitchen.

Matthew told the other three of his need to visit the wheelwright shop he had inherited to check on business there. Jerry expressed a desire to see a little of Salem Town. Hope and Lydia volunteered to be Jerry's guide, and it was agreed they would meet back at the house at noontime. While Matthew saddled his horse, Hope had a hostler harness a horse to their carriage. Asking Hope to drive the carriage, he said she knew where to go, and he did not, but he was afraid they would see he had never driven a carriage before. So while Matthew went toward the village, the other three began their tour of the town. Jerry asked about the waterfront and mentioned he had heard of the Turner Mansion, even in Virginia. He was taken to both places, though the mansion was very near the harbor, so it was really "on the way!" The mansion looked very different from the pictures he had seen on the internet, and he had to remind himself of the many changes the house had undergone throughout its life. He asked to get out of the carriage and walk around the neighborhood. Surreptitiously, he brought his camera out and took pictures of the mansion and also of the young cousins. Being glad he did not have to look through a viewfinder, he hoped each picture would turn out well. Meanwhile, he was on the lookout for a likely place to cache his documents if he had the chance. Being in the presence of Jerry, Hope, and Lydia were ebullient.

Hope, on her part, was happy to be with Jerry, though she knew Matthew would be her steadfast husband. It was just the fact Jerry was exciting and handsome. Aware of her younger sister's interest in their cousin, it surprised her to find it did not engender jealousy for the most part. She knew she couldn't have both men, and she knew Lydia was at the age she would soon be looking toward finding a husband. Though cousins, the relativity was so distant, as to be nonexistent. Imagining Lydia winning the heart of Jerry gave her a pang in her own, for two reasons—Lydia would have Jerry and secondly, she would probably travel to Virginia to be with him, and Hope would miss her younger sister. Lydia, on the other hand, had no idea Hope was attracted to Jerry, and she had to consciously keep from fawning over him. Jerry was attentive to both young women, like an older brother! He thought both of them were attractive, but he also remembered the kiss he had from Rebecca, Matthew's sister, who was nearer to marrying age than Lydia. Reminding himself about changing history, he was adamant about not becoming involved.

Morning passed quickly, and soon it was time to return to the Meacham house. Leaving the carriage with the hostler, the three made their way into the house and found Matthew waiting for them in the parlor. Seeing the adoring looks Lydia was giving Jerry, he let any feelings of jealousy over Jerry and Hope die. He listened to their remarks of the tour of the town and reminded Jerry of their need to get on their way. Hope had left instructions for the kitchen staff to make up a lunch for the two men, to be consumed on the road, so she retrieved it from the kitchen and joined the other three young people at the stable. Lunch had been packed in two bundles, so each was placed in the bags on the back of the saddles. Hope also gave Jerry the letter her grandfather had written to his sister. Soon, all was ready, so the men took their leave. Jerry thanked his cousins for their hospitality and bowed over the hands of each girl, touching his lips to the back of their hand, hoping this was proper etiquette for this time and place. The girls blushed and giggled, then each embraced Jerry, since he was a cousin after all. Matthew drew Hope off to the side and spoke to her, then gave her a light kiss on the cheek. Lydia impulsively bussed Jerry's lips, then stepped back blushing!

"Please return to us, cousin. Write to me, er us, to let us know of your journey home, and then I will write you of any news from Salem."

"Thank you, once more, Lydia. I will see what I can do." Mounting their horses, the two men rode away from the Meacham home. Looking back, Jerry saw both young women waving at them, so he returned the gesture.

Lunch was eaten as they rode, and each was lost in their own thoughts. Jerry wondered what would become of each of the members of the Meacham family. It amazed him to think of the difference between actually seeing his ancestors and the sketchy knowledge he had from seeing the family genealogy. He wished for the time and opportunity to follow this family by living among them for the next three hundred years but knew it was folly. He felt kinship, and possibly more for his cousins, and knew if he possibly could, he would have to travel to a time in their future to get the needed information. He wondered what Hope and Lydia would be like in forty years. Old women to be sure, but possibly already dead and buried, with maybe orphan children left for others to raise. What kind of man would Lydia marry or Rebecca Lloyd? How would the marriage of Hope and Matthew work out? Thinking he would be content to just be a voyeur and chronicler of their various lives, he was deep in thought when Matthew broke into them.

"Jerrold, I have been loath to say anything, but all is not well in this place. There are many feuds between various families, and the church is sometimes overbearing and demanding of their parishioners. The Calvinist influence is strong, and even the banal dinner party we had last night will cause the Meacham family to be castigated by Reverend Witherspoon. He will say it was hedonistic for such an ostentatious thing to take place. In the past, there have been accusations of witchcraft in the surrounding counties, and a few unfortunates have been found guilty and put to death. Now, in our vicinity, we have had a few persons accused, and there are some in prison awaiting trial. There seems to be a sickness of the mind which permeates certain souls, and reason has fled in some quarters. People whom I grew up knowing have distanced themselves from the congregation, and they are suspect. I have told no one about how I found you—without clothes, in the wilderness, lest they accuse you of being a warlock come from hell. I realize you would like to visit your relations more often, and I must caution you to not mix in local affairs. I fear Constance may be accused because some want her property. The local government, I fear, is not above such larceny. If you were staying, I would ask you to court Constance in order to intervene on her behalf. If she were to marry you, there would be much grumbling, and you would not be a popular man, but she would have someone to act as protector. I fear, though, certain people may try to accuse you since you are a stranger and have no real ties. So I would advise you to visit quickly and return to the safety of Virginia."

"But what of you, Matthew? Are you, your family, and Hope's family safe from this hysteria?"

"No one can be sure, but we have always acted neutral and have kept our own counsel about controversial matters. We are minor players, and no one seems to have an axe to grind with us."

"I would like to visit my relations again, but if things are as dire as you say, then I must not tarry. I have met them and carry a missive from Master Jeremiah to his ailing sister, so I suppose you could say my mission is fulfilled. Perhaps I could sail from Salem to Boston and be out of harm's way. I could once more take my leave of my family on my way to the harbor. Do you feel like returning so soon to Salem?"

"I took the liberty of inquiring into outbound ships, heading to either Boston, New York, or farther south. There are a few traveling as far as Boston, but for other destinations, none soon. I would not have you travel overland, as I would not have you set upon once more and possibly lose more than your possessions. As to my returning to Salem, I would ride there each day, if I could, to spend more time with Hope. I'm sure you understand."

"I do, and I am happy for you and my cousin. I wish only the best for you!"

"Thank you, Jerrold. I confess I had thoughts of jealousy to see her in your company."

"Ah, my friend, she is a beautiful young woman for truth. And though I envy you, I would not vie for her. I only hope to find someone like her when I am in a position to court a wife. Here am I, far from my home, with only borrowed clothing. No prospects and not even funds for my passage to Boston! What could I offer any woman? If I were in a position to woo a wife, I would pursue Mistress Bonner, perhaps, or my younger cousin Lydia, or even (and I beg your pardon!) your sister Rebecca! These are all fair maidens, and I just tell you this to demonstrate my ability to choose a fiancé without competing with you."

"Jerrold, I can only say I wish you could tarry here, as I find your friendship fast and true. I am startled by your admission of attraction to my sister, but I must agree she is ripe and soon should wed. I could do worse than you for a brother-in-law. But as I know you must leave, we will speak of this no more. We must make plans to get you away before anything untoward occurs. As to your passage, I suggest we speak to your cousin, Jeremiah, the younger."

As the two companions resumed their journey to Middleton, they continued to plan. Arriving at his unfinished home, Matthew and Jerry unsaddled their mounts and led them to the Lloyd family's home, where they were turned over to the younger brothers for return to their pasture. While at the Lloyd family's home, Jerry noticed Matthew kept an eye on him and Rebecca, just as her mother was doing. Being careful to spread his attentions around, Jerry tried to dispel any concerns of impropriety. After supper, Matthew, his mother, and Jerry sat together discussing the issues Matthew had told Jerry about. Mistress Lloyd, whose first name was Margaret, was a very astute woman whose life on the farm had not dulled her sense of community and religious politics. Having dealt with these things longer than Matthew, her insights were valuable. Though she seldom traveled to the marketplace in the village, she still had enough contacts with neighbors, so her grasp of the local situation was up to date.

"The Parrish girl and her cousin have gotten attention by their antics, and they will probably continue to dramatize the matter. If I were their parents, a switch would straighten them right out! I fear the devil, but these smacks of man-made hysterics. I cannot say it publicly, but I just shake my head at the goings-on. Mistress Goode and Mistress Osborne are no more witches than I am, but I better not talk too loudly or I may end up in gaol. This plays right into the hands of the ambitious Reverend Parrish, and mark my words, if Reverend Witherspoon had young children, I vow he would suddenly have them in fits, with more accusations of witchcraft! I pray we may ride out this storm."

"I know, Mother, so do I! But what should we do about Jerrold? Do we ship him out, let him stay longer, or let him find his way back to his home alone?"

Before Margaret Lloyd could respond, Jerry interjected. "I appreciate your concerns for me, but I think you have to be concerned for your own and Hope's family. I could find my way, and I know now to stay clear of any Indians. If things are as bad as you believe, I think you should be very careful and try to stay on everyone's good side if that is possible!"

"You are a good man, Jerrold. We will talk of this further, but I feel we must retire. Mother, we must take our leave."

Saying good night to the other family members, Jerrold made sure he paid as much attention to Jonathan as he did Rebecca. In a low voice, he told Rebecca he was not going to the river this evening. She blushed slightly and smiled.

"Such a pity, for I must fetch water for the morning."

On their short walk home, Jerry made a decision which could ruin everything he had accomplished, but he felt it would facilitate his returning to his own time without resorting to more subterfuge.

"Matthew, do you feel you can trust me?"

"I feel like I can, sir! What is it?"

"Are you superstitious? Are you open-minded enough to accept things though they may not make sense to you?"

"I do not believe in witches if that is what you mean! I feel I am as open-minded as you are, sir!"

"What would you say if I told you I was not from Virginia but was still one of Hope's relatives?"

"Well, I suppose one could be from somewhere other than where he has told others he was from. If you are not from Virginia, where are you from?"

"I know it is hard to believe, but I am from someplace far to the west of here."

"What is far west of here? I have heard nothing about exploration, except there are many great rivers, lakes, and a great wilderness. What are you saying, Master Jerrold?"

Jerry faltered, unsure if he should reveal his secret, even in elementary ideas.

"Matthew, I don't know if you can comprehend what I am going to tell you. I don't want you to get hysterical and drive me out possibly to the witch hunters!"

"I would not do that, but I have felt something was strange about you ever since I met you, and it was not just because you were not from these environs. Is this something which could hurt me or my family? If it would, you must not tell me, but you must leave."

"It will hurt no one, but you may think me insane, or perhaps yourself, for listening to me. I must tell you, so I can do what needs to be done to complete my journey. Should I proceed?"

"Let us get to the shelter of my home. I would feel more secure there."

Upon entering his home, Matthew lit a fire in the fireplace and put a water kettle on. Then, looking around the room, he seemed to draw strength from his belongings and things familiar.

"Master Jerrold, I await your tale. If it is something dreadful, I pray you to take care with me."

"Matthew, this is not dreadful, at least I believe not, but it may be hard for you to believe or understand. What it is will not hurt you, I promise! The land west of here is vast, much vaster than most people believe. France and Spain have explored it much more than England. Sir Francis Drake sailed south and around this and another continent and visited the area I am from in the late 1570s."

He paused for a moment to let what he had said penetrate Matthew's swirling mind.

"That is just history to you and I. Now, what is history to me, but the future for you, let me tell you briefly. Within a hundred years, the colonists in this new world will fight to be independent of England. There will be a new nation formed, and it will become one of the greatest nations on this earth!"

Jerry paused once more. Matthew looked to be in shock.

"How do you know this? Are you a seer, a prophet, or a demon?"

Chuckling, Jerry continued. "I am none of those. Science in the world you know is not very advanced. As time passes, it will make great discoveries and progress to do many wonderful things which you cannot even comprehend at this time. I am, in fact, a university student, and I am related to the Meacham family through my mother. The truth is, I am from a time hundreds of years in your future. It is just starting to happen, but science has developed the ability to travel through time. I think I am the first to do so. I am about ten generations into the future, and both Jeremiahs are in my lineage. That is why I am here to discover which of Jeremiah, the younger's children I am descended from. Does this sound frivolous to you? All this just to investigate family lineage?"

Matthew was awestruck, and it took him a moment to speak.

"Uh, I am not sure I believe what you are saying. Because I believe you would not willfully deceive me, I am trying to get my mind to understand. You tell me you know the future of this country? You know what will occur in this land? Please…tell me if I marry Hope, and do we have children?"

"My friend, I am not all knowing, even being from the future. If I knew everything, I would not need to investigate my lineage. I can tell you that your family and Hope's family are not involved with the witchcraft troubles coming up. There will be many hanged as witches and more imprisoned, but none of them are people I have met. Reverend Parrish is an historical figure, as is his daughter and niece. As to you and Hope, I know nothing. The records available in my time do not list Hope's marriage or posterity. The Meacham family are not mentioned in history, except for their service in the military when the colonists fight England for independence."

"When does the war take place? Do I fight for or against England?"

"It will be called the War for Independence or Revolutionary War. Most colonists fought against England. I do know you will be too old to fight, as it begins over eighty years in the future. I have no knowledge of how long you live. It would not be good for me to tell you if I knew. It is not right for man to know his destiny! How do you feel? Are you sure you can understand what I am telling you?"

"It is all like I am dreaming, but we are both awake. I have known you long enough to believe you are not insane or at least I am pretty sure you are not!"

"Matthew, I discovered after I arrived I had made an error and should have arrived forty years later. I don't know if I will be successful, but I plan on trying to come back here in forty years."

"But we will both be almost sixty! How are you going to do that?"

"Matthew, I know it is difficult for you to understand, but if I do, you will be almost sixty, but I will still be my present age. If I do come back, and you still live here, I will visit you, but I don't want to cause a riot, so I will come in disguise, so no one who knows me now will recognize me. I will reveal myself to you only. Do you understand what I am saying?"

"Yes, but I am finding it harder to believe. I feel as though I am in my cups!"

"I understand it is not easy to comprehend. I think I should leave soon since you may not act normal around me and other people. Before I go, I want to show you something to prove I am who I claim."

Jerry pulled the camera out of his shirt and showed it to Matthew. Turning it on, the LCD screen lit up, and Jerry scrolled through the pictures he had taken. Stopping on the one he took of Lydia and Hope, he showed it to Matthew.

"What kind of sorcery is this? What have you done to Hope and Lydia?"

"I have done nothing. Just think of this as how we paint portraits in the future. The women are totally unharmed, and they did not know I did this. I would like to take a portrait of you also. I would like one of your whole family, but I cannot reveal this to anyone else. I would be accused of witchcraft for sure! When I do your portrait, it will just take a second, and there will be a bright flash, as though gunpowder has been ignited. Do not be alarmed!"

Aiming the camera at Matthew and framing him in the display,

Jerry pressed the switch and the camera flashed. Matthew jumped and ducked down momentarily. When he saw he was unharmed, he asked to see his portrait. Jerry switched modes and showed him the image. Matthew could only stare at his likeness, as though he were looking into a mirror and see his image greatly reduced and immobile.

"It is truly amazing, Jerrold! This future must be a wonderful place."

"It has its problems, just like the present. I could drive you mad with some of the things men have done. I surely wish I could get a portrait of your family, but I fear they would not keep it quiet."

"Perhaps you would settle for just a portrait of Rebecca?" Matthew said, smiling at Jerry. Jerry blushed.

"I may want one of her more than your brothers, but I am sure you understand."

"Indeed, I do. Perhaps we can get Rebecca to pose for you, and you can do her portrait as secretly as you did for Hope and Lydia?"

"You would conspire with me to get Rebecca's portrait?"

"It could harm no one, and you would have a keepsake of your visit. Now, how could we accomplish this? When did you plan on leaving?"

The two men talked into the night, both keyed up too much to sleep. They did undress but kept up their conversation. Matthew kept asking questions about the future, and Jerry could only answer his questions in general terms and was circumspect in his information.

In the morning, Matthew and Jerry went to breakfast and then returned to labor on his house. By asking Rebecca to bring the men their noon meal, so they would not have to leave their labors to eat at the family home, Matthew set the men's plan in motion. During the morning, the two accomplished quite a bit on the house, and Matthew was confident he would have two extra rooms ready by summer, with the extra help Jerry was adding. He knew Jerry was going to leave within the week, however, so they did the things which required two persons. If Matthew needed assistance after Jerry left, then Jonathan would be pressed into service. Finally, the time came for their meal, and Rebecca was seen coming down the road with a basket on her arm. As she got nearer, Jerry went inside, and Matthew met her, taking the basket from her.

"Stop right there, Rebecca! In this light, you look so lovely, and I vow you would make a lovely portrait in that pose! Hold your hands thus. Now, lift your chin and smile at me. Yes, that is what I think would make a wonderful portrait if we could get a painter to visit."

"Oh, tosh, brother! Such flirtation should be saved for your betrothed. I am immune to such from you, but if Master Jerrold should say such things, I would perhaps swoon."

At that second, Jerry came out the door.

"If I were to say what things, Mistress Rebecca?" Rebecca blushed furiously!

"Oh, nothing, sir!"

"Well, in that case, what wonderful treats have you brought us?"

Jerry looked at Matthew and winked. The pictures had been taken! Jerry only wished he had had aid in taking pictures of Hope, Lydia, and even Constance.

While the men ate, Rebecca looked over the work they had done and finally sat while the meal was finished. She kept looking at Jerry, and both men knew it. When the basket was empty, Matthew handed it to Rebecca. Both men thanked her, then Matthew gently scolded her.

"Be gone, woman, and let men get back to work."

His smile robbed the statement of offense, and Rebecca laughed gaily as she headed toward home. Turning once, she gave Jerry another smile.

Working steadily and skillfully, Matthew and Jerry made even more progress, and when it came time to quit for the day, the two men stood surveying their work.

"Jerrold, I am truly grateful for all the assistance you have afforded me. As I see the house enlarging so quickly, I feel like my life is on the verge of changing quickly also. It has been only a week since I found you, but I feel a kinship which I am not happy to be losing. I will surely miss you! Other than my family, I have been close to no one. I pray I am still alive when next you visit."

"I feel the same, Matthew. I have friends back in my time, but we have shared many things which I have never shared with anyone, except perhaps my family and the professor who helped me get here. I hope I find all in your family and my relatives well when I return."

"When will you leave, Master Tanner?"

"I fear it must be soon. I hoped to visit Salem again, but it would not further my mission, so I have decided not to do so. I feel I must leave tomorrow after supper. I pray you not tell your family until the next morning. I do not consider leave-taking pleasurable."

"I understand. Is there nothing you wish to speak of to Rebecca?

She will be heartbroken, I am sure."

"What can I speak of to her? If I were just leaving for a short time and then returning to stay, there may be things to say. I fear my heart will be heavy also."

"Let us go to supper, my friend!"

All was well with the Lloyd family and their guest that evening. All the children had lost their shyness around Jerry and treated him like another older brother. Games were played, and there were sweets enjoyed. Matthew knew his mother was astute, but it still surprised him when she drew him aside and looking her oldest son in the eyes, she said, "Master Tanner is leaving, is he not?"

"He is, Mother. Tomorrow night, after supper, he will take his leave from my house. He says he will return, but I fear it will be some time before he does."

"He is a pleasant young man, and I know he has an adoring mother somewhere. He is strange in many ways, as though he is not quite comfortable in his clothes and in the life we lead. Do you know something?"

"Yes, my very wise and knowing parent! Sometime, I will try to explain the things he has told me. It is difficult for me to fathom all the things he says. I know but one thing—he wishes no harm to anyone, least of all you, your children, nor his relatives in Salem. He is a good and true friend, and as you know, I have had none."

"Yes, I see that, and I perceive he is a loving person. The only thing I fear is the affect his leaving will have on your sister. I feel she sets her cap for him despite his open professing of only a short stay. There are so few men to choose from, and she despairs, even now, of becoming a spinster. But at her age, I also felt the same!"

"Rebecca will find a husband, even if I have to take her to Boston or New York. I will not have my sister pine her life away!"

"You are much like your father, Matthew, which makes me miss him more keenly. Let us rejoin the family."

Upon their return to Matthew's home, they discussed the labors of the next day and what they hoped to accomplish. Jerry knew Matthew wanted to talk about things which would happen in his future, but the young colonial was too polite to bring up the subject. Finally, Jerry gave him a quick overview of some of the history he could recall. Telling him about the Revolutionary War and the organization of the colonies into states and a little about the government which would come about due to the winning of independence from England took much of the time. Touching also on the westward migration, he told a little of what some of Jeremiah's own descendants would do to help colonize the western lands. Keeping all information vague, he feared the knowledge could possibly harm Matthew if he were to speak of it, amid the present witch-hunt hysteria. Matthew did ask Jerry if he had a fiancé in his own time, and Jerry assured him he did not. Finally, both became quiet and eventually sleep overcame them.

Upon arising the next morning, both men already anticipated the sadness of Jerry's impending departure. In the short week Jerry and Matthew had spent together, a natural affinity had formed. Jerry wanted to give his friend something to remember him by, so he went and dug up his hidden cache. Bringing it into Matthew's home, he took one of the food bars and opened the foil wrapper. Having watched Jerry do so, Matthew was intrigued by the brightness of the foil, but when Jerry broke the food bar in two and gave half to Matthew, the colonial was confused. Jerry took a bite of his half and chewed. Hesitantly, Matthew followed suit. As the sweet taste of the bar exploded in Matthew's mouth, his eyes grew wide, and he smiled broadly.

"So this is what you eat in your time? It is quite good, but wouldn't you tire of this taste?"

Grinning at his companion, Jerry said, "This is just a small bit of what we eat. We eat all the things you do, plus much more! We eat meat of all varieties—beef, lamb, pork, chicken, turkey, fish. There are vegetables and fruits in my time you have never heard of, but I am sure you would like! This would usually be a 'snack,' or small meal, for when we are out walking or hunting or relaxing and do not want to cook a meal. We have storage boxes which keep things cold or even frozen, as though they were left out in freezing weather. There are many things in my time which we take for granted, but which people living now cannot even comprehend. I want you to have these other bars. There is nearly a dozen, but you must keep them hidden from others, or at least unwrap them, because this wrapper is very advanced and could be interpreted as witchcraft. I fear to give you more of which I have, as they could not be explained to the people of this time."

"If you cannot give these things to me, could you at least reveal them to me?"

"I can do that! Here, let me show you!"

Although he didn't have much more to show, Jerry unveiled each item as if it were a precious possession. First, he showed Matthew the plastic ziplock bags. He imagined the colonial would think nothing of such a mundane item in Jerry's time, but Matthew made much of the nearly transparent bags with their air and watertight closures. Postulating a dozen uses he could make of them, his longing for them nearly bordered on avarice. Next, came the first aid kit, which fascinated Matthew with the adhesive bandages and cloth tape. He was already familiar with ointments, but the tube was new to him, and the purported healing properties of the antibacterial salve sounded wonderful to him. Jerry was so tempted to leave the kit behind but was fearful lest someone see the Band-Aids or if someone were to be saved by the salve, which could upset history. In the end, he pressed the tube of ointment into Matthew's hand with the admonishment to use it sparingly, only when in dire need, and above all, only in secret. Matthew took his gifts and put them in a cache he had built into an inner wall. The foil wrappers and tube would protect the precious articles from deterioration. With that task completed, the two went to breakfast.

At the completion of the morning meal, Matthew again asked if Rebecca would deign to bring dinner to his house. She agreed. Once Matthew and Jerry returned to their building task, they worked with a will, attempting to do as much as possible that day! As noontime approached, Matthew told Jerry he was going to take a walk after they ate, giving he and Rebecca some time alone. The look passing between the two men had unspoken meaning. Matthew was sensitive to the feelings between the two, but at the same time, he was silently asking Jerry to be proper and tender with his sister. On Jerry's part, his look said he would be a gentleman and not take advantage. As they looked up, they saw Rebecca and her sister Rhoda carrying the basket between them as they came toward the house. Matthew told Jerry quietly that at the proper time, he would invite Rhoda to go for a walk with him.

Dinner was a simple but plentiful meal, and the four shared what was in the basket, unlike the day before when Rebecca had eaten at home. They ate in the shade of a tree in front of the house and made small talk about a number of subjects. True to his word, upon completing the meal, Matthew got up and asked Rhoda if she would accompany him for a walk to settle their meal. Looking at Rebecca and Jerry, she saw the pleading look from her sister, so she accepted the invitation. That said, the older brother and younger sister walked away from the house, leaving Jerry and Rebecca still sitting under the tree.

"I don't understand why he did that, but I am glad he did! This is the first time we have been alone and not down by the stream."

"Yes, and I have all my clothes on, and I am not wet or cold!" Jerry said, as they both laughed.

"You knew Matthew was going to leave us alone, did you not?"

"Yes. It was planned previous, but I just learned of it just before you arrived."

"Is he giving you leave to court me, I hope?"

"Nay, but not for lack of desire. You would make any man a wonderful wife."

"But not for you, I fear!" Rebecca said with a sob.

"Ah, fair, Rebecca, do not cry! You know I am not staying and may not return before you are long wed! If I were to tarry, it would be my desire to court you. I regret I cannot do so. I will sorely miss your vivacious mien."

"You speak strangely! I sometimes lack understanding of your words. I pray you are being kind."

"For a surety, I am being highly complementary, for I find you much to my liking, but I cannot partake!"

"You are leaving, are you not? And soon!"

"You are very perceptive, and you act very mature."

"I am the age most women marry, but there is no man for me, I fear."

"As I said before, give it a little time. I think your mother and brother are already looking."

"Oh, Jerrold, I shall never forget you! You gave me my first true kiss, and I feel no other man will win my heart as you have. I shall wither and die in your absence!"

Rebecca began to cry. Jerry arose and pulled her to her feet, taking her in his arms and comforting her as best he could. She continued sobbing as he made soft, soothing sounds while stroking her hair. After a minute or so, her sobs diminished. She sniffed her nose and wiped tears from her cheeks. Looking her in the eyes, Jerry leaned down and kissed each eye to take away her tears, then kissed her nose, which caused her to begin giggling quietly. By the time she looked directly at him and was smiling, he leaned to kiss her once more, but this time, he touched his lips to hers. With unaccustomed passion, Rebecca returned his kiss fervently. Amid pounding hearts and gasping breaths, the two lovers pulled back from each other with something akin to wild fear in their eyes.

"Oh, Jerrold! I feel so jumpy inside! A kiss from another man can never be that wonderful!"

"I beg your pardon, Rebecca. I should not have taken advantage of you! That kiss was a kiss for lovers and not for you and I."

"But I do love you! I knew I loved you when I first saw you!"

"We must be calm and not lose all propriety! I will not naysay your declaration of love for me, but you have to resign yourself that I am not destined to be your mate! Sweet Rebecca, I envy the man who takes you to wife. Now, calm yourself before your brother and sister return, lest they think I have ravished you in their absence."

"I shall try to be calm on the outside, but my heart is breaking inside."

"As is mine, I assure you!"

As Matthew and Rhoda came into view, Jerry and Rebecca were standing close under the tree, which had shaded their dining. Matthew looked at both and saw the anguish in his sister and the sadness in the face of his friend. The two girls gathered up the remains of dinner and started back toward their home.

"All is not well, is it?" asked Matthew.

"As well as expected, she suspects I am leaving soon and almost begged me to stay. She is certain she is destined to be a spinster, but I told her to be patient. I told her you and her mother were searching, even now, for a suitable husband who will win her heart and give her a blissful life."

"You are correct in that we are beginning to look around us to see if there be a suitable mate for her, but we cannot be certain we will find one without going farther afield. That is our problem and not yours, my friend. I trust she did not put undue pressure on you to stay?"

"No more than I put on myself! But it is folly to even contemplate such a course. I must leave! I do not belong here."

"I understand. How will you return? Should I bring my horses in and saddle them?"

"That will not be necessary. I will simply walk into the forest a short distance and signal my mentor to return me to my own time if he can. This part of our grand experiment has never been accomplished from such a time difference. If it is not successful, you may be saddled with an adopted brother who knows many things but will perchance be hanged as a witch!"

"If you cannot leave, then you will become my brother-in-law from Virginia! There will be overjoyed women in my family tomorrow! As much as I pray it could be, I know you have a mission to fulfill, so I wish you every success."

"Thank you, Matthew! I know you feel so in your heart. I could do worse than becoming a member of your family, but my own mother and father will mourn my loss, and my professor may be charged with what amounts to witchcraft in my own time!"

"So things remain the same, eh?" Matthew said, smiling.

Supper at the Lloyd family home was somber by comparison to the night before. Rhoda, Jonathan, and Daniel were oblivious of Jerry's impending departure, so it was a normal evening. The remainder had heavy hearts. Jerry made an effort to spend some time with each family member and tried to refrain from being too close to Rebecca. Enjoying a quiet moment with the mother, he expressed his gratitude for her graciousness. She, in turn, thanked him for the labor he had donated to help Matthew and made a special point to thank him for being a true friend to her son. She also made an oblique comment concerning his proper relationship with her oldest daughter. When it was time to leave, Jerry shook the hands of the two younger boys, gave Rhoda an embrace, and was pulled into a motherly hug by Mistress Lloyd. Rebecca held back and followed Jerry out the door. In the darkness of the night, she flung her arms around Jerry and kissed him avidly, then ran back into the house, crying softly. As the two friends walked toward Matthew's home, the light filtering from the house was cut off as the door closed.

"I wished I could have taken portraits of your whole family but could not think of a way to do so!"

"I understand. Jerrold, I want to thank you for your help and for your friendship. I pray I may live to see you again. Forty years you say? That is a long time, and who knows where I will be or what I will be doing? If I do not see you, then I pray your quest has been worthwhile."

"In forty years, you may not even remember me. But I hope to see you also and have you tell me how the time has gone for you and your family. If you can, will you write down the family information from Hope's family and also yours? If you feel you will not last the time, would you bequeath the information to 'Jerrold Tanner' to be claimed at an undisclosed time?"

"I would be honored to do so in order to help you make all this sacrifice worthwhile."

As they came to Matthew's home, they entered and lit the candle. Everything Jerry was taking with him was already packed and waiting. Looking at each other, the two strong men suddenly embraced. This was not foreign to either, as it is the way of men who have shared things and formed a bond or for family members.

"May Godspeed, Jerrold!"

"May the Lord bless you and your family, Matthew."

Picking up his pack, Jerry walked out the door and up the road in the direction of his arrival place. Not trusting his ability to find the exact spot where he arrived, Jerry just walked a quarter mile or so off the road and set his packet down. Undressing and folding his clothes to fit in the packet and removing his boots, Jerry felt the cool breeze of the night on his naked skin. When all his possessions were inside the packet, he took one last look around. Half expecting to see someone watching, he was nonetheless struck with an overwhelming feeling of loneliness. Heartsick at the thought he may never again see his newfound friends, especially Matthew, Rebecca, and Hope, he steeled himself to proceed with his plan. Feeling inside the packet for the homing beacon, he pressed the switch to activate the device, then stood back. In the dark, he could not see the packet clearly, but he sensed it disappearing within a minute. Saying a silent prayer, he hoped at least the camera would be intact upon arrival at the lab. Taking a deep breath and uttering a prayer for himself, he felt for the subcutaneous beacon on his thigh and manipulated it into operation, then waited!

12

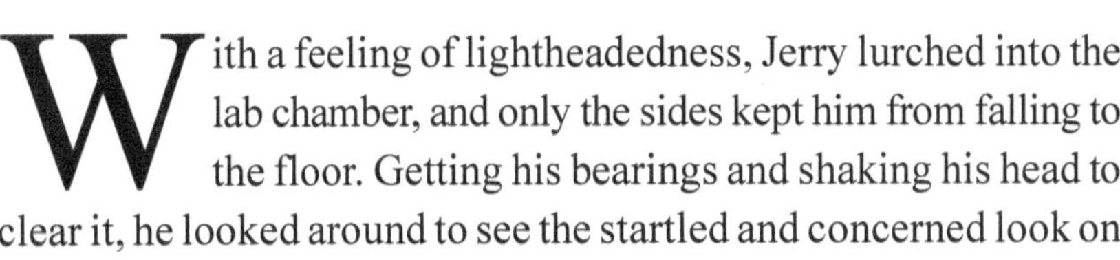

With a feeling of lightheadedness, Jerry lurched into the lab chamber, and only the sides kept him from falling to the floor. Getting his bearings and shaking his head to clear it, he looked around to see the startled and concerned look on Professor Bill Blanchard's face.

"Welcome back, Pilgrim! Are you okay? Do you need anything?"

Drawing a deep breath, then exhaling it, Jerry nodded at Bill but did not speak immediately. Stepping toward a nearby chair which had his robe draped on it, Jerry put shaking arms through the sleeves and drew it about him, belting it about his waist.

"Yeah! I'm okay! I didn't think I'd miss all the slang terms and contractions we take for granted. I tried very hard to concentrate on not using them in Salem."

"So you really made it to Salem? Massachusetts? In the sixteen hundreds?" Bill asked, anxious to hear all the details.

"Yes! Your machine worked pretty well. No! It worked wonderfully! I landed in the wilderness just east of Salem about ten miles, and I was only about eight months late on the time we aimed for. That should give you a benchmark for calibrating your time machine."

"I'm trying to come up with a fancier, more scientific name for her, but was too worried while you were gone to really concentrate. How long, objectively, did you spend in the past?"

"I was there for a week roughly. How long have I been gone from the lab?"

"I set my stop watch when you left, and I just remembered to check it! Let me look. Oh, if we subtract the last minute or two, you have been gone for three hours and forty-five minutes. I wasn't sure if time would track, or in other words, if you were there for a week, would you be absent from here for a week? We never really experimented with that. I wonder if there is a formula involved."

"That will take further investigation, and I have an idea how to do that. I want to go back!"

"What? You just got here! What've you got yourself into? Is this going to change history?"

"No, Bill, it's not like that. I don't mean 'go right back' to the same time! I mean I have to go back to the same area but about forty years later."

Talking into the wee hours, Jerry related his experiences to his professor. Having nothing to hide, he told his friend everything, even his attraction to his cousins and Matthew's sister. Bill was enthralled with everything his student told him and grilled Jerry extensively to glean as much information as he could get. About thirty minutes into their discussion, they were startled by the sudden appearance of the clothes packet in the portal. Jerry rushed over to the bundle and dug out his camera. Downloading the images, both men were thrilled with the quality of the pictures, even the ones Jerry had taken of his cousins surreptitiously. Bill agreed with Jerry's appraisal of the beauty of all three girls and was also wild about the authenticity of fresh pictures of seventeenth-century architecture. Jerry eventually got around to telling Professor Blanchard about why he needed to return to New England at a later date. Bill was not sure it was wise going to the same place. It could raise too many questions as to why he had not aged. Jerry adamantly doubted anyone would even recognize him, and if that were really a danger, he could go in some type of disguise or even have a plausible explanation, like he was the son of the original Jerrold Tanner. In forty years, it was incomprehensible anyone would remember the fine details of anyone's appearance.

Finally, they came to an agreement to allow Jerry the opportunity to return to gather additional information. He had the written information Lydia had scribed for him, but it would not hold up as an official document. The more they discussed the need for records and why, they came to the conclusion it was not important to be able to prove the authenticity of such records. The information was for Jerry's family records only, and they were not trying to claim lands or property. On the forms in the *Book of Remembrance*, there is a place to indicate the source of information, and all they had to write was family records. It would be accurate and truthful. No one would ask the details of how the data was collected! Next week would be the time of their next excursion into time travel. History was not going anywhere!

It was approaching four o'clock on Monday morning, so Jerry put his contemporary clothing on and went home. He had a class at one in the afternoon. Bill Blanchard had a class at 9:00 a.m., but there were always teaching assistants to cover such things. Bill would take to the cot he kept in his lab and leave a note for his TA, who came in at 8:00 a.m. Plans were made for the two to meet again the following Tuesday since Jerry worked at the furniture store on Monday. The mental shift, due to the time difference, had Jerry's brain in a turmoil and was enough to keep him awake until nearly 7:00 a.m. At last, he fell into an exhausted, dream-laden sleep. He missed his 1:00 p.m. class but made it to his next at three. Disorientation was still affecting him, as he brought himself back up to speed in the modern world. Realizing things had been much slower in Salem, he felt acutely the anxiety inherent with the times.

Coming home after class, Jerry went to the kitchen and was confronted by his mother. Looking him up and down, she continued with her tasks but soon turned back toward him and spoke.

"Honey, are you all right? I know you've been working really hard on your school work and also your part-time job. I hope you're not getting sick. You look thinner and tired. I heard you coming in late last night."

"Mom, it wasn't late last night but early this morning! Dr. Blanchard and I got caught up in our research and didn't quit until nearly four. He slept in his lab, so at least I got to sleep in my own bed! I expect him to look worse than me. I'm okay, Mom! Nothing's wrong, a couple good night's sleep won't cure. Don't worry, Mom."

"Your professor is a physics teacher, right? I hope you aren't messing with things that will blow up and hurt you or burn down buildings or something like that?"

"We don't do anything to cause explosions, Mom. That would be chemistry! Besides, that kind of thing is against university rules."

"Scientists do things against rules all the time!"

"Oh, Mom, don't worry! You only have to worry if I come home and you can hear me but can't see me!" Jerry teased his mother, smiling as he said it, so she knew he was fooling.

"Oh, you! If you were younger, I'd send you to your room for a while!" She sounded serious but was smiling, too.

Going to the refrigerator, Jerry searched for something to eat before he had to leave for the store. Finding some things, he remembered from last time he looked, he had to remind himself it had not been a week but just overnight. He ate some celery, cheese, and an apple. There was tuna mixed for sandwiches, so he built one for himself and put it in a sandwich bag and laid it on the counter so he could pick it up on his way out of the house. Giving his mother a peck on the cheek, he went up to his room to put on working clothes. As he left for work, he reassured his mother and said hello to his father, who was coming home as Jerry was leaving. Work was light and uneventful, for which Jerry was thankful. He was finished by ten and went right home and went to bed.

Tuesday morning was very lazy for Jerry. He lay abed until almost eight, then got up and showered. He marveled at the simple things he always took for granted. He had showered on Monday, but he was on autopilot, so it never registered on his conscious mind. But this morning, he reviewed the memories of taking baths in the cold stream in Massachusetts, using no shampoo and very primitive soap; no deodorant; no aftershave lotion. Then he went down to breakfast, and remembering the simple foods he ate while in the past made him very aware of the richness and variety of the foods he ate in his own family kitchen. Young Jerry Tanner had been sensitized by his trip to the past so he took hardly anything for granted. He had been humbled greatly, and even worse, he could not rid his heart of the ache of loneliness and emptiness. He had never been in love but imagined how he felt about Rebecca was probably pretty close to what it was like to be "in love." He also felt the pangs of missing his friend Matthew and his cousins. Thoughts even arose about what had become of Constance Bonner! Had she found a suitable husband before the courts took her late husband's properties away or had she been removed from her house and had to accept what the courts gave her from the sale? Chuckling to himself, he thought he was acting like a person addicted to soap operas, who was suddenly deprived of watching them.

Tuesday classes were mundane, and he could hardly wait until he could meet with Bill Blanchard in the lab. At last, he was able to walk over to the physics building and go the lab assigned to Professor Blanchard. When he arrived, there were a half dozen students milling about, finishing up their assignments. Patiently, he paced around the lab, noting the time portal and associated equipment were draped and placards warning dire consequences if disturbed. Catching Bill's eye, he sat at a lab station and thumbed through a textbook, waiting for the students to leave. After about twenty minutes, the lab was occupied by just Bill and Jerry.

"Well, is the weary traveler caught up on his sleep? Have you come to your senses and decided not to try such foolishness again?"

"Yes and no! Yes, I've caught up on my sleep! No, I still want to try it again!"

"Good! I'm sorry to say I'm afraid to go myself, but I'm hooked on the concept of others going for me. My main fear, however, is I may strand someone in another time, or worse, get them killed in another time. Either way, I have to explain why I have missing associates, and where are they? The authorities won't even be smart enough to ask 'when' are they!" Giving out a near hysterical giggle, Bill continued, "I could tell them to look for human remains in 'such and such' a location, and they would be about 'so many years old'!"

"Bill! You aren't going off the deep end about this, are you? I'm taking the real risks, and I've left you the letter! Of course, I can see why not having a 'corpus delicti' may leave some doubt as to the veracity of your story! Come on, Bill, it'll all turn out great, and you'll end up with the Nobel Prize in Physics!"

"More like I will end up in prison, as the girlfriend of some guy named Bubba! No, I'm okay, but all day yesterday, I had to keep trying to convince myself how my spatial/temporal utilitarian displacement linear yoke would be a boon to mankind and not a curse!"

"What? You're going to call your time machine STUDLY?"

"Uh, yeah! Pretty clever, don't you think?" Bill said, smiling, or more correctly, smirking!

"Well, I have to say you aren't getting all uptight about it if you can think up a crazy name like that!"

Looking injured, Bill said, "It's not so crazy! It's an apt name, and I just robbed some think tank geek of his commission for thinking up an acronym when this thing goes public, or at least is revealed to the military, who is paying for all my work!"

"I guess I can live with it if you can! Now, what do we have to do before our next jump? I hope my clothes will still be in style, though I think I should clean them before I go again. They may get wrinkled in the bundle, but I'd like them to not smell as badly as they did when I finished wearing them. I'm tempted to take some deodorant with me, but I don't suppose I should!"

"No, but I suppose a small container of body wash/shampoo

would not be a bad idea…something with very little scent. I don't want to ship a footlocker with you! That might be a bit hard to hide."

"Yeah, I know. I won't take as many food bars, and I will need a new tube of Neosporin. Is there a digital camera without a flash, which can take pictures in low light? I can't think of anything else I dare take with me, though some kind of weapon may come in handy."

"I don't want you killing anyone!"

"It would be purely for self-defense! I guess just a pocketknife would be enough. At least I could cut someone and maybe dissuade them a bit. Besides, it would be a tool also in case I need to cut rope or something."

"Okay, just a pocketknife. A small pocketknife, please!"

"You got it! What I really wish for is to be wearing all the clothes which would fit in for any given time. I don't want to attract attention with zippers and all that, but I don't feel good going without underwear. Commando is not my style!"

"It was probably pretty normal back then! Not everyone had the money for such frivolous finery."

"Yeah, well, you try going without underwear for a week, and you'll know how I feel!"

"I know a drama professor who claims to have done research into historical clothing. Let me check with her and see if she's done as much in-depth research as she claims. I'll talk to her tomorrow and maybe have answers for you on Thursday. Now, do we want to keep the spatial settings exactly the same? Do you want the place I sent you to or do you want the place I retrieved you from?"

"I think you better send me to the same place you sent me before. The place I left from may be settled forty years later. Also, I think I know why I couldn't find the packet when I arrived. Did you notice the packet arrived back here about thirty minutes after I did? I probably left the area before it arrived the first time. Maybe we should send it about thirty minutes before you send me. That way, it will either be waiting for me or it will arrive within a few minutes of when

I do. I'll just wait a while for it, and then I won't appear to the locals in my birthday suit. It's really embarrassing, even though it was a man and not a woman. In those days, I would have probably been pitchforked to death for being indecent! And another thing, let's try to get the time of year closer. It was pretty cold when I showed up naked!"

"Yes, my prima donna! Just kidding! I imagine it was a bit uncomfortable, both physically and esthetically. I'll also check into getting another digital camera, but no promises. I'm on a pretty tight budget. The camera you used last time was my personal camera."

"Oh. Okay! Do what you can."

Shortly thereafter, both men left and locked the lab. Jerry went home and did some research on the internet. He tried to see if he could determine what had changed, historically, between 1692 and 1732. It dawned on him to check the family genealogy to see what he could find out about where people were born and where they died. He knew the elder Jeremiah had died in Salem in 1696. The younger Jeremiah had died in Windham, Connecticut, in 1743, so Jerry would probably not see him. He was more interested in getting a list of the births and deaths of his children with any offspring, which he could connect to his known lineage. He reminded himself he was not being as cold and mercenary as it seemed. He was but a shadow in their lives, neither interfering with, nor hopefully, changing their history. He was also interested in what became of Matthew and Hope, and, of course, Rebecca and Lydia. As an integral part of his research, he also tried to see some pictures or descriptions of their clothes for that period. Everything he saw was generic, probably what they wore in England and may not reflect what they wore in Massachusetts. With a feeling of unrest, Jerry shut down his computer and went to bed.

When Thursday came, Bill had a book of clothing pictures for various periods of history, and some were helpful, except there was no way they could get period clothing made on such short notice, even if they had the money. The wardrobe department of the university boasted about how many costumes they had, but then you realized they made the costumes to "appear" authentic. In reality, they were made of synthetic material and designed to be seen from a distance but would not pass close inspection. Jerry and Bill resigned themselves to being stuck with what they had and hoped Jerry may be able to acquire something when he got to his destination. Currency was still a problem. No one having such historic articles were going to loan them with the near certainty they would never recover them. Looking up Hal Jarvis, his history professor, Jerry quizzed him about the currency used in the colonies and what type of trade goods were readily negotiable. Hal began looking at Jerry shrewdly.

"You're going to time travel, aren't you?"

Jerry felt the blood suffuse his face. He wanted to tell Hal everything but wanted to talk to Bill first.

"Uh, I'm just doing some further research, Hal!"

"Uh, huh! Sure, you are! I know the syllabus of every history professor at this university and information like you're asking for would not fit any of them. Jerry, what's going on?"

"Let's go talk to Bill and maybe he can answer some questions!" So off they went to the physics lab run by Professor Blanchard. Once there, Jerry explained to Bill what Hal was doing there and told him what he had been researching. Bill looked at Hal, and after a few seconds, swore him to secrecy! Hal was only too willing to swear, as both these men were friends; Bill Blanchard had been for many years. Giving Hal a quick synopsis of what they had experimented with and what the outcome of these exercises had produced, he finally told him about the jump to Nevada and then the jump to Salem. Hal was flabbergasted and wouldn't stop asking questions. This was understandable, considering history was his forte, and he had more of a vested interest in the findings, whereas Bill Blanchard's interests were from a scientific perspective. They eventually showed him the photos Jerry had taken in Salem. On the verge of asking to be another time traveler, Hal was anticipated and cut off by Bill.

"Hal, it'll be hard enough trying to explain a missing student! Just think of the furor a missing history professor would cause. And you have a family, man! What'll become of them? It's bad enough Jerry's parents would be deprived of a son. You're a husband and father! I think you better do this vicariously through Jerry. You may want to give him an additional agenda on his next jump…"

"He's going to jump again? Soon?"

"As I was saying, you may want him to do something additional, but his first priority is a continuation of the main reason he went the first time. This is just further research. Now, do you have anything to add which may make it easier for him to get around? I believe he was asking what commodities were negotiable, so maybe we can send some with him. And don't say a bushel of wheat or a pregnant ewe!"

"Let me see what I can do! I may be able to think of something. Salem is a seaport…hmm, uh, yes! I've something to add. I happen to have a small number of pearls I collected when I was younger. I dove for them myself and never did anything with them. They're not really gem quality these days, but as a salable commodity in the time period Jerry's going to, they would bring something, perhaps enough to buy clothing items and maybe enough to keep him eating and housed. Jerry is supposed to be from Virginia, and he can say he traded for them with sailors who sailed along the coast of the southern colonies and even some of the tropical islands. It's not as though he has to show a bill of sale in those days. Possession was the main thing. Unless someone accused him of stealing them, he shouldn't have any problems. I'll dig them out and bring them to the lab. I have them in a leather pouch I made, so it looks authentic enough. Anything else?"

"Do you have a compact digital camera fast enough to take pictures without a flash? We need something he can take photos with but not give himself away!"

"Yes, I have such a camera. I'll bring that, too, but I get to keep the pictures on the memory card after you copy them to your computer. Deal?"

"Deal!"

By the time the trio finished their discussion, Hal was nearly manic. He dashed off toward his office. Bill and Jerry talked a few more minutes, mostly to comment on their new "partner!" They laughed at Hal's enthusiasm, but not in a mean way as they could relate! Parting, the two agreed to meet again on Saturday evening for a dress rehearsal, so to speak! Jerry had work, so went home to eat and change. Bill stayed at the lab, tweaking, primping his brainchild, and talking affectionately to STUDLY.

While Jerry was working at the furniture store on Saturday, he was visited by a hyper Hal Jarvis. Carrying with him a backpack, he pulled Jerry off to the side and opening it, he pulled out a camera and two spare batteries. Laying these down, he also produced a leather pouch which was a little worse for wear but definitely seemed authentic for the colonial period. Opening the pouch, he poured out about a dozen pearls. They were obviously less than perfect, but may still provide much needed funds. Fishing once more into the depth of his backpack, he pulled out a much-worn buckskin shirt with fringes on the sleeves and across the breast. Having no tags, it appeared to be homemade.

"In my younger days, I was so into history, I tried to live it somewhat. I used to camp during the summer and fall, trying to live as much off the land as our ancestors did, and I managed to do pretty well. I learned to cure my own deerskins and made this shirt myself. I know it's not the greatest, but I think it will pass as something from the era you are traveling to. It should fit, and I have a few other things I have collected or made myself. I had to dig all these out of the garage, so they may be a little musty. Here is a larger pouch you can use to carry things in and a hand-forged knife and scabbard I came across. I have a flintlock, but it's probably too modern."

"Bill doesn't want to arm me because he's afraid I'll kill someone who could become important. The knife will be a tool, and the rest will come in handy. You don't happen to have a pair of hardsoled moccasins, do you? The boots I have are not very comfortable for walking."

"I made a few pair of moccasins, but I have a hand-tooled pair of boots which may fit you! Why don't you come to my house when you get off work before you go to the lab? I was going to bring these to the lab tonight but just couldn't wait to show you!"

"Hal, I really appreciate the loan of these things, and I'll try to take good care of them and bring them back with me. I sure hope those boots will fit! Why don't you put these things back in your pack and bring them tonight?"

"Okay. See you there."

When the three friends met at the lab on Saturday evening, the anticipation within the group was nearly palpable. Bill had his equipment in top shape; Jerry had his research in a small packet available for sharing; and Hal brought his backpack again. Laying his precious ante to the project down, Hal made sure all articles were addressed, so they could be ooh'd and ahhh'd. Handing a pair of boots to Jerry, he told of having them made by an experienced but amateur leather craftsman. He normally only made leather accoutrements for himself, but Hal had talked him into some outside work. The boots were a reasonable fit, and the addition of a pair of wool socks would make them comfortable. They were not factory made, so should pass. Jerry tried on the shirt and found it fit loose but not sloppy, and he would wear a linen shirt he had beneath the buckskin. The strapped pouch slung easily over his shoulder, and the knife and scabbard hung from a rawhide strap he tied in a square knot around his waist. He still had the pants from his first jump, but he would need to continue going without underwear until he could procure some in Salem or learn to do without! Unless he could afford to buy headgear, he would go hatless, though the climate may allow him to get by. So this had really been a dress rehearsal! He felt much better equipped than last time, but he still had to travel naked and hope he met up with the packet at his destination. Everything was packed for travel, with the addition of more food bars, renewed first aid kit. Packing the camera and batteries in ziplock bags was a precaution they hadn't taken the first time, but did so now! All was in readiness, and tomorrow they would meet again. Not wanting to miss a thing, Hal insisted on being present when Jerry left the lab for Salem.

Sunday, after church, Jerry had a nice relaxed meal with his parents and his older brother and sister-in-law, who lived across town. Conversation was mundane for Jerry, as he was keyed up, but he held up his end of it and so much wanted to tell the family what was going on. If one looked at it subjectively, Jerry was older than everyone thought due to his spending one week in the past. While everyone aged less than four hours, he had aged a week! After dinner, Jerry told his family he was going to the physics lab to do some experiments. Again, everything seemed so normal to his parents and sibling, but Jerry was aware he may not return home this night, and who knew how long he would actually live in the past this time. Having to make his departure as normal as could be, he just told them not to wait up for him, wherein his mother reminded him of his need for proper rest or he'd get sick. Of course, he agreed with her, telling her thanks and that he loved her!

Upon his arrival at the lab, Bill Blanchard saw him and remarked, "I'm glad you're here, Jerry! Hal's about to drive me nuts! He almost has a rut worn into my floor, pacing back and forth like an expectant father! You can relax now, Hal. Jerry's here!"

Rushing toward the young man, the history professor had a look of relief on his face. Jerry just looked at him and smiled.

"Relax, Hal! As the guy said in that old movie *The Time Machine*: 'We have all the time in the world.' The past isn't going anywhere! Besides, I'm not late. It isn't even eight yet!"

"I know! I'm just excited! I wish I were going, but Bill had a point, so I'll just have to wait for you to get back, hopefully with a bunch of good pictures! Try to get pictures of people doing everyday things and not just buildings!"

"Yes, Professor. Maybe I should get the camera out and see if I know how to operate it, and hopefully it will be quiet. People may wonder why every time I'm acting nonchalant, there is all this clicking and whirring coming from my direction!"

"Good idea!"

Almost making a pest of himself, Hal seemed to be everywhere and doing all he could to assist! A look from either Bill or Jerry, and he would suddenly back off and apologize. When they had the packet in the portal, Bill checked his settings one last time. Consulting his watch, he energized the portal and the packet winked out of sight! A collective sigh rose from everyone, especially Hal. As the thirty-minute mark approached, Jerry took off his contemporary clothing and donned the robe. This was a common occurrence for everyone but Hal, and he watched interestedly. When it was down to the last couple minutes, Jerry said a silent prayer, then removing the robe and throwing it across the same chair he had used before, he calmly walked to the portal. Everyone said "good luck" to each other, and Jerry gave Bill a final nod. As STUDLY hummed and whirred, Jerry ceased to occupy the portal. With a sigh from Bill and an expletive from Hal, they began their wait!

Having learned from experience, Jerry was on the balls of his feet when he blinked into existence in another time and place. He was still a bit lightheaded, but he did not fall down or stagger. Blinking his eyes a couple times, he slowly gazed around him. It was broad daylight, and he immediately saw the packet at his feet. Congratulating Professor Blanchard on his accuracy, he stooped to pick up the bundle. Taking a more careful look at what was adjacent to his arrival site, he tried to imprint the image of his location in his memory, so he could hopefully leave from the same location. Nothing looked familiar, though he did not really expect it to, if he were, in fact forty years later than his last sojourn to what he hoped was still near Middleton, Massachusetts. Donning the clothing he had brought; he repacked the bundle and hid all but what he put in the shoulder pouch. He kept the beacon which had been with the bundle in the pouch, just in case he had to send his clothing back in an emergency and from a different location. The knife in its scabbard felt comforting to him, and the boots were comfortable, as he had hoped. Taking his bearings, he strode off in the direction of Middleton, he hoped.

As he walked on, he began seeing evidence of settlement encroaching closer to his arrival point and made a mental note to himself that if he returned at an even later time, he should pick another point further from habitation. Nothing was familiar yet, and he tried to remember how far from his first landing he had seen the Lloyd homes. The areas of cultivation were much vaster, but he found a road and followed in the direction he felt was correct. The day was warm, and he guessed it to be late spring. Seeing a man in the field, near a fence, he approached. The man seemed as interested in Jerry as Jerry was in him.

"Good day, sir! May I enquire if I am on the road to Middleton?"

"Aye, you be."

"Is the home of Matthew Lloyd near?"

"Aye, just a mile or so further on. We don't see many walking this road, especially from that direction. Might I ask where you are bound from?"

"I rode a wagon from Wakefield, then got off a way back. I thought I knew where I was heading but got off the track and ended up in the woods."

"Aye, it happens! Just head that way, and you'll see it along the road about a mile, like I said."

"I am obliged to you, sir! A good day to you."

"Aye, and the same to you!

Continuing on down the road, Jerry hoped his accent and manner of speech was not too odd! Passing several homes with cultivated fields, he recognized the Lloyd family home but was not sure if it was still inhabited by the family. Spotting a house he recognized as Matthew's, he quickened his stride but slowed to see if anyone was about the fields adjacent to the house. Seeing no one, Jerry went to the door and politely knocked. A short moment later, the door was opened by a young woman Jerry guessed to be in her twenties.

"Pardon me, mistress, but is this the home of Matthew Lloyd?"

"It used to be, but he moved back into the ancestral home yonder," she said, indicating the direction Jerry came from.

"Oh, thank you! Pardon me, again, mistress, but may I be so bold as to ask if you are a relative?"

"I am, sir. I am the wife of Reuben Lloyd, youngest son of Matthew."

"Congratulations. I know the family, and it is a great one. Do you know if Master Lloyd is at home?"

"He is, but it is not a good time. His wife is gravely ill, and the family surrounds her. I am here only because of my children."

"I am saddened to hear Mistress Lloyd is ailing. I shall inquire at the home to see if my visit is convenient. Thank you, mistress!"

Hurriedly, Jerry retraced his steps to the home he had spent time in just last week. To think the home had actually seen forty years since he was here last was incredible. At the stoop, he lightly tapped on the door. It took a couple minutes for anyone to respond to his knock. Eventually, a man in his late thirties opened the door and looked at Jerry questioningly.

"Pardon me, sir, but I have come to see Master Matthew Lloyd, and I realize it is not a good time for the family, but I have come far to see him, and I know he would want to know I am here."

"Would you wait for a while, and I will converse with my father. May I request your name, sir?"

"I am Jerrold Tanner from Virginia."

"One moment, Master Tanner." The man looked very pointedly at Jerry, then quickly went back inside.

While he waited, Jerry looked around the outside of the home and saw where repairs had been made a number of times, and a form of ivy had nearly covered the walls. Looking out upon what used to be open fields, he now saw it was fully cultivated, and off in the distance, he saw a number of cattle.

"Jerrold?" Jerry turned at the voice.

Seeing a much-changed Matthew, he knew it was still the same man. Heavier now, and his hair was almost totally grey, but the eyes were still as expressive as he remembered.

"Matthew! I am sorry to arrive at such a bad time. I assume your wife is Hope and none other. How is she?"

"Jerrold, you amaze me by being the same as you said you would be. I know it is not witchcraft, but it is hard to believe I have lived these many years, and you have aged not at all! Yes, Jerrold, it is Hope, and she is at death's door, I fear. I would normally say she would be glad to see you, but the shock may be more than she can endure. Let me go and prepare her. Jerrold, there have been no secrets between Hope and myself. I told her many years ago about your secret. She seemed to sense the truthfulness of it and did not question your return some day. Perhaps this will give her some peace, and it may rally her, so she can be your hostess once more in life. Please come into my home."

Upon entering the dimly lit home, Jerry could almost sense the original family he had known here. Looking about, he could see the many changes wrought by the intervening years and imagined them as Hope's own mark on Matthew's mother's home. A few older children were milling about in a somber mood. The man who had answered the door came to Jerry.

"Sir, let me introduce myself. I am Jerrold Lloyd, and I was named for a friend of my parents, Jerrold Tanner, also from Virginia. Would he be your father?"

"Uh, yes! That is correct. I have come here to bring greetings from my father and to let your parents know all is well with him."

"All present here, today, are my brothers, sisters, nieces, and nephews. Everyone! This is Master Jerrold Tanner, and his father is the person for whom I am named. He comes to visit from Virginia."

A number of Matthew's descendants greeted Jerry and told him how they were related. There was a strong family resemblance. Matthew's looks were apparent in the men and boys, and a couple of the women and girls had a hint of Hope's beauty. One girl reminded Jerry of Rebecca and wondered if she were a daughter. Before he could inquire, Matthew returned and ushered Jerry into a bedroom, and he asked those in the room to leave them. Bringing Jerry to the bedside, he looked down on the pale visage of a mature Hope. Much older now but still exhibiting the beauty Jerry remembered from so recently. Her eyes were closed, but as though sensing his presence, they opened. A wan smile came to her mouth, and she whispered,

"Jerrold. Matthew always knew you would return, and I tried to have his faith. It is so good to see you, though you are unchanged, and I think I am dreaming of our short time together all those years gone by. What he told me was so difficult to fathom, and at times I wondered if we had been bewitched by you. When you disappeared from our midst, I was not surprised, but Lydia was much vexed and pined for you for some time, as I know Rebecca did."

"Hope, do not tire yourself. You must get well so you can enjoy your family for many more years. Is there not something I can do? What is the source of your sickness?"

Matthew answered for her to save her exerting herself further.

"It is a wound from working with the animals, and it has become septic. We have tried all the herbal remedies we know and poultices taught by the Indians, but nothing seems to help. I despair of her life. Is there nothing you can do, my friend?"

Jerry had thought about things many times, listening to the admonitions of Bill Blanchard, but in the end had secretly put a supply of penicillin tablets, which had been prescribed for him, but he never took. They were approaching their expiration date, and he reasoned they could come in handy if he were injured, never dreaming he would use them for anyone else. But if they could help Hope, then he would gladly administer them to her. Reaching into his shoulder bag and rummaging in the first aid kit, he found the bottle and opened it. Shaking two tablets into his hand, he asked,

"Do you have water?"

With elation in his eyes, Matthew sprung to the bedside table and poured liquid into a cup. Handing the cup to Jerry, Matthew stepped away from the bed, allowing Jerry to raise the weak woman into a semi-sitting position. Placing the tablets at her lips, he bade her to take them into her mouth, then raising the cup to her lips, had her swallow, washing the tablets down her throat. Then laying her back onto her pillow, he said,

"This is medicine from my time, and it should heal her, but I must continue to give her the treatment for a few days. She will recover but not overnight. It will take a week or so."

"Will you remain that long, Jerrold?"

"If I can, but if I leave before a week's time, I will leave the medicine for you to give to her."

"Thank you, Jerrold! I was sorely afraid I would lose her, and that would be unbearable. I have lost so many in my family, and I do not wish it to happen to my beloved wife."

"Has she been feverish?"

"Yes, and when she is thus, she is addled and speaks strangely."

"I think it is normal."

Jerry felt Hope's forehead and detected a fever. Digging into his first aid kit again, he took out two aspirin tablets and once again raised her up for her to take the pills.

"Are you a physician in your time?"

"No, I am a mathematician, almost! These are common treatments in my time. They are not foolproof, but I hope they will help your wife and my cousin. The medicine I just gave her will help with the fever. She needs to drink liquids, either water or perhaps tea."

"I will make sure our daughters are told. They had attended her this past week since she became ill."

"You say it is from a wound?"

"Yes."

"Could I see the wound?"

Going to the bed, Matthew drew back the covers and pulled Hope's nightgown up to expose her calf. The bandage on her calf was fresh, but her husband unwrapped it. Revealed was an angry-looking wound which was suppurating. Judging by the amount of pus on the bandage, the infection was advanced, but Jerry did not think blood poisoning had set in yet. Again, delving into his bag, he brought out the fresh tube of antibiotic ointment. Matthew recognized the tube and stated,

"Ah, the wondrous healing salve. I made the container you gave me last for many years, and it saved my family many times." Applying an ample amount to the wound, Jerry stepped back so Matthew could reapply the dressing.

"That should help heal the wound. I pray I gave her the medicine in time to bring her back to full health."

"At least she now has a better chance than she did without you, my friend. I am indebted to you once more but to a much greater extent!"

"It is what friends are for, Matthew. I am just glad for the chance to try and help your family. I think it best if she is allowed to rest and let the medicine go to work. I will give her more tonight! And do not forget the liquids."

Giving one of his daughters instructions as to his wife's care, Matthew ushered Jerry out of the bedroom and outside the house. The two men talked for an hour or so. Matthew brought Jerry up to date on the last forty years of his life. He was surprised to hear Jerry had only lived a week in his own time. Mistress Margaret Lloyd, Matthew's mother, had lived until 1703. Jonathan lived in Peabody, just northwest of Salem. Surprisingly, he had married Lydia Meacham, and they had six sons. Daniel had gone to sea at sixteen, signing on a whaler, but had been swept overboard during a storm before he saw his twenty-first birthday. Rhoda had married Isaac Meacham, one of Hope's younger brothers—one Jerry had not even noticed when he was at the Meacham home. Isaac had moved to Windham, Connecticut, to be near his father. He and Rhoda had a son, two daughters, and a number of grandchildren. Matthew told Jerry he and Hope had two sons, two daughters, and at last count, ten grandchildren. None of Matthew's children had married into the Meacham clan.

"What of Rebecca, Matthew? How fares your oldest sister?" With a saddened face, Jerry's colonial friend responded,

"Jerrold, my friend, Rebecca was very sad at your departure. She grieved and pined her life away. She lived for less than two years and never accepted suitors, though our mother and I tried to find her a husband. She died as she feared she would, a spinster! Although you were only in her life a week, she loved you beyond all reason. I hold you blameless in all ways, Jerrold! You were kind, caring, and did not delude her or take advantage."

As the two men sat on the front porch in silence, they both shed tears of sorrow.

At dusk, the family assembled and had a prayer for Hope, and then a family dinner was served. Spending the evening together, the family talked of their experiences as a family. Jerry thought it sounded like a wake and spoke to Matthew about it. As the patriarch, Matthew directed the family to be more joyous in their reminiscences. It worked and soon the family was laughing at little things each remembered about other's antics. Preparing a bed on the floor in the living room, Jerry had declined the offer of sleeping in a bed. Reminding himself he was younger than most of the family, though he had been their father/grandfather's contemporary, he refused to take another's bed. Before retiring, he gave Hope another penicillin tablet and more aspirin. She was wide awake, and he spent some time talking to her.

Telling Jerry about how Rebecca was one of her maids of honor at her wedding, Hope added the fact Constance Bonner had been her matron of honor. By that time, however, Constance had found a husband from Boston, whom she could control; directing him to sell off her late husband's property, the proceeds which she used to move back to Boston, where she lived out her relatively short life in a manner to her liking. She had been taken by one of the frequent influenza outbreaks to sweep the area, dying the same year as Matthew's mother. For the rest of the short conversation, they talked of Rebecca. Hope admitted to Jerrold of her attraction to him and also to her sister Lydia's infatuation, but they had been momentary, while Rebecca's love for him had been acute and unrelenting. Rebecca had confided in Hope of the fact she and Jerry had kissed a few times. Admitting she could think of no other man but Jerry, her agony over losing him was overwhelming. The tragedy of her death haunted Jerry, and he began thinking he should have stayed in Salem and never returned to his own time. Finally, Jerry urged Hope to sleep. Standing ready to care for her during the night, one of her daughters plied her with water.

Early the next morning, Jerry was awakened by the normal sounds of a busy household. Most everyone was up and doing. After he had dressed and washed, he was offered breakfast. The men of the family were already out doing chores, assisted by the younger boys. Household chores were being accomplished by the women and girls. After eating, Jerry went into the bedroom to check on his patient. When he arrived, she was being fed by another daughter or possibly a daughter-in-law. Knowing it would take a couple days to see much improvement, he was nonetheless surprised with her upbeat countenance. Figuring it was her positive outlook, despite her wan look, he chose to join in her happiness.

"So how is my favorite cousin this morning?" This caused a look of interest from the family nurse. Jerry decided he should guard his tongue, so added, "At least, that is what my father called you!" Jerry had clued in both Matthew and Hope last night as to his posing as the son of the original Jerrold Tanner.

Hope caught on and replied, "Your father was such a sweet and caring cousin. I pray you take after him in all ways!"

"That is my prayer, also!"

"I feel rested but still weak. I fear your potions will not work, but at the same time, pray they will!"

"It will take a few days before you notice any great improvement, but the potions are in your system by now. Speaking of which, it is time to take another. I would also like to see your wound."

Guarding his belongings, Jerry kept his shoulder bag on his person at all times. Reaching inside, he took out the bottle of penicillin and shook out a tablet. Handing it to Hope, she placed it in her mouth and washed it down with a draught of water from the cup at her bedside. Allowing Jerry to pull back the bedclothes, she let him lift the hem of her nightgown and unwrap the dressing on her calf.

"I need some hot water and a cloth to bathe the wound."

"Marjorie, would you please get the things your cousin asked for?"

"Yes, Mother!" The young woman left.

"So she is your daughter?"

"She is my youngest and come to stay with me while her husband Stephen remains on their land. Three of the children here are hers. My sons are Jerrold and Reuben, and my daughters are Elizabeth and Marjorie. It is joyful to have family about you, especially when one is ailing."

"Yes, I see."

When the things were available to Jerry, he bathed the wound to clean it. The hot water was soothing to Hope, and she relaxed under Jerry's ministrations. Looking at the wound critically, Jerry decided it looked a little better, and her fever seemed to have broken. The redness had been reduced somewhat; the ointment treating the infection topically, while the penicillin fought it internally. Reapplying the salve to the wound, he asked Marjorie to redress the wound. When Hope once again had the bed covers up to her chest, she asked Jerry to sit with her. Pulling a chair to the side of the bed, Jerry let Hope carry the conversation as she told him of her marriage and children, relating anecdotes about them and demonstrating her justifiable pride in her family. Thinking of his own life with his parents, he hoped he had not disappointed them too much. While Jerry was telling Hope his thoughts, she drifted off to sleep without replying.

Leaving the room so she would be undisturbed, he became the center of attention among the girls and women in the house. Wanting him to tell them about Virginia and his life there, they said they grew up hearing about a cousin of their mother's, who had visited from Virginia. Now, his son had come to visit. He had little new to tell, but since none had heard him before, it was all new to them. There were a couple of young women near his own age, and he was very careful not to encourage their interest. His heart still hurt from hearing of Rebecca, and he wanted no repeats! Soon, it was time to prepare dinner for the family, especially the men who were out laboring. Jerry felt at loose ends, so he went outside. Strolling up the road, he decided, on the spur of the moment, to visit his bathing place. Cultivation had cleared the land right down to the banks of the stream, and he found the trees and brush which had screened him from view were gone. The stream was not as swift now since the spring runoff had ended. The place he had bathed still existed and had been much used for getting and carrying water to the homes nearby. His mind replayed the times he had met Rebecca at this place, and his heart beat leadenly as he recalled her sweet smile and the feel of her lips on his. Suddenly realizing he had returned as much to see Rebecca as for anything, he was much saddened. He had prepared himself for her to be older and married and a mother, but he had never thought she would be long dead! Seeing activity at Matthew's home in the distance, he plodded back.

After dinner, Matthew stayed at home and let the others return to the field. He and Jerry spent a short time with Hope, who had awakened and been fed by another female family member. Soon, Matthew led Jerry to the back of the house, where he had once helped Jonathan carry a deer so it could be skinned and prepared for food to feed the family. On the bench which sat against the back wall of the house, the two men sat, middle-aged and young, but once close friends and peers.

"Jerrold, I have kept the records you asked me to keep for you. Hope was very diligent in her correspondence with her brothers and sisters. She wrote down each birth, death, and marriage. I have it in an oilskin pouch, and it is ready for you when you wish to see it."

"I truly appreciate what you have done for me, Matthew! It is still difficult for me to see you as you are because I still see you as a man my own age, working beside me to add to your house. I find myself wishing I had been courageous and stayed here. Perhaps Rebecca would still live today, and maybe we would be brothers-in-law! My heart aches, and I know not what to do about it. I know what I would like to do."

"What is that, my friend?"

"I would like to go back to my time, then come back near the same time I came at first. What I would do then, I know not, but I have many options. Whatever I choose to do may change the course of your history, but only from the perspective of Rebecca not dying, hopefully. I must think on this more fully. Understand this, though, if I change things, you will never realize it. If I go back and prevent her from dying, you will just know your sister is still living, and you will have no knowledge of her 'not' dying! Do you understand me?"

"I believe I do, but it is very confusing. Trying to think of it is much like the buzzing in my head from too much wine. What I think you are saying is, if Rebecca did not die when she did, I will never have knowledge of her dying at all, so it will be just as if she were always here."

"I think you understand the concept. Could I look at the family history you kept for me?"

"Let me get it."

Going inside, Matthew was gone for a couple minutes, then returned to the bench and handed Jerry a bundle wrapped in oil-cloth. While Jerry unwrapped the documents, Matthew waited to see if his efforts pleased his friend. Jerry looked at the names and dates, and mentally arranged some of the data into family group sheets and pedigree charts. Elation rose within him as he saw that Hope's young brother Samuel had a son named Samuel, who in turn had a number of sons, one of which was Joshua. This completed the pedigree chart and answered one of the main mysteries Jerry's dad had about their ancestry.

His mission, for all intents and purposes, had been completed. He could go back anytime, taking these documents with him! Offsetting his emotional high was the knowledge he was missing an important aspect of his time-travel—he had lost someone very dear to him. It must be love, but it was bittersweet because he could not share that love with the one person who engendered it.

Jerry thanked Matthew effusively, showing he was very pleased with the effort to maintain the record over the past forty years; all due to a simple request between friends. In his heart, however, Jerry felt the lead weight of loss. As a form of therapy, he began asking his friend to tell him everything he could about Rebecca and what she went through from the time he had departed until her final days. Thinking it would be cathartic, it instead made him more morose. That it caused him pain was a given, but he felt a guilt within himself no one else would assign him. Academically, he had made no promises to Rebecca and even tried to dissuade her from attaching anything to their relationship, but it gave him little solace.

Spending his days around the house of Matthew and Hope Lloyd was his pattern. He once visited the graveyard, which served the village of Middleton, to see where Matthew's mother and sister were buried. Looking upon the marker for Rebecca, he wondered how her life would have turned out if he had never come to this time. Inadvertently, he had fallen into Bill Blanchard's greatest fear about time travel. He had not murdered anyone, and he had not saved anyone's life, but he could see now how his mere presence may have been a factor in the premature death of a woman who could have borne many children. This made him think of how he was treating Hope and hopefully saving her life, but he rationalized she was beyond childbearing age, so he should be safe!

Further discussions with Matthew and Hope (who was feeling better each day) brought him relief by finding out no one he knew had been implicated in the witchcraft trials which were taking place even while he was visiting the first time and had ended within a year's time.

The inhabitants of Salem Village had been so repentant they changed the name of their community to Danvers, which Jerry already knew.

Reverend Witherspoon had not lasted long, being overshadowed by the notoriety of Samuel Parris, the first ordained minister of Salem Village. By spring of 1694, the reverend and his son, Roger, had moved to Boston, ostensibly so the reverend could accept a position with a new congregation. After the hysteria of the witch hunts had died down, things were quiet, and this was when Matthew and Hope had been betrothed. Her father's new wife, Deborah, had stepped into motherhood well and did not delay in bearing Jeremiah more children. With the assistance of Hope and her family, Mathew had increased the acreage he cultivated and within a couple years was producing enough crops to sell in Salem, and Hope began having their children. At the present time, Matthew was a prominent man in Middleton, and his family farmed a large portion of the tillable land in the area.

Finding no real reason to delay his return to his own time, Jerry had many discussions with Matthew and Hope. In addition to his outlining basic future history, he talked of his desire to return to a time when Rebecca was alive. The colonial couple could see Jerry was fixated on seeing her once more and perhaps preventing her from wasting away. He tried to explain how he may change their lives if he did so. Of course, one of those changes would be Rebecca may still be in their lives if she did not die from something else. But the other possibility could be he would not be here to help save Hope from dying of sepsis. Long debates took place on this subject. He was reluctant to make any further changes to history but felt so strongly about wanting to save Rebecca, even if it meant saving her so she could marry someone else and having his children. Still, he did not want Hope to die for something as minor as a cut on the leg. Through all the discussion, no real solution or determination was reached.

After two weeks, Jerry felt he had to return. The official statement made to the rest of the family was their cousin from Virginia had to return to his studies and his parents. There were many offers to provide transportation to Salem, Boston, or other points along the way, but Matthew and Hope supported him as he declined all offers. They told everyone Jerrold was an adventurous sort and took pleasure in finding his own way, as his father had forty years earlier. That he chose to leave at night rather than morning seemed odd, but he simply told them he wished to get a start early the next morning, without awakening the household for farewells. It seemed to make sense to them. Having depleted his supply of penicillin on Hope, he left the remainder of his antibiotic salve to Matthew, who knew well its value. Not forgetting to fulfill Hal Jarvis's request for lots of pictures, he had conspired with Matthew to conceal the camera so candid pictures could be taken of the entire family in all sorts of situations. He also took pictures of the graveyard and especially Rebecca's headstone. Although he had not ventured as far as Salem, he felt he had sufficient evidence of colonial life in the early 1700s. He had transferred the digital images he had taken on this last trip to this camera, and since Hope had not known about him until later, when her husband had filled her in, he showed them to his cousin. She was thrilled to be able to see the pictures he had taken of her and her sister, Lydia, when they toured Salem. She also made appreciative sounds of the "portrait" of Rebecca. Sighing, she became very wistful before pulling her mind back to the present.

After dinner, as was becoming his pattern, he said his farewells to the family. Then, with Matthew and Hope, he walked up the road a way. Shaking the hand of his friend and getting an embrace and a kiss on the cheek from his cousin, he told them they may never see him again, or they may not remember him visiting them at this time, if he decided to change things. It was a very anxious time, and their relationship seemed so tenuous. They longed for an assurance of some sort but knew not what to expect. With a wave of his hand, Jerry turned and continued up the road until he felt like he could turn into the comparative wilderness. In his bag were a few artifacts he had been given, and he carried the oilskin pouch with the written family history. It did not fit in his shoulder bag but would fit inside the packet. He had not used the pearls, had not purchased clothes, and was still confused about what his next step would be.

Arriving at the place, he had hidden his packet, he took a look around to make sure he was unobserved, then he disrobed, packed his bundle, and activated the beacon. Waiting but a moment after the packet disappeared, he activated his own beacon and held his breath.

14

Remembering to flex his knees, Jerry made a good, stable landing in the portal. By the time his head cleared and he could chance looking around, he saw Bill and Hal awaiting his first spoken word.

"Well, it never gets easier! Glad to see you two, and hope you haven't been too nervous!"

Leaving the portal, he went to the chair which held his robe and put it on once more. Not being anxious to expound about his trip, he waited for his companions to ask the questions. Of course, Hal did not disappoint by asking the standard, "What did it feel like?"

"Hard to explain! I guess you could say it's like going on a carnival ride or an elevator. How long was I gone?"

All business, Bill glanced at his stopwatch and answered, "Four hours, twelve minutes! How long were you there?"

"Two weeks to the day," Jerry answered just as professionally.

"Well, that gives me two points on my graph. Did you have any trouble finding the clothes packet this time?"

"Nope! It was waiting for me. I was almost standing on it!"

"Great! Now we have a pretty good lock on animate versus inanimate for a jump that far. We may be able to work out a formula. Did you cause any disruptions? You know what I mean!"

"Not this time, but I may have uncovered an inadvertent one from last time."

"What was it? Tell me!"

"Bill, it is kind of a tender subject, so let me tell it in my own way."

"Okay. Shoot!"

"I told you about the girls or women I had contact with on my last jump. I told you about my two cousins and the young widow and also about the sister of my friend, Matthew."

"Yeah, I remember. What happened?"

"This time, I didn't see my younger cousin or the widow who had died. My older cousin, who married my friend, was fine, but older of course. She and Matthew had four children and have ten grandkids so far."

"Okay. What else! I have a bad feeling."

"It's not bad, relatively speaking. I may not have changed things."

"What? Tell me what you did!"

"Remember I told you about Matthew's sister, Rebecca?"

"Yes. Go on!"

"Well, I tried to discourage her from getting a crush on me. I made no promises to her. I told her I couldn't stay!"

"But as I remember, you did kiss her a couple times, right?"

"Yes, but it was just a little kiss, not a deep kiss, and I didn't even have my arms around her but once!"

Hal Jarvis decided to cut in at this point.

"A kiss may not mean much now days, but back then, you didn't usually kiss someone until you were engaged, and sometimes not until you were actually married! That kiss could have been the same as proposing to the girl. Man, you can really stick your foot into it!"

"Hush, Hal! Let me talk to the boy! So you didn't make any promises, and you didn't have sex and make a baby, so what's the big deal?"

"She fell in love with me, and when I left, she was so despondent she just withered away and died within two years! Her mother and brother tried to get her to marry someone from the area, but she didn't know I was from another time, and she thought I would love her enough to return from Virginia, for heaven's sake, because that's where I told her I was going! Anyway, I think I may have changed history by keeping her from marrying and having children!"

"It could have happened that way, but I don't want you to have such a high opinion of yourself, Big Boy! She could have died from any number of things and not had children!"

"Can we chance it?"

"It'd be clearer cut if she'd committed suicide, but to…how'd you say it…'wither away?'…that's more nebulous."

"Her brother said she pined away for me until she got sick and died! I think it's pretty clear. I feel awful!"

"So what can we do about it? We can't change history, again, if we really changed it to begin with. Well, you know what I mean!"

"I don't know!" Jerry said miserably.

"As I've said before, we have time. History isn't going anywhere. What else do we have?"

"What about the pictures? Did you take pictures?" Hal reentered the conversation.

"Yeah, but we have to wait for the packet to arrive, just like UPS or FedEx!"

"Oh, yeah, I forgot! How many did you take? How much did you get for the pearls?"

"Relax, Hal! I took about a hundred pictures, but I didn't go anywhere, except right around Matthew's place. I took a bunch of candid shots of his family doing what families did back then! I never went back to Salem, so I never tried to barter for clothes. So I still have the pearls. Of course, it means I have no additional clothes either. The only thing new I brought back is the family history I asked Matthew to keep for me. It's everything I originally went for, so my mission is complete. Oh, and I brought back a few small artifacts, just so you have something tangible for your history. I just feel so guilty about Rebecca, I feel like I need to do something but haven't figured out what yet!"

"We'll sleep on it and discuss this more, later! Ah, there it is, the packet!"

Rushing over to the portal, Hal beat the others to the packet. Unwrapping it so he could get to the camera, he dropped the oilskin package to the floor and brought out the shoulder bag. In rummaging through the bag, he took out the pill bottle. Bill saw it and snatched it up. Reading the side of the bottle, he looked questioningly at Jerry. With a sheepish look on his face, he confessed.

"Come on, Bill, I just took them with me in case of an emergency for myself! But when I got there, my cousin Hope was very sick from an infected leg wound. I just couldn't let her die! Her whole family was there, to be with her when she died. It broke my heart to see the anguish on their faces. She is too old to have more children, so I figured it would be okay! I gave her the medicine and used the Neosporin on her leg. It took a while, but she recovered, and Matthew was very grateful, as was Hope. I did a good deed and hope I partly made up for letting Rebecca die! So just shoot me! I did what I thought was best, and I tried to keep in mind what you've taught me! Of course, if one of their kids or grandkids had been sick, I probably would have done the same!"

"Damned do-gooders!" Bill grumbled, but his smile eased the sting.

By this time, Hal had the camera and was reviewing the pictures on the LCD screen. Excitement was evident in his expression. Pausing occasionally for a longer period at a particular picture, he acted like a kid with a new toy!

"These are priceless, Jerry! They will be great in a slide show when I cover colonial America!"

"Yeah, and how're you going explain where they came from? You can't tell anyone they're authentic!"

"I know!" moaned Hal.

"I guess you could always say they're still shots from a movie or maybe from a tourist village like Colonial Williamsburg."

"I'll think of something! These are too good not to be seen."

"Remember your pledge of secrecy!' Bill Blanchard reminded his fellow professor.

"Yeah, yeah!" complained Hal.

"It's getting late or early, depending on how you look at it! Let's get those pictures copied to the computer, so Jerry will have a copy for himself."

After the pictures had been downloaded to the lab computer, Jerry uploaded his own copy to a flash drive, so he could take it home. The clothes packet and bag were stowed away in the lab. Jerry dressed in his own clothes and taking the documents Matthew had given him, he said goodbye to his friends and left for home. Bill and Hal were not far behind him, only taking time to shut things down and locking up the lab. Jerry was keyed up, so when he got home, he went to his father's study and took a look at the family genealogy book. He did not make changes but mentally filled in the blanks in the pedigree charts. Trying to figure out how he was going to explain the source for this new information, he was looking over the other lines of the chart. Suddenly, his eyes grew large at what he saw. He rubbed his eyes, as if disbelieving what he was reading. Sleep would not come for the rest of the night.

Jerry was up and in the kitchen when his mother appeared to make breakfast.

"Well, what's this? Since when do you get up so early on a Monday, dear?"

"Uh, just couldn't sleep, Mom. The experiments in the physics lab were pretty rough, and I can't get them out of my mind. I'll check with the store, and if they can do without me tonight, I'll get to bed early."

"That's good, honey. I don't want you to get sick so you miss any classes and can't go to work. What do you want for breakfast?"

"Uh, nothing, Mom. I already had a bowl of cereal, and I'm good! When will Dad be down?"

"He's out of the shower and will be down shortly, I'm sure."

"Okay! I need to talk to him before he goes to work."

By the time Stewart Tanner entered the kitchen, Jerry was ready to burst, but the demeanor of his father left no doubt he was in a hurry and had no time to talk. Jerry was quick to interject before his mother said anything.

"Dad, I need to talk to you tonight. Maybe we could talk after dinner. I'm going to try to get out of work tonight!"

"Okay, son. If it's that important, maybe we should talk now, but I'm running late."

"Tonight is all right. Have a good day at work, Dad. See you later!"

After his father left, Jerry returned to the study and pored over the family history. Rummaging through the journals in the file cabinet, he found nothing on the ancestor he was interested in. It was too far back for most journals. The ones his father had were mostly from the mid-nineteenth century up to the mid-twentieth century. Pondering on the things he had discovered, he sat for another hour, then got up and got ready for his first class of the day. Before leaving home, he called the furniture store, talked to the manager, and got approval for missing work that evening. Monday classes went well, even though he was preoccupied. Finally, his last class was finished and he went home.

Usually, he was not home for dinner on Monday, so his mother had prepared a salad and had fresh-baked rolls. When his father arrived home, they sat and ate. Not wanting to make his mother feel left out, he edged into the subject he wanted to discuss with his father. He went over again the dead-ends his father had come to in his family history research. He talked first about the Meacham line and this piqued his mother's interest. They discussed how the hole existed in linking the ancestors in New England with their descendants who eventually joined the westward tide. He told his father of his frustrations of not finding anything in Salt Lake City to shed light on the missing information. Nodding his head, Stewart Tanner was wondering where his son was heading. This was very familiar ground and, to his mind, was not accomplishing anything by simply talking it out. He had to have additional sources of information. Finally, he came right out and asked, "Son, I know all this, and I felt pretty sure you would get nowhere in Salt Lake, but I let you go so you could get experience in family history research. Now, what has you in such a sudden frenzy about the missing information? It's still going to be missing until we find another source! What's on your mind, son?"

Carefully weighing his words, he said, "Dad, I have the information, but you may not agree it is credible, and you may not like what I did to get it!"

"What? What do you mean you have the information? And, if you have it, why wouldn't I think it's credible? And lastly, what did you have to do to get it? I can't imagine how getting this information could be done illegally!"

"I didn't say it was illegal. I just said you may not like how I got it!"

"Okay. Let's take this from the top. What does the information say?"

This was something Jerry could act upon, and he had the material he had from Matthew on the sideboard inside a folder.

"I have written records which list the births and deaths of all the children of Jeremiah the elder, and his son, Jeremiah the younger. I also have the children of the younger's offspring, as far as 1742, which lists the son who matches up with our lineage. It goes Jeremiah, Jeremiah, Samuel, Samuel, Joshua, with a birth date which works out for being the same Joshua who was Mom's great-great-great-grandfather!"

"Let me see that, please?"

Handing his father the folder, he waited for him to examine the written records. Not realizing he was actually handling paper and ink which was really over three hundred years old, he used his experience reading the spiderweb-like handwriting of the seventeenth century. Just as Jerry had, he was mentally arranging the names and dates into a family group sheet and finishing out the pedigree chart. Looking at his father's face, he was buoyed up by the joy he saw. He could almost forgive himself everything because he so wanted to please his father. Finally, Stewart Tanner looked up from his reading.

"This is wonderful, son! I can see why you wanted to try to explain. I don't know where you got this, but it explains a lot. This paper, and the handwriting almost makes me believe you just got this from your mother's ancestors and brought it right home!"

"Well, something like that!"

"What do you mean? How did you get this information? I have hunted and hunted for years, and you just stumble onto it? It doesn't make sense unless there are suddenly new sources you found on the internet! Is that it, son?"

"Not exactly, Dad! I didn't find it on the internet. It took a little more effort than that and the help of a great man. Almost as great at you, Dad!"

"Don't go buttering me up, young man! Am I going to regret being given these records? Are they stolen from some long-lost archives, somewhere?"

"No, Dad! Honest!"

"Okay, then, what's it going to cost me to keep these or to even let me copy them?"

"Nothing! No. They're yours and the family's, of course."

"Son, what's the bottom line? How'd you come by these and why are you being so evasive?"

"The bottom line, Dad, is I got these records by doing something completely different and thinking outside the box, as you like to talk about. I don't know quite how to tell you and Mom about it!"

"Well, as usual, you should start at the beginning and move forward! Should we remain sitting down for this?"

"It wouldn't be a bad idea."

So Jerry began at the beginning, about how a college history assignment had begun his journey into the unknown. He brought them along slowly when he began talking about his association with Professor Blanchard. He spent a long time going over his hypothetical discussions with Hal Jarvis and how he was advised to approach his physics professor when he began this semester's classes. Tentatively, he took his parents into the theory of time travel, and the paradox Bill Blanchard was scared to death about! Finally, he talked about the lab experiments with furniture and rats. He soft-pedaled his participation in the experiments and his travels into the past. Finally, his dad caught up and made the quantum leap he was afraid to broach.

"So, you actually took a trip into the past?"

Jerry's mother sputtered but was speechless. Having difficulty comprehending what her youngest son was saying, she just kept quiet and let the men discuss things.

"Yes! At first, it was just a day or so, and it was just between the lab and home. Then, we had to do something more ambitious, so we sent me one hundred years into the past and to the desert outside of Las Vegas—Pahrump to be exact! I was gone from the lab only a few minutes, and it all went well."

"Did you get hurt in any way from your, uh, traveling?"Jerry's mother, always the pragmatic one, asked.

"No, Mom. I felt a little lightheaded for just a second or two."

"So, when did you get the documentation?"

"It's a little involved, and you'll have to let me tell it without interruption. Afterwards, you can ask me questions!"

Launching back into his narrative, Jerry explained how they cautiously planned every step of the venture with historic and topographical research; attempting to find period clothing; taking precautions by adding food bars and first aid kit; the addition of the camera, with the need to keep these modern things hidden. His remarks about having to travel naked was a small sticking point for his mother, but his insistence that it was necessary because of the physics allowed him to continue. His constant remarks about the prior experimentation before he was ever allowed into the machine was more to reassure his mother he was taking no unnecessary risks than for information purposes. By the time he finally got around to talking about his first jump, he had their undivided attention.

Telling of his developing friendship with Matthew and his family and his trip to meet the Meacham family had them wanting to ask questions, but he repeated his request to hold all questions. He lost his mother, at first, when he explained his need to jump again, at a later date, but she finally saw the reasoning, and he continued. When he told of his return to the past and his treating Hope's infected leg, they were amazed, but when he told of Rebecca and her death, they were saddened.

At last, he was able to talk about how he obtained the family records and his almost immediate return to his own time. Finally mentioning the pictures he took opened things up for questions. Of course, his dad asked to see the pictures, but before he could get up to bring his laptop computer out, his mother stopped him, demanding he answer her questions first. A lot of her questions were just to get amplifying information, so he patiently filled in the gaps for his parents. One line of questioning was to find out more about his relationship with Rebecca, and he assured her of his proper conduct when dealing with her, except for the addition of the kisses! Just as Hal had, his mother remarked about how kissing probably meant more in those days than they do now.

Getting up to bring his laptop to the kitchen table, he let his parents talk while he was gone, so he was not surprised such discussion brought additional questions. While setting up the computer, they asked for more information on the Meacham family and their life amid the witchcraft hysteria. Answering them as best he could, he began showing the pictures in chronological order. The first, from Salem, showing the buildings and his cousins elicited more questions. When he got to the ones he took forty years later, they were enthralled with the depiction of colonial life close at hand. When the pictures were shown, and questions and answers had dwindled down, Jerry asked, "Well, what do you think about all this? Do you believe I actually traveled in time?"

His mother was the first to answer, "I don't know, dear, but I'm glad you're back, safe and sound! I'm not sure I believe in time travel, but it surely sounds believable! But what I don't understand is if you were gone for a week the first time and two weeks the second time, how come you were never gone from home overnight?"

This question dictated he explain objective and subjective time and temporal displacement. It was beyond his mother's understanding, but his father kept nodding his head, so he hoped he was getting enough to eventually explain it to his wife.

Then, his dad weighed in with his opinion, "I have to say, son, that is quite a tale, and if I hadn't read the information you brought back and seen the pictures, I would be asking if you're on drugs!" His smile robbed his remarks of any offense.

"I know it sounds far-fetched, like something out of a science fiction movie, but I know it's real, and I know what I know. I also want you to know something I discovered in our records, and it was there before I jumped."

"What's that, son?"

"Take a look at your Tanner lineage. What do you see as far back as you've went?"

"I know my direct lineage has its earliest records in Massachusetts, around the late sixteen hundreds. So what?"

"Dad, what is the name of your earliest ancestor? Where was he born?"

"His name was Jerrold. He was born in Virginia, but no birthplace or date, but his records indicate he would have been born around 1674. He would've been around nineteen when he married."

"That's right, Dad! What's his wife's name?"

"Rebecca Lloyd!" His father paused, thinking, "Oh, my Dear Lord! You're not suggesting…?"

"I'm not suggesting anything, but it makes sense in a way!"

"What are you two talking about? What is all this drama?"

"Don't get all upset, Mom, but all this may be an example of the paradox I was telling you about—the one which gives Professor Blanchard nightmares!"

"I must be dense, so will someone spell it out for me?"

"Look, Helen, we're not saying it's real, but it's so coincidental! If Jerry hadn't come back from the past and if he'd married Matthew's sister, he could be our first Tanner ancestor!"

"Hrmpf! That's so ridiculous! How can he be his own ancestor? I think both of you are off your rockers or on drugs! Don't you go jumping around in time any more, young man! Do you understand me?"

"Helen Louise Tanner, let's be reasonable. If I follow Jerry's line of reasoning and if I believed in this 'paradox' thing, then I think I am about to lose a son."

"What?" Jerry's mother screamed. "I refuse to let you do anymore of this…this…this time travel! I won't stand for it!"

"Mom? Don't you see? If what Dad and I suspect is true. If I don't go back, ever, and I die in this time, then this whole line of Tanner will never have existed. In fact, if I don't go back right now, while I'm still nineteen, or if Rebecca dies before I go back, then this Tanner line won't exist! I don't understand all the whys and where-fores, but I think I have just realized my fate!"

"We don't believe in fate, dear!" his mother said, again, pragmatically.

"Call it what you want, but I think this is what I'm supposed to do."

"Wait! I don't know if this makes sense, but there couldn't be a future in the past! Someone had to start the line, but it was in the past long before you were even born, how could it happen this way? Oh, I am so confused! My head is starting to hurt!"

"I don't know how to explain it either, unless there's some sort of alternate universe, and in it, I went back and changed history by marrying Rebecca and had a family instead of letting her die as a young woman! In that case, there is a universe out there where this line of Tanners does not exist! I'm as confused as you are, but I believe if I don't go back and marry her, you and Dad will not exist. Since you do exist, I did go back!"

"What if there was another Jerrold Tanner from Virginia who showed up in Massachusetts and married this Rebecca, and you're not needed in that time at all?" interjected Stewart Tanner.

"Okay, but it seems too coincidental and are you willing to take a chance by not letting me go back to stay?"

"So, if we stop you from going back, do we just sit here and wait to blink out of existence? I don't believe that!"

"Dad, I don't know what to believe! I think I believe I set in motion a chain of events by going back and meeting Rebecca. I don't know for sure if 'I' was the cause of her not marrying and dying childless. I don't know if our ancestor, Jerrold Tanner, married the Rebecca Lloyd I met. There may be more than one Rebecca Lloyd in Massachusetts and more than one Jerrold Tanner, who was from Virginia, and settled in Massachusetts! I'm really just as confused as Mom! I was just doing what I thought I had to do, for the good of our family—our ancestors and our immediate family. I don't want you or Mom or any of us to have never existed! I don't think we will ever know for sure!"

"It's like the old question, if a tree falls in the forest and no one is there to hear it, does it make a sound?"

"Yeah, Mom, kind of like that!"

"Well, what do we do?" asked the family patriarch. There was a long moment of silence, then Jerry spoke, "I guess I should talk with Professor Blanchard, though it wouldn't affect him either way, I suppose. He could still go on with his experiments in time travel, but he may be so scared he destroys STUDLY!"

"Studly? What on earth is that?"

"Oh, just the acronym he thought up for his time machine. I don't remember what it stands for. It really doesn't matter anyway. We just call it that to make it easier than saying 'time machine.'"

"When are you going to your professor?"

"I doubt he's in the lab tonight, so I guess it will have to be tomorrow."

"I guess there's no real hurry in making a decision as long as you're still 'about' nineteen! Let's 'try' to get some sleep and then talk again tomorrow after you and the professor talk. Okay?"

"Okay."

16

Despite the pronouncement for sleep, there was little actually done in the Tanner home that night. On Tuesday morning, everyone was up but groggy, so a somber mood pervaded the house as each prepared for their day. Stewart Tanner went to work; his wife did her normal housework; and Jerry went to his morning class. All were preoccupied and anxious for the evening to arrive. Jerry went to the physics lab between his classes. Bill Blanchard was there, but he was overseeing the running of lab exercises by some students. Letting Bill know he needed to talk, he was directed to the office, where Bill promised to join him as soon as he could.

"So, my footloose friend, what's on your obviously addled mind?"

"Bill, I have to tell you something my family and I have discovered, and it may be part of my travels."

"Don't tell me you carried some dread disease back and gave it to your family?" Bill said, grinning.

"No, but this is serious!"

"Okay. Sorry. What's up?"

So, again, Jerry began at the beginning, and as his narrative progressed, the professor got more and more serious. At one point, he began pacing behind his desk, as he and Jerry discussed the finer points of what the student had related to his mentor. After the main points were covered and the suppositions began, Bill kept giving Jerry squinty-eyed looks.

"No offense, Jerry, but I may have been better off choosing a straight-out history meddler! Things may not be as complicated, philosophically speaking, of course. So cutting to the chase, you believe you have to go back to your Rebecca to save her from dying of a broken heart and giving her a whole passel of kids, so your present family will not blink out of existence! In other words, you are your own ancestor?"

"In a nutshell, that's about it!"

"And you subscribe to the theory of alternate universes or realities and figure if your family exists, then you 'did' go back and do what I just said?"

"I'm leaning in that direction, Bill, but I'm not one hundred percent sold."

"I'm with you, kid!"

"So, what do you think we should do?"

"I'm sure you're aware I won't be affected, regardless of what we do, so I have no vested interest professionally. In a way, I do feel responsible since without STUDLY, you wouldn't have gone back in time. But then again, if we follow your theory, I, or someone else, 'had' to invent a time machine, so you could go back and become 'your own grandpa!' Kinda makes me feel like a rat in a squirrel cage! But, as your friend, I feel just like you—on the horns of a dilemma!"

"I don't know what to do! As you've always said, the past is still where we left it, but if I affected the past, it can get out of hand! What came first, the chicken or the egg? Or in my case, did I create my own lineage or what? Do I just let Rebecca be dead and hope my family and I don't disappear? Did the Jerrold from the alternate reality come to this reality, in the past, and create my ancestral line? And am I expected to go to his reality and return the favor?"

"Let me throw this out, just for grins and giggles. In one instance, you decide you like life just as it is and go on living it, ignoring the past. What happens? Or another slant on the same theme, I destroy STUDLY, and you are 'forced' to stay here and you live out your life, but with a guilty conscience, and you hate me forever! What then?"

"Well, in both cases, since I live out my life here, it proves I haven't upset history by my actions. But those are just scenarios which may not be viable."

"You think too damned much like a scientist! I think we have beat this pretty much to death! What do you want to do? First, answer me this, if you decide to go back, are you doing it for your family or because you love Rebecca?"

"I don't know if I love her. I didn't get to be with her very long, but I think about her almost every waking moment. Of course, I would also be doing it for my family, I think!"

"Bah! You just talked in circles! You didn't answer my question, just like a politician!"

"I don't know how to answer your question!"

"You're toast, my fine, young friend!"

"I feel like burnt toast! Can we take a couple days? Maybe something will come along to help me decide."

"Okay, the past isn't going anywhere! Unless another meddler changes it!"

"Could you hurry and invent a way to clone me, so I can stay and go?"

"Yeah! Good luck with that!"

So, Jerry went to class, and Professor Bill Blanchard returned to his students. However, both had their minds on the "matter of time."

At home that night, Jerry filled his parents in on what he and Bill had discussed and how they agreed to let it alone for a couple days. Afterwards, Jerry and his dad went to the study to pore over the family history, looking for some clue to help solve their dilemma. Prayers, of the fervent variety, were said by all in the Tanner home that night. Reconciling science and religion, or more specifically, time travel, and religious beliefs was difficult, but rationally, if human scientists can invent things, using the laws of physics, then surely the Almighty, who ruled those same laws, was capable of utilizing the same principles, but his Wisdom chose not to do so.

Online, Jerry looked for records from the 1690s, but there were very few documents to survive. Of course, there was no US Census! Searching the records of DAR archives was of little help because it didn't go back that far either. The only real help came from church archives of births, christenings, and marriages. He found records of Jeremiah Meacham marrying Deborah Browne and also where Matthew and Hope had married, but there was nothing about Rebecca or Jerrold. Within his mind, it raised the question: If he went back now and married her, would the records then be there if he came back and looked them up? A real conundrum!

Jerry couldn't face attending his classes on Wednesday, so he dropped in on Hal Jarvis to get his input on the matter. Sitting in Hal's office, Jerry brought him up to speed on what Bill and Jerry's parents were all thinking about. Without addressing the matter at hand, Hal did a little daydreaming.

"If I knew, at your age, what I know now, I would love to go back and live during that time period, traveling around and seeing how things really were back then. Then I'd come back here and teach what I lived and not have to just regurgitate what some clueless scholar wrote in a textbook, thinking he knew all there was to know! Hell! If I were younger and not married, I'd go back and say I was Jerrold Tanner and 'be' your ancestor!"

"I don't think it would work that way!"

"Of course not! Your Rebecca would never believe I was you, so we'd never be married, and I couldn't be your great-great-great… well, you know what I mean. Sorry, I can't come up with any better ideas for you."

"I appreciate all you've done, Hal. I enjoyed talking to you about this since you really started it all. But I guess it's up to me to make the decision."

"Yeah, I guess I was the instigator, and I hope you don't hold it against me!"

"Of course not! All this happened 'after' I turned in my semester paper."

Bidding his teacher and friend a good day, Jerry walked slowly home, pondering, as he saw it, his real options.

At home, he had the house to himself. His father was at work, and his mother was running errands. This gave him solitude he really didn't want because his mind went freewheeling, and the number of scenarios which came to him were distracting. Trying to simplify things, he categorized his options—go back or don't go back! Of course, each of these options had their own subcategories. If he chose not to go back, then he foresaw himself spending his life playing "what if?" Before his trip into the past, he felt he had mapped out his future pretty well. College was a given! Raised by parents who were conservative but erudite, he and his brother had their lives channeled toward a college education, though their course was not dictated. Choosing to pursue a degree in architecture, his brother had finished his degree and was busy trying to establish himself in the profession. Jerry was thinking seriously about being a teacher of mathematics but hadn't totally committed yet. Lately, not surprisingly, he had considered switching his major to physics. Right now, he just didn't know!

What if he did go back to New England? What would he do with his life? He could always help Matthew farm, but he'd never considered farming as a vocation. In actuality, he already had more education than most schoolmasters of the seventeenth century, but the bulk of his knowledge was based on facts and theories not even dreamed of in that time. Teaching would be difficult—to constantly be on guard, lest he teach things which had not come to pass yet! If not teach, then what? Knowing nothing about being a merchant or even a tradesman, like a carpenter or wheelwright, he wondered how he, alone, would live, to say nothing of supporting a wife and family! With all his education, he felt ill-equipped to survive in the world he had visited twice! Oh, Rebecca! How fainthearted he felt. Sunk into the depth of depression, Jerry fell into a troubled sleep, filled with images of Rebecca and colonial Massachusetts.

Waking his youngest son for dinner, Stewart Tanner could see his son had not slept well. Before going downstairs, Jerry and his dad discussed the matter once more.

"Son, I don't claim to understand everything you're going through. I can give you my take on things, but the decision is yours. I'll back you up however you decide, but I don't believe this family will cease to exist if you don't make the right choice. I truly believe we're here to stay! If you decide to go back for this girl, Rebecca, I can kind of understand that, but I would counsel you to be cautious. Just because our recorded ancestors have similar names to you and this girl you met, it doesn't mean you're your own forefather! The world abounds in coincidences, and I would hate you to change the course of your entire life just because of a clerical error or a true coincidence. Look at all the Jeremiahs and Samuels in your mother's genealogy!"

"So, you're saying I shouldn't go back?"

"No, not at all. I said I'd give you my opinions, but I'm not trying to sway you either way. You may not be twenty-one yet, but you're a man in my book. I'm just trying to make you aware of all the possible options, misconceptions, and repercussions, as I see them."

"Thank you, Dad! I appreciate it."

Still without a decision, Jerry went through the remainder of the week following his normal routine of school, work, and homework. Friends and family knew he was preoccupied with a huge decision to make, so knowing the stress he was under, they remained supportive without being intrusive.

Unbeknownst to Jerry, events were occurring around him which would come to light at a later date. His friends, specifically—Hal Jarvis and Bill Blanchard—felt strongly enough about him to lend assistance in his adversity. Long discussions were held between the two university faculty members. At one point, they called Stewart Tanner to ask his opinion and get his input. Finally, they were confident they were taking the best course in aiding their young friend. In one respect, Hal Jarvis felt he was getting the opportunity of a lifetime, but it was of collateral benefit to the history professor. Deciding it was in Jerry's best interest and though totally against Bill Blanchard's ingrained fears, the two decided to send Hal into the past to assess the state of affairs in and around Middleton, Massachusetts! Having calibrated STUDLY, they felt a time one year after Jerry's first trip would be best.

Due to age and the sedentary lifestyle of academia, Hal could not fit into the clothes Jerry had used. Deciding they were beyond trying to be authentic, they used the costumes from the drama department. Anyone observant enough to notice the difference in fabric and wanting to cause trouble would just be avoided in the future. Not totally confident of his ability to get around in that time, Hal was still intent on carrying out his assignment. Choosing to plan the jump for Sunday evening seemed almost traditional to Bill. The clothing packet was packed for Hal, with a couple additions, in case things were critical. Bill had come up with a refinement to his beacon. Instead of imbedding the beacon under the skin, he had imbedded it into a couple mouthpieces he got from the physical-ed department. You simply put the mouthpiece inside your mouth, then clamped down on it, and it would not fly out, nor be swallowed during the journey. The beacon was set to allow ten seconds to get it into the mouth after activation. Hal became hyper with apprehension, which was readily discerned by Bill, who tried to calm him, suggesting he might suffer a stroke or heart attack. Being only forty, Hal gave his friend a scowl and a rude gesture, which lightened things considerably! When all was ready, a final mission review was held. Professor Blanchard wished his friend luck and stood by the controls of STUDLY. Professor Jarvis stepped into the portal and, with a final glance around the lab, gave a nod. His trip began, and he hoped the clothing packet, which had been sent thirty minutes prior, would be waiting for him, having no wish to be seen naked.

chapter

19

Being older, less physically fit, and ignorant of the effects of time travel, the scholarly Hal Jarvis stumbled and sprawled out on his face when he came into 1693 Massachusetts Colony! Lying facedown on the humus of the forest floor, the earthy odor reminded Hal of his vegetable garden. Letting his head clear and getting his bearings, the professor immediately saw his clothing packet off to his left. Rising slowly, as he took stock of his present physical condition, he removed his mouthpiece and then bent to retrieve his clothing. Since he had no intentions of staying in this time long enough to expose his underwear, he brought it along. Feeling odd in breeches and stockings, he nonetheless did his best to act the part of a colonial gentleman. Looking at the sky through the trees, he estimated it to be late morning, and the weather was pleasantly warm, so he must have arrived in early summer. Having replayed in his mind all of what Jerry had described of the Middleton countryside, he donned his shoulder bag and struck off in what he hoped was the right direction. It took him about twenty minutes before he began seeing cultivated land and then a house or two. When he saw the two homes belonging to the Lloyd family, he recognized them from the photos Jerry had taken.

Deciding to visit the home of Matthew first, which he and Bill had planned, he approached the front door. Realizing Matthew may be out working away from the home, he determined to at least check the house. Knocking on the door, Hal waited to see if anyone was home. Hearing someone approaching, he took mental stock of what his first words to someone from the past would be. Caught completely off guard, he was found speechless when a young woman of perhaps eighteen or nineteen answered the door.

"Yes, may I help you, sir?" Came the puzzled voice of the young woman.

"Uh, um, uh, is Matthew Lloyd at home?"

"Yes, just one moment. Would you care to enter?"

"I beg your pardon, mistress, but I shall remain here."

"As you wish, sir!"

Leaving the door ajar, she went into the interior of the house. Hal had not prepared himself for the patterns of speech he would encounter, so he was playing catch-up, racking his brain to not make any glaring grammatical errors, so he would not appear low class. It took but a minute or two before a brown-haired young man came to the door.

"Yes, sir? How may I assist you?"

"Uh, Master Lloyd, I would like a moment of your time to speak with you in private, if it is possible?"

"Yes, of course! Let us walk away from the house, sir," Matthew said tentatively but moving away from the front door.

"I am Master Jarvis, and I am a friend of Jerrold Tanner!" Hal felt he suddenly had all of Matthew's attention.

"Yes, Master Jarvis! I had not hoped to hear of Jerrold for many years to come. Are you from, uh um, the same area Jerrold is from?"

"This is why I asked to speak to you privately! Yes, I am from your future. I was Jerrold's history professor at the university Jerrold attends."

"I pray my friend is well, Master Jarvis?"

"He is but is heavyhearted."

"Why is my friend troubled?"

"I must tax your understanding, Matthew! I have to explain things you may not be able to fathom."

"That is what Jerrold told me also, and I believe I managed to remain sane."

"Admirable, my boy! Now, I have to further tax your sanity!"

"Go on."

"Jerrold told you he would visit you in forty years! To you, that is far in the future, but to Jerrold, it was a matter of choosing to appear at that date. He visited you and found things going well for you and your wife, Hope. I fear to tell you more about your future."

"Then I do live to see Jerrold once more? That is a comfort to me. Pray tell me why he is troubled?"

"How fares your sister, Rebecca?"

"Ah, there is a different kettle of fish, as they say in Salem! She has not been well since Jerrold took his leave last year. She has refused to entertain courtship of several would-be suitors. She is industrious in the household but will not travel outside our close environs. She is, truthfully, nearly sick unto death. She gave her heart to Jerrold, though he was very proper with her and made no promises. How does one read the mind or heart of a woman and fully understand them?"

"The mind of a woman is still a mystery in my time, Matthew! Tell me, is she in good health or has she declined?"

"She is pallid and takes little nourishment, so her clothing hangs on her frame. Why do you ask so many questions of my sister?"

"When Jerrold visits you in your future, you will tell him of your sister's passing within two years of his departure. It shook him to his very foundation, and he is, at this moment in his time, contemplating returning to your time and staying, so that he can marry Rebecca and possibly extend her life."

"That would be great news for us all, as we have much affection for him and would enjoy his return! But I see it cannot be an easy decision, for he has his future in his own time! His intentions to sacrifice all for Rebecca is commendable, but I feel it could embitter him in time!"

"Matthew, you are wise beyond your years, and I see why you will succeed! Let me tell you why I have come to your time and tell me if you approve."

Speaking at length, Hal Jarvis outlined the plan he and Bill Blanchard had hatched. It was an ambitious plan which had far-reaching effects and consequences. Matthew had chances to interject opinions and ideas, and after an hour of conversation across the road from his home, Matthew invited Hal to take dinner with he and his wife. The professor readily accepted, though he would have preferred eating with the entire Lloyd family, as Jerry had done. Upon entering his home, Matthew introduced Hal to his wife, Hope. Being a father himself, he recognized the sign of impending motherhood on the young woman, though she was not showing that much.

"Forgive me for being bold, but I congratulate you two on your future child. I am the father of six, so I am familiar with the outward signs."

Blushing, Hope was happy for the recognition, as she wanted the world to know she was expecting!

"Thank you, sir! I perceive since my husband has said you are friends of Jerrold, you are also from our future. Are the rigors of childbirth any less in your time?"

"Many of the dangers women endure in your time have been alleviated in mine. Most of the deaths in both mother and child can be prevented, and there are potions to relieve some of the pain inherent in childbirth!"

"I would like to have my child in your time then, as I am fearful for the life of my child. Tell me, if you can, about my future as a mother!"

"I know not about how many you conceived, but I do know you ultimately have four children who grow to adulthood and have families of their own."

"Only four? My mother had many more!"

"I only know history and not all the details. Perhaps you and Matthew decided to have only four!"

"Perhaps. I am sorry to be ungrateful for the glimpse into our future you have given us!"

"That is quite all right!"

Dinner was a pleasant diversion for the Lloyds. Other than

family members, they had few visitors, and to have one who knew Jerrold Tanner was an exquisite treat. Hal Jarvis, who revealed his given name was Harold, tried to be aware of everything he told them. Telling a few anecdotes about his own family and a few about Jerry's, he kept them enthralled during a meal of mostly meat and vegetables. Being the height of the growing season, their garden provided a good supply, if not a wide variety. Most were root crops, and he was conscious of the lack of tomatoes, which he knew were considered poisonous at this time in the colonies and England, though they had been eaten in Spain and Italy for many years. They would come into wide use in the next half century. Hal could tell Hope was anxious to ask more questions, so he finally asked her what she wanted to know, allowing his knowledge of details in their life was limited.

"Is my first child a boy or a girl?"

"I only know your oldest child to grow to maturity is a boy!"

"How many of each do I bear?"

"I only know when Jerrold visited you in 1732, you had two boys and two girls, and you had grandchildren. That is all I can tell you."

"I'm sure by the time Jerrold saw me again, I was an old hag!"

"Fishing for compliments, my wife?"

"Jerrold, or Jerry, as I know him, says Hope is still a handsome woman at nearly sixty! You are still a handsome and able man at the same age. Still actively engaged in farming, you will be successful, with your sons and sons-in-law helping you. Now, I feel I say too much! One of the follies of being a history professor is the habit of expounding too much on history!"

"My wife, I must take Master Jarvis to meet my mother and the rest of my family. Master Jarvis, other than my overly curious bride, only my mother knows of where Jerrold actually came from, so we must be discreet about what we say in front of the others. I fear Rebecca has been kept in the dark. I fear her knowing would make her even more morose."

Matthew led the way up the road to the other house Hal had

recognized. Upon entering, Matthew called out to his mother, telling her he had brought a guest. Mistress Lloyd came into the living room to greet her new visitor. Being a perceptive woman, she waited for further information about Hal Jarvis. She noted his manner of dress and looked closer at his clothing. Hal looked around to see if any of the other family members were within sight. He saw no one. He decided to take a chance and reveal himself to her.

"Mistress Lloyd, I am a close friend of Jerrold Tanner." This elicited an immediate response from the matriarch of the family.

"How does he fare? I pray he has not passed!"

"No! He is well and knows nothing of my journey to visit your family."

Hal spent a few moments briefly informing Matthew's mother about Jerry's dilemma. He revealed to her what the fate of her daughter would be if no one intervened. Mistress Lloyd didn't seem surprised about the impending death of her oldest daughter. Again, she was very perceptive.

"What are your plans, Master Jarvis? Can you save my daughter?"

"I believe I can, but there are conditions which may not be to your liking!"

Hal then told Matthew's mother about his plans, with Matthew adding what his own thoughts had been on the matter. Mistress Lloyd took the information in and sat stoically. Having lived a harsh life on the colonial frontier, she had endured many hardships and was not one to wring her hands over things which she could not control. In the end, she was in agreement with Matthew and Hal.

"Since we three are conspirators, of a kind, would you call me Margaret?"

"So, Margaret it will be, and I am Hal, or Harold, but I prefer Hal!"

"Hal, when do you want to reveal your plans to my daughter?"

"I have made this journey for the sake of Rebecca and Jerrold, but being a history professor, I am deeply desirous of seeing Salem, both the village and the town, and perhaps the harbor. I have the ability to save images of people and scenes, and I would like to take advantage of Matthew to take me to these places. I have some pearls which may be of value, and I can compensate you for your sacrifice. I would have to find some merchant in Salem willing to give me goods or cash in exchange. Matthew, would you be willing to take me to Salem? After I return from Salem, I will reveal to your daughter what my plans are, and we will see if she is willing to travel with me."

Plans were made for the journey, and Hal was invited to eat with the entire Lloyd family. When he was introduced to Rebecca, she gave him a look of barely concealed contempt and said in a low voice to her mother, "I cannot marry an old man, Mother, so please do not give him any hope of me doing so."

Her mother laughed and told her Master Jarvis was already married and had six children. She added he was there to go with Matthew to Salem. After that, Rebecca was much more pleasant, though she was still noticeably depressed.

After spending the night in the spare bedroom on the floor, Hal took an early morning dip in the stream. Being summer, it was much warmer than when Jerry had taken his bath the first time. He had also brought his own soap! Breakfast was prepared by Hope, and afterwards, the three went out to find Jonathan had hitched a horse to the family carriage. Hope had asked Matthew if she could go to Salem with them, and he had agreed since she had not seen much of her family since the wedding. Hal was surprised with the mode of transportation but had to admit it beat walking or riding a horse. He knew he would be stiff from bracing himself against all the rocking and rolling the carriage went through as it bounced down the road, but his excitement about the journey was enough to offset the expected suffering. Making sure he had a record of this trip, Hal took pictures of Matthew and Hope, this time with her full knowledge and pictures of everything else which caught his eye. Having found a way to conceal the camera in his clothing and still take pictures, he happily clicked away. They may not be framed perfectly, but he could always deal with the imperfections later with Photoshop.

They had started early, so the trip to Salem was not hurried. Since they felt they couldn't take advantage of Hope's family by expecting them to put the three up for the night on such short notice, they planned to return to Middleton later in the day. Their first stop was the waterfront, where Matthew and Hal haggled with a merchant for supplies Matthew could use and a quantity of cash money in exchange for the pearls. Hal was anxious to return to his own time with cash to be used in any subsequent journeys, but he shared some with Matthew, for which the young man was very grateful. Cash money was a rare commodity but could be a major advantage when bargaining for goods and services. After the harbor, with a short tour to allow Hal to take pictures, they went to the Meacham home, where they were a welcome change of pace.

Deborah Meacham had one child already but was already expecting again. She was overjoyed to hear of Hope's impending happy event! The two women spent a long time, like two hens, exchanging information about motherhood. Lydia hovered, waiting for a chance to speak to her sister. While the women were engaged, Matthew took Hal on a walking tour of the neighborhood, which included the divi- sion between Salem town and the village. Figuring this was a once in a lifetime opportunity, the history professor took as many detailed photos as he could, without arousing the interest of the natives. Hal kept expecting to see some modern convenience, camouflaged to hide it, as he had seen numerous times in Old Williamsburg. Reminding himself this was the "real deal," he was again grateful to Professor Bill Blanchard! Finally, it was time for the trio to begin the journey back to Middleton. It was a pleasant drive back, and they arrived in time to have supper with Matthew's family.

After supper, as the family gathered in the living room, the matriarch took the floor to make an announcement. Of course, what she told the family was a slightly altered version of the truth but true nonetheless! What she said was, Master Jarvis is a good friend of

Jerrold Tanner (which caused Rebecca to perk up noticeably!) and was here to inquire as to the health of Rebecca, and perhaps persuade her to accompany him to Jerrold's location. This announcement caused quite a stir among the siblings—Rebecca and younger. Beside herself with joy, the seventeen-year-old began sobbing and had to be comforted by Hope. Of course, the others wanted to go, too, and had to be reminded of the need to stay and help with the household. Margaret Lloyd asked Rebecca to go with Matthew, Hope, and Master Jarvis to discuss things at Matthew's home, while she tried to get the three remaining children in check. Nearly dragging the adults out the door in her excitement, Rebecca had to be restrained from running to the other home!

Inside Matthew and Hope's small home, the four people sat on makeshift furniture. The eyes of Rebecca had taken on a shine one would expect of someone fevered. With increased respiration and flushed countenance, she sat with expectation on her face!

"Did he send you to get me?"

"He doesn't know I am here, but he has been much troubled with the thought of you. Please allow me to explain."

At this point, it became the task of trying to reveal the reality of things, without making her feel surreal or insane. Each of the three adults took turns laying the groundwork of this reality. She was agog for most of the preliminary foundation and felt a suspicion they were just talking as to an addled person. The provincial mind of Rebecca Lloyd was not accustomed to thinking of such esoteric subjects as time travel. And the idea of someone from her far distant future coming to her time and capturing her heart was far outside her normal realm of belief. It took the other three nearly an hour to get her to believe Jerrold Tanner was not from Virginia in the sixteen nineties. Thinking back, she remembered some of his strange use of words, and she began to see what they were telling her was possible. Asking many questions, which helped to fill in the chinks of her understanding, she finally began reconciling her belief system with how things had happened as they did. The strange speech, the tanned skin, and the seeming unfamiliarity with mundane things she noticed in passing, but was too infatuated at the time to see the flaws. Hal took a chance and showed her the picture Jerry and Matthew had conspired to get of her outside in the road. She remembered the circumstances and could see how it had occurred. She was enthralled with her picture in a tiny frame and did not even think of the technology behind it. Her simplistic acceptance of everything did not fool Hal. He knew she would eventually have to come to grips with the anachronistic nature of things between herself and what Jerrold represented.

Once she accepted Jerry was from the future and had traveled back to her time to research family lineage, she finally realized why he was not at liberty to stay and be with her. His mission was not merely traveling to return to school but to return to his own time and family. This epiphany allowed her to go forward with what Hal was saying about Jerry and his dilemma. He gave her a brief outline of why Jerry was troubled about leaving her. She immediately offered a plausible explanation.

"I have a cousin, my father's brother's daughter, who is named Rebecca, also. The family lives in Peabody, just north and east of here. There was no real affection between my father and his brother, so there is very little communication, but I heard she has recently married a fisherman who sailed off the Outer Banks, which I heard was near Virginia. Perhaps she and her husband are Jerrold's forebears?"

"A plausible explanation, but I believe he looked for a record of marriage."

"Oh, I doubt she is living near her family, as she was looking for an excuse to leave home. They are the heathens of our family, and she may have been married by some itinerant preacher or some magistrate of a small village and then left the area. If I had the time, I could send a post and perhaps gain some information about her husband from her sisters. They are notional, so they may not want to tell me anything!"

"I don't think it will be necessary. The fact there are coincidences in names should be enough, perhaps, to set Jerry's, er, I mean Jerrold's mind at ease."

"So, you call him Jerry in his time? But if he finds out he is not meant to come back here to be his own forebear, then he may not want me after all!"

"No, I think he is as smitten with you, as you are with him!"

"Smitten?"

"It means infatuated, taken with, a great affection for. I forget about words and their usage, through history, though if anyone should, it is I."

"Do you think he loves me?"

"He once said he didn't know what love was, but if it was how he felt for you, then it must be love!"

"I am not set in my mind in this matter. You are taking me to your time, and I will get to see Jerrold? I mean Jerry? How am I to act in your time? I will be lost in your world."

"I admit, you will suffer what we call 'culture shock,' but if you have a patient teacher, and they take things slowly, you should be able to adapt. I am concerned about the sicknesses in my time. I fear you will need inoculations to combat them."

"In-knock-you…what?"

"I'm sorry. It is medicines given by injecting them under your skin. It should be safe. I'll have to consult my brother-in-law, who is a physician. He can advise me. I will be your guardian for a while. I want to surprise Jerry but still give him a chance to make his decision."

"I pray he is not angry with me for coming to his time."

"I'm more afraid he will not be as proper in his reception of you, as things are not so…uh, how do I say it…rigidly moral in our time. I fear you will think we are all too earthy for your sensibilities. You may ask to return almost immediately."

"Jerrold was very proper with me. It is I who was…earthy…as

you say. I saw him naked…twice!"

Blushing furiously, she looked sheepishly at her brother, who had raised eyebrows…and a smile.

"It was all innocent! I was drawing water from the stream, and he had been bathing! He tried to be very proper and covered himself immediately, really!"

The adults laughed at her discomfort, and she saw they were not censuring her. She was a woman grown in her time, although just shy of eighteen.

"When are we going to travel? How do we travel?"

"Before I go into that, I have to tell you something which may upset you!"

"What is that?"

"When we travel, we wear no clothes!" All colonial eyes were on him and wide open.

"So…*that* is why I found Jerrold naked the first time! I always wondered about it!"

"Yes. It was his first time, and we had not perfected the delivery of the clothing packet! We now know to send it ahead, so it is there when we arrive. That is also why we do not arrive and depart in public."

"And that is why Jerrold and Jonathan were able to find some of his belongings when they went hunting the next day. Many things are becoming clear to me. But you should not see my sister naked, sir!"

"I was going to get to that! I suggest you and your wife accompany us to the spot from where we will depart. You will chaperone us and take a cloak or blanket to cover Rebecca until just before she actually departs. We will pack a few items of clothing for her to don after she arrives at our destination, but she will be able to take very few possessions—only her most prized items."

"Will I never return to this place? Will I never see my family again?"

"It is possible you may return, but it is not my decision. My friend who invented this apparatus we use may find it too risky to keep using. He is afraid we will make an error and inadvertently alter time and change all we know! He has allowed us to make this change, and I must tell you, Rebecca (your brother, mother, and Hope already know this), but if I did not come here and offer to take you to Jerry, you will die within a year, wasting away, we presume from a broken heart!"

Looking totally shocked and very sober, the young woman paled.

"Oh, my! I must admit, I had no will to live, without an assurance he would return. I fear I would have expired in due time, as I have spurned the sustenance my mother attempted to give me. I know I have been obstinate and disrespectful in many ways. I feel ashamed, but I could see nothing except my misery. I must beg her forgiveness!"

"Your mother is a very astute and understanding woman. She has lived these past years without her husband, so I'm sure she is acutely aware of how you feel. Luckily, she is a strong woman and has her children to live for.

"But let me finish my instructions for our travel. To save time, perhaps you should pack at home, as will I, then each of us wear a cloak only, if I may borrow such? I will send the clothing packets on before, then you will be sent on first. My friend is expecting you and will have a robe for you. You may be slightly lightheaded, so do not be alarmed when you find a man holding a robe out to you. I will depart after you and will arrive a short time after you do. I will also have a robe handy, so there may be a short period of discomfort as we see exposed skin, but we are adults."

While Rebecca and Hal had dominated the conversation, Matthew and Hope had patiently stood by and listened to all that was said. Finally, they had the chance to ask their questions.

"After you have gone, how do we know when to expect you back?"

"You can't, as far as I know! You will only know when we arrive on your doorstep, so to speak! I hope that is not disconcerting for you."

"Since we are changing history now, could it mean Jerrold will not visit in forty years?"

"Did he ask you to collect the information for him on Hope's family history?"

"Yes!"

"Then he will still arrive to get the information. The only thing which will change is your sister will not be present, unless he brings her with him, in the revised future, but she will not die next year, in your time. I know this is confusing for you as it is for me! There are so many things which may change, and I know not how to explain it. We just live our life as it comes. I pray those who travel in time will not destroy other people's happiness!"

"That is my prayer also," said Matthew, and it was echoed by both Hope and Rebecca.

"What do we do now?" asked Rebecca.

"I realize it will be difficult, but we should retire for the night. You have to take leave of your mother and siblings. As far as your brothers and sister know, I am taking you to Virginia to be with Jerry. If I have my mind correct on this, you may be able to visit your mother at such a time as to be aged as you would be, if you were really going to Virginia. This could really upset things since Jerry visits you forty years into your future, but he has only lived for one week in his time. I believe he posed as his own son, and luckily, it seemed to pass unnoticed, though at that time, Hope only had knowledge Matthew had shared with her. Now she has all the same knowledge Matthew has, though she first learned of it when you two were married. If Rebecca returns…oh, never mind! It is so confusing! It makes my head spin!"

"I try not to think about it! I will just live my life as it comes, as you said!" remarked Matthew.

"I should like to see your time, Master Jarvis! It may be frightening but exciting also!" Hope interjected.

"Again, I must remind you. I have no say in such matters. Any invitation to visit the future will have to come from Professor Blanchard!"

"Ah, Blanchard is not an unknown name in Massachusetts. Perhaps he will desire to visit with his forebears!" teased Hope.

Escorting Rebecca to her home, Matthew and Hal not only bid Margaret a good night but also gave her a brief update on what had been discussed at Matthew's. As they walked the short distance back to Matthew's home, Hal remarked diplomatically, "Forgive me for such boldness, but your mother is a handsome woman and about my age. If I were not married, I would be tempted to ask to court her. I hope it does not offend you, Matthew!"

Chuckling, Matthew confided, "My mother told me last evening it was a pity you were a married man, as you are also to her liking. I must insist you act properly toward my mother, sir!" His smile robbing the demand of any rebuff.

Upon rising the next morning, Hal decided against another bath, though he felt he needed one. Rationalizing he would be home before the day was out, he pretended he was out camping. Matthew was already in his fields, and Hope gave him what was left over from their breakfast. Walking out into the field, he photographed Matthew from a distance using the zoom on his camera. He also took additional pictures of the two Lloyd homes. In the interest of posterity, he went to the Lloyd family's home and asked Margaret if he could take her "portrait." Not realizing what was entailed, he explained it to her and showed her some of the pictures he had taken on this trip. Not understanding the technology did not prevent her from noting the detail in the pictures, so she would not allow pictures of her to be taken until she had changed clothes and groomed herself.

With all the children engaged in work outside the home at that time, she sat in her living room, reclined on a divan. Looking almost regal, Hal took great pleasure in posing her and taking a dozen shots. Afterward, he showed her the pictures, and as is human nature, she was overly critical of how she looked in the pictures. Obtaining permission to take the portrait of her children, using the same camouflage he utilized in Salem, he sought them out where they worked at their assigned task. In so doing, he had opportunity to come in contact with Rebecca, and she lost no time in questioning him about their travel plans to reassure herself she was actually going to where Jerry lived. As apprehensive as she was, it took a great deal of reassurance!

Everyone was at dinner, as it was planned to announce Rebecca's departure. It was short notice, but the adults thought it best to proceed in this manner. Jonathan, Rhoda, and Daniel were not only very excited but also at a loss for the short time they would have to spend with their eldest sister before she left. With the departure of Rebecca, Rhoda would be alone in her own room, which both excited her and made her sad, because she had grown up in the same room with her sister. The boys had gained more space in their room when Matthew had moved into his own house. Rebecca tried to keep back her tears, but they flowed frequently. It was a greater adventure than her siblings could even imagine. Of course, there were promises to make return visits, though the adults doubted this would occur. The children were told their oldest brother and sister-in-law would take the carriage and see them on their way.

After dinner, Rebecca went to her room to pack the few things she decided to take with her. She found it difficult to explain to Rhoda why she was leaving the bulk of her wardrobe at home. She simply told her sister she was limited in space and weight for the journey, which was essentially true, and she would get new clothing when she got to her destination, which was also true. Magnanimously, she gave Rhoda everything she was leaving behind, though it would be a few years before the clothing would fit. Rebecca brought her small bundle out to the living room and sadly made her farewells to her brothers and lastly to her mother. The leave-taking was more poignant for mother and daughter, with their knowledge of the true nature of the journey. What mother is able to easily bid a child adieu, knowing they may never see each other again! During the final goodbyes, Matthew had harnessed a horse to the carriage and had it parked in front of his front door. The travelers went into Matthew's home and changed into their cloaks, putting their clothing with the rest of the baggage. When all was onboard, the four travelers climbed aboard. Fortunately, the road took a turn not far from the home, taking them out of sight of the house, so within a quarter mile, the carriage could be swung off the beaten track and into the forest. By the time they found the spot Hal decided was his arrival point, they had traveled out of view of civilization.

Combining his and Rebecca's clothing into one packet, he made sure he had removed both his mouthpiece and one he had brought for Rebecca. Instructing her how to insert the mouthpiece into her mouth, he found it a little large for a woman and made a mental note to have smaller ones on hand in the future. Sending the clothing packet ahead was fascinating for all present when it blinked out of existence in their time. Next, it was Rebecca's turn, so being a gentleman, Hal closed his eyes as he activated the girl's beacon mouthpiece and had her insert it into her mouth. He then stepped back as Hope took the cloak from Rebecca. It took only a minute for Rebecca to blink out. Hal had tried to instruct her on what to expect, but his experience was limited, so he hoped she was not hurt when she came into the portal in the lab. He took a couple minutes to express his gratitude to his hosts, warmly shaking the hand of Matthew and embracing Hope. He then stood back and activated his beacon and put it in his mouth. Hope had turned around, so he shrugged off the borrowed cloak and closed his eyes.

20

Eyes still closed, Hal stumbled into the portal and almost fell out as he tried to get his balance. Taking a quick look around, he saw Rebecca being comforted by Bill Blanchard, who was introducing himself and trying to reassure the young woman all was well. Rebecca had eyes as big as saucers, as she took in all the sights so new and beyond her ken. Hal quickly donned the robe which was nearby and hurried over to Rebecca, who visibly relaxed when she saw a familiar face. Holding her hand, Hal talked soothingly to her and again introduced Professor Blanchard to the colonial girl, adding a testimonial or two about Bill's being the inventor of the apparatus which had had such a great impact on her life. Still very much in awe of her situation, Rebecca was slightly hyperventilating, and Hal had to calm her down even more. Her first real question was when she would see Jerrold! Both men were not surprised and chuckled. Realizing how foolishly she was acting, the young woman took on a look of chagrin. The men had to tell her it was what they had fully expected her to ask, and she should not feel embarrassed.

Now Hal had accomplished his mission, he became apprehensive of how he was going to pull off the rest of the hat trick! He had primed his wife for Rebecca's arrival by simply saying he was hosting an exchange student for a short time. He told his wife the girl would be backwards in many things but would understand English well. He told her, however, the girl would not understand most colloquialisms and slang and was almost totally ignorant of modern conveniences. His wife had quipped how she must be from the moon or mars, if it were so. Now, he had to deliver this innocent girl to his home and convince his wife she was a perfectly normal seventeen-year-old but would not know the first thing about what to do in a modern house. He thought it best to try to tell her the truth, and though his wife was a professional, she may not be so open-minded about such a scientific breakthrough as time travel. He expected her to say, "Oh, sure, and I'm Betty Crocker!" Whatever, he had to get Rebecca acclimated a little so she would not go off the deep end before she saw Jerry again, and then she could lean on him for support during her cultural transition. He reminded himself there were many precedents, such as war brides from Japan, who had a great deal of culture shock with which to adapt.

By the time Bill and Hal had Rebecca soothed, they gave her clothing to put on in the restroom adjacent to the lab. Upon walking into the room, she could not understand what everything was, so the two educators…educated her…as to the modern conveniences in a bathroom. Although they didn't see, they figured her long stay to dress was due to her trying out the faucets, and they know they heard the toilet flush a number of times. When she came out, she had a very pleased look on her face. Professor Jarvis was not looking forward to teaching her about life in a kitchen! Hal handed Bill his digital camera, asking him to download the pictures to the lab computer and then return the camera to Hal for his personal archives. When they left the lab for Hal's home, Bill Blanchard wished him luck and asked to be kept informed as when she would be reunited with Jerry, as he wanted to be present.

Being just midnight, since Hal was not in Salem as long as Jerry, he still had a disgruntled wife to deal with. Once she saw Rebecca though, she became the gracious hostess of a young lady. She took the small bundle from the girl and showed her the guest bedroom and was amused with Rebecca's reaction to a modern bedroom. After getting her guest into bed, she went back to her own and interrogated Hal.

"Has the poor girl been raised in a hovel? I can't imagine what she's used to if our simple furnishings impress her so! Hal, where did this girl come from?"

"Betty, what I tell you is in strictest confidence. Do you understand me?"

"What? Is she in some kind of witness protection program or some such?"

"No. Listen to me, and I'll tell you things you may not believe or understand. But it's confidential!"

"Okay, okay!"

"You know Bill Blanchard, and you've met one of my students, Jerry Tanner."

"Yes."

"Well, they've been working on one of Bill's little experiments…"

"You mean they created her, like in that movie *Weird Science*?"

"No! Betty! Just listen, and you'll learn everything I know!"

"Okay!"

It took a lot of retelling and backtracking and blustering on his part before his wife thought she understood what he was saying. Not that she believed it all, but she believed 'he' believed it!

"So, you want me to believe that poor girl in the guest room is straight from sixteen ninety-three Massachusetts, and she has never seen anything like indoor plumbing and modern kitchens and such? How did she react to riding in the car?"

"I walked to the campus because I knew it may freak her out to see a car, so we walked home, too!"

"Oh, My Lord! What were you thinking, bringing her here? It's like bringing home one of those 'wolf girls' you see on the covers of the tabloids!"

"I told you! If we hadn't done this, Jerry was seriously, and I mean seriously, thinking about going back to her time and staying there! Bill and I didn't want that to happen either!"

"But what if she had a kid who grew up to be president for Pete's sake?"

"I told you! Jerry went back forty years later and found out she died two years after he was there the first time!"

"So, you figured you'd go back just before she was on her death bed and rescue her! Is that right, Sir Galahad?"

"We did it for Jerry and her, not for Bill and I!"

"She's a pretty thing."

"Yes, and younger than our kids! My motives were honorable, Betty!"

"I know, dear. I'm just teasing you, you big old softy! But I have to go to work tomorrow, and so do you! Who's going to…babysit her?"

"I've got my TA to take my classes, and I've asked Jerry's mother to come over. She's as freaked out about this as you are! This could be her future daughter-in-law! She's the only woman other than you now who knows anything about the time travel stuff! Jerry told his parents about it when he thought he may have to leave them."

"Well, I'm glad you've got a chaperone, just to protect yourself."

"Me, too! I have to tell you, honey, her mother was attractive, too! She's our age and a widow!"

"Hmmm. No more time traveling for you, buster! Got it?"

"Yes, dear!"

It took a while, but the Jarvises got to sleep. In the guest room, Rebecca had heard the murmur of voices raising and lowering, and she suspected she was the topic of conversation. Looking around the room, she was amazed with the things she saw. All the fabric which made up the bedclothes, the drapes, and the linens in the ensuite bathroom were so finely woven, she wondered how they were made. She looked for a candle or lamp to make it light enough to explore but hadn't seen Betty Jarvis flip the light switch, which plunged the room into semidarkness. The bathroom had a small nightlight, which supplied enough light for her to explore the bathroom, again trying out the faucets. She let the hot water tap run long enough to get the water hot, nearly scalding her hand. Feeling the softness of the towels and wash clothes, she climbed into the bathtub and lay down. Being an intelligent girl, she realized what it was used for but did not turn on the faucets. She had seen mirrors, though not so finely made. Thinking she could take the nightlight, like a candle, into the bedroom, she pulled it out of the socket. When the light extinguished, she didn't know how to plug it back in, so she left it on the counter. Going back into the bedroom, she decided Master and Mistress Jarvis would help her figure these things out in the morning. It still took her a long time to fall asleep.

Hal called the Tanner home early the next morning. Jerry's mom answered the phone and was immediately updated on the status of Rebecca. With butterflies in her stomach, she wanted to know when she should go meet Rebecca. Hal told her she could come over right away if it was convenient. He didn't tell her he was nervous about being alone with her in case someone visited. Rumors would spread like wildfire if someone knew he was in the house with a young woman, not his own child and his wife not at home!

Answering the front door, Hal was pleasantly surprised in Helen Tanner's appearance. Still lovely at nearly fifty, she had kept her slim build.

"Hello, Mrs. Tanner. Glad you could come over!"

"Oh, call me Helen! No use being so formal. You're Hal, correct?"

"Yes. Thanks for helping me deal with this."

"It's quite all right! Is the girl up yet?"

"I was about to check in on her. I heard her moving around in her room a while ago, so I guess she's awake."

Showing the way upstairs, Hal went to the guest room and knocked lightly. Hearing a faint, "Come in," he opened the door. No one was in the bedroom, but there were sounds coming from the bathroom. Helen Tanner took over and went to the slightly ajar door and peaked around it. Sitting in the bathtub was a lovely vision of female beauty. Of course, she was naked but was low in the tub, shielding her body from view.

"Hello, I'm Helen Tanner, Jerry's mother. You must be Rebecca Lloyd. I've heard so much about you. May I come in and assist you?" Waving Hal out of the room, she indicated she'd see him soon. Entering the bathroom, she took a towel off the rack and approached the tub.

"Have you had a chance to bathe yet?"

"N-n-n-no! I am not familiar with things and just barely got the water to flow into this beautiful basin."

Going over to the medicine cabinet behind the mirror, Helen looked for shampoo to wash her hair. Finding a small bottle, she took a washcloth off the counter and went to the tub. Gently directing Rebecca in the use of the shampoo and soaping up the cloth, she watched as the innocent girl washed herself. Upon the completion of her washing, Helen let her rinse herself, only interfering when she failed to get all the shampoo out of her hair. Rebecca's light brown hair was long enough to reach part way down her back. Assisting her to stand, Jerry's mother gave her a towel to dry off her body. Unashamed in front of this matronly woman, she allowed Helen to show her how to drain the tub and rinse it out. Finding a robe on the back of the door, Helen let Rebecca don it and then found a comb to pull through her hair. Rebecca knew how to comb her hair but was fascinated with the fine teeth of the comb. Soon, her hair was free of snarls, and she looked radiant with her face shiningly clean. In the vanity, Mrs. Tanner found a new toothbrush and toothpaste. Through pantomime, she taught Rebecca how to brush her teeth and rinse out her mouth. It was amazing to Helen how clean her teeth appeared despite being unfamiliar with teeth cleaning. Soon, she was ready for dressing.

Opening the door to the hallway, she stuck her head out and saw Hal pacing back and forth.

"What do you have for this young lady to wear, Hal?"

"I thought she could wear some of the clothes my daughters left in the closet. I hope they fit. I'm not sure what is there. If nothing fits, she brought a couple dresses with her. I don't think she brought any underwear, and I know they did not have brassieres in her time." Hal flushed at this last statement.

"I'll see what I can find."

Ducking back into the room, Helen went first to the dresser to see what it contained. One drawer contained lingerie, but she just chose a pair of underpants, deciding she could go without a bra for now. Directing the colonial girl to don her first pair of underpants, the girl was surprised they felt silky to her skin, though they were rayon or nylon. While she was doing this, Helen looked through the other drawers and had gone to the closet. On the clothes rod hung a wide variety of clothing for all seasons. Finding a dress, she thought would fit, she showed the girl how to put it on. Buttons were somewhat familiar, but these were much smaller than she was used to. The zipper totally flummoxed her. With the assistance of the older woman, the zipper was closed. Directing her to the mirror on the dresser, she let Rebecca view herself in clothing from the twenty-first century. Of course, Rebecca had no idea what century she had come to. She just knew she was going into the future, following the man who had her heart!

"You're a very lovely woman. I understand now why my son speaks so highly of you."

"Thank you, Mistress Tanner. I hope Jerrold is glad to see me. When will that be?"

"It won't be long, dear. I'm sure if he knew you were here, we could not keep him from you."

"Then why do you keep us apart?"

"In our time, there are many sicknesses which were not present in your time, and we must do things to protect you from these, so you will remain healthy. Mr. Jarvis is going to arrange for you to see a physician, who is his brother-in-law, and get him to…"

"In-knock-you-late me, right?"

"That's right, dear! I know everything you see around you is very strange, but you will get used to it in time. Now, let's go see if we can get you something to eat for breakfast!"

With a look of appreciation, Hal watched the women come out of the bedroom. Escorting them downstairs, he took them into the kitchen. Rebecca was so enthralled by everything, her eyes just shone.

"Everything is so beautiful! Everyone must be wealthy in your time!"

"No, dear. There are poor among us, but even what little they have is so different from what you are accustomed to seeing, it would still amaze you, I'm sure!"

As Hal opened up the refrigerator, Rebecca recognized eggs and correctly assumed the gallon jug of white liquid was milk. Getting the bread out of the refrigerator to make toast, Rebecca asked to see a slice of bread. To her, sliced bread really "was" amazing. She praised how white it was but couldn't wait for toast. She had to try a slice right away! Asking her what she normally ate for breakfast, she started naming foods and dishes neither adult was familiar with. Having never seen sliced bacon before, nor sausage links, she asked to try one of each. Accepting two fried eggs, she was like a "kid in a candy shop!" Everything interested her, and she looked about her, asking numerous questions about all the items most people take for granted. Watching Hal cook on the stove, she asked where the fireplace, the chimney, and the wood box were. Toast was new to her, though she had eaten overcooked bread. Giving her a glass of orange juice, Hal hoped the acidity would not upset her system. Deciding he could give her something from home, he brewed a cup of tea for her, but when he gave her sugar to put in it, she didn't know what to do with it. Explaining how it would sweeten the tea, she tried a spoon of sugar on her tongue, letting it dissolve there. A widening of the eyes showed she was surprised with the sensation of sweetness. Four or five spoons of sugar went into her tea, and after stirring it, she took a sip. It must have been to her liking, because she soon drained the cup. After trying everything they gave her, she soon decided she was full and just sat in a daze. Watching Hal clean up the kitchen, she saw him putting the dishes in the dishwasher and asked why he was putting the dishes away dirty. Chuckling, he explained how the box he was putting the dishes into would clean them, she asked if anyone washed their dishes anymore. He assured her they did, but this was a "labor-saving" machine.

Glancing at the clock, Hal picked up the phone and dialed a number. The call was answered on the other end and he asked for Bennett. When he was connected to his party, Hal began his conversation.

"Bennett, you're not going to believe what I'm about to tell you…"

While Professor Jarvis was on the phone, Helen Tanner took Rebecca into the living room and they talked, mostly about what the girl saw in the living room. When Hal finished his call, he joined them. Telling them they had an appointment in an hour's time, he began to explain a few things about what she would see and how she should react to these things. Explaining how all her questions would be answered in time, she was asked not to scream or act overly surprised when she saw something new. He also told her about some tests his brother-in-law wanted to run on her. Although he was a doctor, his specialty had been microbiology and serology. He wanted to do tests on her blood and take skin and hair samples. He also wanted to take X-rays. As intrusive as he felt this was, it was a small price to pay for discretion on the part of the doctor. Helen was asked to escort her into the exam room and be with her throughout the tests. The name they would use was Rebecca Jarvis, and she was to pose as his niece.

The trip to the doctor's was nothing compared to getting Rebecca into an automobile for the first time. Luckily, the car had a bench-type front seat which allowed Helen to sit on the outside and have Rebecca sit between her and Hal. It was a wonder the blood pressure and pulse readings weren't off the chart from the apprehension the young colonial woman had shown during the short ride. Dr. Bennett Shumway was aloof at first until he began examining Rebecca. Soon, he was nearly fawning over her. He took blood nearly the second she stepped inside the exam room, then he left the room. Going directly to his lab, he had put a slide of her blood under his microscope and examined it. Excitement grew almost immediately. This was pure, untainted blood from three hundred years ago, and the differences he saw were astounding. It would be a shame to vaccinate her for all the childhood diseases any normal child would be inoculated against before the age of five. He couldn't give her all the vaccines at once, so he planned a schedule. Some would make her slightly ill, and he didn't want to compound her discomfort. He would start her out with diphtheria, pertussis, and typhoid, then in a week or so, measles, mumps, and rubella. Then a week later, chicken pox and polio. Lastly, would come her smallpox vaccination. What this meant was, he would be destroying her pure, innocent blood and contaminating it with all the antibodies people seemed to need to survive in this world. It saddened the true scientist in him. He decided to wait until he had fully tested her blood.

The blood work was what Hal was interested in, so he stopped Dr. Shumway before he gave the young woman a pelvic exam. The X-ray was allowed, which was the extent of additional tests they were allowed to run. Getting a promise of test results, the three left the doctor's office and went back to Hal's home where they let Rebecca calm herself from all the culture shock she was experiencing. While the young woman rested, Helen and Hal discussed the topic of when Jerry would be told of her presence in their time. The next day, Jerry had physics, and maybe it would be the best time to break the news when all the principles could be together—Jerry, his parents, his two instructors, and Rebecca! Hal put in a call to Bill, and Helen called Stewart at work. It was agreed they would come together at the lab during Jerry's lab period. Now, Rebecca just had to be entertained for the next thirty hours!

Deciding there were things she wasn't ready for, they kept her away from TV, music, stores, and more car rides. Since Jerry would be working on Monday night, Stewart joined his wife and Betty Jarvis for dinner at the Jarvis home. Rebecca was the guest of honor, but she wanted to be involved with the preparation of the meal. They had chosen a roast, potatoes, and carrots for dinner, with a flan for dessert. Figuring this was as close to home cooking for her they could come up with, they allowed her to peel the potatoes and carrots. Betty and Helen got acquainted as the three women worked together in the kitchen. Constantly being amazed about some new aspect of life in the kitchen, Rebecca remained in awe the entire time. The older women kept things low key and tried not to overwhelm her. Laboring at familiar tasks was therapeutic for Rebecca, albeit it strange to be cooking in such strange surroundings. As women will do, they talked as they worked, and the two older women kept asking the colonial about her lifestyle. Being naturally gregarious, the girl was made to feel at ease by the two other women. Of course, she had her own questions, so there was a general exchange of information. Dinner was a pleasant time, and they had tea with their meal to make things seem more familiar for Rebecca.

After dinner, the Tanners took their leave, while Helen promised to pick Rebecca up the next morning and take her to the Tanner home, so Hal could teach his classes. After the Tanners left, Betty had Rebecca try on clothes to establish a wardrobe for her. Luckily, the clothing in the closet was not that far out of date. Betty reluctantly introduced the girl to bras, though she would have preferred to take her to a shop to be professionally fitted. The old brassieres her daughters had worn were still in the drawers, and she tried a couple different ones on the girl. Although they were a reasonable fit, the colonial found them restrictive and uncomfortable. She asked why women would wear such things and was told about the natural sagging of breasts with age and childbearing. Thinking of women in her time, Rebecca remarked how she understood the difference in women's appearance, with and without one. She preferred to go without for now. The two women continued to talk about many things, comparing similar experiences, but from the perspective of different eras. Talking past midnight, Betty realized suddenly how tired she was. Excusing herself, she bid Rebecca a good night. Falling asleep was not so difficult this time for either woman.

Morning found Rebecca trying out the bath tub again. She normally took only one bath a week, but since the tub was available and hot water seemed limitless, she could not resist the temptation. When Hal knocked on her bedroom door and got no answer, he stuck his head in the room. Hearing splashing sounds from the bathroom, he called out to Rebecca so she would know breakfast was ready. Replying she would be down shortly, he fled to the safety of downstairs. Promising herself a long soak next time, she reluctantly got out of the tub and dried off. Draining the tub and rinsing it as she was shown yesterday, she dressed in another dress which had caught her eye. Remembering the underpants, she donned them and put on a pair of sandals she had found in the closet.

By the time Helen arrived to pick up Rebecca, she had finished breakfast and helped Hal clean up the kitchen. She was delighted with how clean everything was, as she was used to fighting the dust and dirt which was prevalent, constantly filtering into everything in her mother's home. This was how she imagined a palace would be, and though much smaller than a palace, in her mind, it still dwarfed her own home! Thanking Hal Jarvis for breakfast, she went with Helen Tanner, though not excited about being in an automobile again. Luckily, she only had a few blocks to travel. The young colonial woman was amazed with the well-groomed yards and lush lawns she saw on the trip. It was as though bare earth was not allowed to show. When Mrs. Tanner drove into her driveway and activated the garage door opener, the startled girl thought they would crash into the door. However, almost immediately, she was riding into the garage, and the door was closing behind them. Head whirling from all the new sights, sounds, and technology, young Miss Lloyd was in a daze. Helping Rebecca out of the car, Helen led her into her kitchen, and another world of shiny appliances and clean surfaces.

Trying to entertain the girl, Helen took her on a tour of her home. Constantly awestruck, Rebecca felt almost physical pain trying to fathom every new thing she saw. A great many things were familiar to her, as to function, but the modern version of things took some acclimation. Wondering if it were proper, Jerry's mother showed Rebecca his room. Without telling the girl who lived there, Rebecca inhaled deeply and stated, "This is Jerrold's room, is it not? I recognize his smell, though I was near him only a few times and only for a moment!"

"Yes, this is my son's room. I hope he doesn't mind me showing it to you."

As though walking on air, Rebecca drifted around his room, taking in the sight of everything associated with Jerry's life. All at once, she saw something which took her breath away. Tacked to a bulletin board on the wall was an enlargement of the picture Matthew had posed her for. With swelling heart, the girl was near to tears, thinking Jerry would think so much of her to have her likeness on display. Sinking down in front of the desk, Rebecca began sobbing.

"Oh, my dear, don't cry. I know you've thought for a long time about how he may feel about you. This may be an indication, but it'd be better hearing it from his own lips."

Attempting to stifle her sobs, Rebecca was handed a tissue to wipe her eyes with. This was something else new, and she had to be shown how to use it to dry her tears. Sniffling and looking sheepish for her emotional display, she gave Helen a tentative smile.

"I am sorry! I am just overwhelmed Jerrold would want to have my portrait in a place of honor in his room. I feel he may love me, as I know I love him."

"We'll see, my dear. This evening, we'll get to see how much he thinks of you."

For the remainder of the day, the two women roamed around the house, as the younger assisted the elder in her household chores. In her mind, Helen felt this may become a common thing if things turned out the way she suspected they may. After lunch, it was obvious the young woman was tired, so Helen suggested she take a nap. Asking permission to take it in Jerry's room, she was given permission to do so. Knowing Jerry would be home before going to the physics lab prompted Helen to awaken her early, so she could be taken back to the Jarvis home. She had just returned when Jerry came in and went straight to his room to drop off his book bag. Preparing dinner, she heard her son's feet on the stairs.

"Mom, has anyone been in my room?"

"I've been in and out all day looking for dirty laundry and putting the clean clothes away. Why? Is something missing?"

"No. It just feels like someone has been in there, poking around, and my bed isn't the way I left it."

"I may have messed it up when I was in there. I'm sorry, son."

"No big deal, Mom. I was just wondering. So what's for dinner?"

At dinner, the conversation was on a variety of topics. It was obvious they were staying away from the decision Jerry had yet to make. When his father asked him what his lab period was going to be on tonight, Jerry wasn't sure what Professor Blanchard had on the agenda. The question, however, reminded Jerry of a conversation he had with Bill earlier in the day.

"Uh, Professor Blanchard suggested I invite you to the lab tonight to let you see STUDLY. Bill thought you may feel better about things if you could see where I spend a lot of my time."

"That would be nice, dear, but I don't like the name of his machine! It seems vulgar and disrespectful!"

"Helen, it's just an acronym. Acronyms are all the rage, especially in anything dealing with the government! Son, I think it's very nice of your professor to invite us. What time should we go?"

"My lab starts at seven, so I guess you could go the same time I go. You probably won't want to stay as long as I will, so we should take separate cars. Okay?"

"Sure, son."

23

By the time dinner was cleaned up and the dishwasher loaded and started, it was time to go, so they drove separately to the campus and parked in student parking at the side of the physics building. Escorting his parents into the building, he showed them around a little before taking them to the lab. Bill was working around his invention and turned toward them as they entered. Although Bill and Stewart had spoken on the phone a couple times, they had never met face to face. Jerry introduced his parents to his professor, and they made small talk for a few minutes before Bill asked Jerry if he was ready to begin an experiment. Answering in the affirmative, he awaited direction from his mentor. Bill explained to the Tanners about the need to travel in time naked. They said they already knew about the nudity part of Jerry's adventures. As though it just occurred to him, he let slip the fact Jerry was not his only human time traveler. Jerry immediately became very curious as to who else had jumped. Bill acted nonchalant about it, but Jerry pressed him for details.

"You know how crazy Hal's been about your jumping back into the past. He's pestered both of us for all the information we could give him, and he let us use all the stuff on the last jump you made, just so he could feel involved! Well, after you came back and was thinking about going back permanently, he started browbeating me about letting him go back before you screwed up history!"

Bill smiled as he said this, so they all knew he was teasing.

"So…did you let him jump? And without telling me, so I could give him some pointers? Bill! How could you do that to me? You know I should have been told!"

"Listen, Jerry, my boy! You were walking around here in a daze, your chin dragging on the ground, and wringing your hands! I did what I thought best for STUDLY and for you!"

"Uh, sorry, Professor!"

"Quite all right, my boy! To answer your question, yes! He jumped. Not for long, but he went and came back without breaking his neck I might add! He's not as agile on his feet as you!"

From off in the hallway.

"I heard that, you old crackpot! I'll get better with practice! Hello, Jerry. I've met your parents. How are you folks doing tonight?"

Without waiting for a reply, the history professor took a packet out of his coat pocket and pushed it toward Jerry.

"Look what I brought back! I cashed in those pearls while I was there and bought a few things, then got the rest in currency, so we won't have to go back penniless next time!"

"You actually got to Salem and bargained with some merchant to get cash? You've got to be kidding me, Hal!"

"I kid you not, boy! I even met your friends, and Matthew helped me get to Salem, where I met your relatives."

"You did? When did you jump? I mean 'when' into the past did you jump?"

"I jumped about a year later than you did your first time."

"Did you meet Hope, and Lydia, and Rebecca?"

"Yes. Hope was married to Matthew, so I saw them in the home you helped Matthew build on to. Lydia was there in Salem when we visited. And, yes, I met your Rebecca!"

"How was she? Was she well? How did she look?"

"Whoa, boy! Don't get all hyper? You sound like I did when I first heard about your jump. I had a wonderful adventure! Matthew and Hope were gracious hosts, and I met his entire family. Hope was expecting their first child by the way. I brought you something you might like to have!”

“You did? What is it?”

“My wife has it in the hallway. Betty? Will you bring Jerry's gift in now?”

Entering the lab first, empty-handed, Betty looked at the group. Jerry was about to ask what was up, but in an instant, he saw a modern young woman enter behind Hal's wife. Wearing a dress and sandals, she looked like any other modern woman until he looked at her face, then his heart nearly halted mid-beat. Looking nervous but smiling shyly, he still recognized the beauty of the colonial girl who held his heart captive when he returned to his own time. His eyes had nearly worn out the picture he kept in his room, and he always carried in his memory the many images he engraved on his heart. Feeling tears filling his eyes, he moved in her direction, fearing he would lose her in his momentary blindness. Seeing Rebecca moving toward him, he saw the tears running down her beautiful cheeks. Coming together in a crashing embrace, they cared not who saw them. Across time they were reunited, and nothing would stifle their display of affection for one another! Giving Rebecca a kiss so gentle but with such unmistakable emotion, the five adults felt justified in their orchestrating this reunion. Both Helen and Betty gave out sighs of compassion, as they remembered their own courtship. Pulling back from their kiss, each looked into the face of the other, still amazed at their being together again.

“Well, Jerry, how do like your present?”

Turning toward the adults, both young people smiling so broadly they feared their faces would split.

“I'm so grateful, Hal! I don't know what to say except thank you!”

“I am also very grateful, Master Jarvis. Thank you! Thank you all! You have been so gracious to me and helpful!” Rebecca gushed.

“You're both very welcome! All of us felt the pain and anguish you were going through, Jerry, so we came together to help you. Of course, this is only the beginning! We wanted to get you two together to see how you felt about each other. Now, we've a pretty good idea, but there are still a lot of hurdles to get over. You'll have to decide 'when' you're going to live. When you decide, there will be additional decisions. We are here to help and to advise if you want.

Stewart Tanner added, "We don't want to influence you, but your mother and I are quite impressed with this young lady, and I do mean lady! She's so unspoiled and so lovely, we'd enjoy having her in the family."

"Thanks, Dad! Thanks, Mom! Not to put a damper on things, but I think Rebecca would prefer I court her for a while so we can know each other better. I only wish her family could see us together."

It was Bill Blanchard's cue to enter the conversation.

"I may be able to help with that, but I don't give frequent flyer miles, and at the rate people are learning about STUDLY, I may have him taken away by the government!"

Everyone agreed it would be catastrophic for such a thing to happen, so all reaffirmed their vow of secrecy, and the Jarvises said they'd talk to Dr. Shumway.

Keeping his arm around Rebecca, Jerry felt possessive about a woman for the first time in his life. Although propriety dictated the colonial girl remain at the Jarvis home, it was more convenient to move her to the Tanner home, as Helen was at home more than Betty and could be a chaperone. It was more to keep neighborhood tongues from wagging than having any doubt of the moral fiber of the two young people. Telling Rebecca, she should pick up the clothes Betty had accumulated for her, Helen added she would take her shopping for some new things. At that moment, foremost in the women's minds was how this innocent, colonial girl would react in a department store or even a grocery store the first time!

Bill Blanchard directed a question to Hal.

"Hal, I wanted to discuss the pictures you took while you were gone. Some of them were more interesting to me than others. Could I have a few words with you?"

The two professors walked off to one corner of the lab for their confab, as the others continued to socialize.

"I took the liberty of looking through the file I downloaded from your camera and came across a group of pictures you took of a woman you had pose for you inside a home. Who is she Hal? She is a handsome woman!"

"I guess I have to apologize to you, Bill! I thought the only figures you were interested in was on a mathematics table. Yes! She is a handsome woman. For a few moments, I kind of wanted to be an unattached man."

"Well, damn it! Who is she? I'm an unattached man, and I want to know about her!"

"Patience, my old friend! I will reveal all. That woman is Margaret Lloyd, the mother of Matthew and Rebecca. She is a widow, and according to Jerry, she never remarried and died of influenza in 1703."

"Hal, you and I have known each other for a long time, and you've never seen me take much interest in women. My science was my mistress, and I managed without female entanglements. It was not because I didn't care for them, but just never found one to catch my attention. I had my fair share of coed crushes to deal with, but they were too young for my tastes. I saw a woman in those pictures who suddenly caught my attention! I can't get her out of my mind."

It was dark by the time everyone left the lab. Rebecca, though wanting to take in every new sight and sound, was oblivious to the world about her. Sitting beside Jerry in his car, she was about to burst with emotion. Desire to be in his company had been the focus of her life for over a year. The constant ache in her heart had killed her appetite and haunted her dreams. Now, at long last, she was within touching distance of the person who had invaded her life and captured her heart. Even the propriety she had been reared with did not prevent her from touching him, even if it was only his arm. Seat belts prevented her from being right next to him, but she endured the separation, knowing it was just momentary, and she would soon be in his embrace once more.

Telling his dad and mom he wanted to take Rebecca to the local drive-in restaurant to treat her to a shake, he said he'd be home within an hour. His mother said it would give her time to get the guest bedroom ready. Arriving at one of the local hangouts for high school and college-aged kids, Jerry was a little apprehensive, but he felt he just had to be seen with Rebecca. Having been extremely shy in high school and the start of college, he suffered a great deal of ribbing from friends and not-so-friendly acquaintances he had grown up around. Being more mature now, mostly as a result of his time traveling, he felt like being more outgoing. Never having been on a real date, unless he counted the junior high dance he had been driven to, and picked up afterwards from, by his parents, he wanted to see how it felt, and he was dazzled by the beauty of his date tonight! Getting out of his car and opening the passenger door for Rebecca, he took her hand and walked into the restaurant.

Inside, the people who knew him just stared! Figuratively speaking, their jaws were hitting the floor and not a word was said to him as he found an empty booth. Before arriving, he had asked Rebecca to let him order her something he was sure she would enjoy. Still in awe of everything and proud to be seen with Jerry, she readily agreed. Wanting so badly to be walking down the streets of Salem on Jerry's arm, she felt a little out of things in this modern world, but she knew she would be safe with Jerry. As soon as the waitress had taken their order for two shakes, he saw one of his college classmates approach the booth.

"Tanner! This must be your sister or cousin, right?"

Rebecca responded before Jerry could.

"I am not his sister or cousin, sir! I am his fiancé!"

"You're kidding me, aren't you?"

Being confused by the use of slang, she didn't know how to respond.

Jerry found his voice.

"Roberts, this is Rebecca Lloyd from Massachusetts! She is, in fact, my fiancé!"

"Holy guacamole! You've been holding out on us! If he ever breaks up with you, Becky, just let me know!"

Walking back to his table, the guy named Roberts filled in his tablemates, and there was a lot of derisive laughter. Jerry ignored them.

"I'm sorry, Rebecca! Some of these guys can be real jerks!

"Are you speaking a foreign language? I hardly understood what he was saying! What is a 'holy gwaka mow lee?' Why did he call me Becky? And what is a jerk?"

"Uh, we've developed a new set of words and expressions which would make no sense in sixteen hundred Salem. Becky is a nickname, a short name for Rebecca. A jerk is a person who doesn't speak respectfully. And holy guacamole is like saying, 'Oh, my heavens'!"

"It may be harder to learn the language than to get used to all these…things…people use to ride around in and wash their dishes and cook their food!"

Delivering the shakes, the waitress gave the couple a smile but commented, "I haven't seen you with a girl before, Jerry, but you made up for it! Your lady is quite lovely! Puts a lot of the women who come here to shame."

"Thanks, Ruth! This is Rebecca. Rebecca, this is Ruth. She always treats me better than the others."

"Glad to meet you, Rebecca! Jerry is a sweet boy, er, I mean man! Always treats me nice and never goofs off!"

"It is a pleasure to meet you, uh, Ruth! It is kind of you to say I'm pretty!"

"She's real polite, too! You kids enjoy the shakes. Yell, if you need anything else."

Waiting for directions on what to do with her shake, Rebecca eyed the container and the paper-wrapped tube. Ignoring the straws, Jerry took the plastic spoon provided and dipped it into the shake, then raised it toward his companion's mouth.

"Taste it! See if you like it!"

Cautiously, the colonial girl opened her mouth and allowed Jerry to push the spoon inside. The cold and sweetness exploded in her mouth. Eyes wide, she let the shake dissolve and warm up in her mouth before swallowing the milky confection.

"Oh! That is delicious! What is it? What is it made of?" Realizing everything was new, he took pains to explain basically what a shake was made from, she was intent on remembering the ingredients, though many she had never heard about. Ice cream was unknown, but she recognized milk and sugar. Strawberries were known, but she had little experience with tasting them. She finally decided it didn't matter what was in it. She liked eating it, though the coldness was new to her. Not knowing how the richness of a shake would affect her digestion, he had ordered small shakes, so it didn't take them long to finish them. Trying to get every tasty drop of the shake out of her cup, she still tried to be polite.

So that was the beginning of Rebecca's life with Jerry, far from her childhood home. Jerry took her to many places and tried to explain beforehand what was going to happen, so she would not feel embarrassed. Careful not to put this innocent young woman in situations which would open her to ridicule, he sheltered her from the seamier side of his world. Continuing his college classes, he left his girlfriend in the care of his mother, where she learned about keeping a modern house. She still was not introduced to television and more sophisticated conveniences, since it was too much too soon. Jerry made their betrothal official by buying her an engagement ring. It was a simple one, but she was thrilled. A betrothal in her time didn't always include a ring unless the family was well-to-do. Always happy to see Jerry return home, her mood around him was mostly buoyant, but there were times he caught her gazing into nothingness and sensed she missed her family…and her time. The things he and his family had always taken for granted were still all new to her. Being used to reading, the family picked out books which were classic and suitable for her unsophisticated mind. She wasn't backward in any sense, but the changes in society over the three hundred plus years since her time were somehow crude and vulgar in many instances, and the Tanners were concerned she may become jaded by assimilating some of this material.

Hal Jarvis had talked to Jerry and his parents about what his brother-in-law had concluded from her blood test. He was fascinated with the number of antibodies she already had and felt she could survive not taking the inoculations. He cautioned them, however, to not expose her unnecessarily to any sick person, since viruses had mutated into newer strains not present in her time. The weight she had lost from not eating and sleeping was regained. She spent an hour or two with Jerry each evening, and she felt the normal urges of a young woman, just as Jerry did, but they were careful not to let things get out of hand. Finally, Jerry realized Rebecca had been there an entire month. He had to make the next move. So he wanted to talk with her and see how she felt about things. A picnic was planned. Helen Tanner helped Rebecca prepare and pack a lunch, while Jerry and his dad packed a small camping table and chairs. Planning to go to a park a little way out of town, he hoped it would not be too crowded. Leaving late in the morning, they were there well before noon, so they set up their table and lay a blanket on the lawn. Still amazed at the lush lawns, Rebecca sat on the blanket and riffled through the blades of grass with her hand as she waited for Jerry to join her. After settling beside his fiancé, Jerry looked at her and for the thousandth time thought of how beautiful she was. Giving him a shy smile when she caught him gazing at her, she wanted to tell him everything in her heart but could not find the words. Instead, he opened the conversation.

"Rebecca, you know I love you, don't you?"

"Oh, yes, Jerrold, you show me how much all the time. I am so happy to be with you."

"Is there something missing…something which would make you happier?"

"You make me happy, and this ring you gave me makes your intentions clear. I look forward to marrying you and someday give you children. I have dreamed of this for so long. I want nothing more than to be your wife, Jerrold!"

"Is there nothing more I can give you?"

"I wish I could show my ring to my friends and family to tell them of my happiness and about how wonderful my fiancé is to me! But I understand this cannot be because I chose to come here to be with you! It is the sacrifice I was willing to make, even when I thought it was just to Virginia I would be going. I knew I could not be with my family and friends and would have to make a life wherever you were! I loved you that much, Jerrold! I still do, so here I am, in a strange land, trying to learn so many new things! But I am with the man I love, so I console myself with making a life here, in this time, with your kind parents and your other friends. So I can only say you have given me much, and I will be content with my new life and hopefully to be a new wife soon!"

"Rebecca, I have never loved anyone before. I didn't know what love was until I met you! I didn't know what to do! I was still undecided when my friends and parents decided to make the decision for me. They did it out of love and with romance in their hearts! I'm glad they brought you here, and it's been wonderful this past month, but I fear you're not totally happy! There are so many new things in my time for you to learn. If I had decided to return to your time and court you, it would have been difficult for me there, too, but it may have been easier. I would still have all my knowledge of modern things and may be able to improve the lives of your family, though I know very little about farming. I want to ask Bill to send you and I back so we can visit your family. I know it would make you happy, even if it is for just a short time. One of the advantages of going back in time is we can pick the time to visit and be pretty sure what is happening, but we don't have the same choice when it comes to going into the future. The future still holds all the mysteries of our life, and we don't know what will happen. I believe the only restrictions we have for going back to your time is to appear after you left. I don't know what would happen if we went back and you were there, in your past and in your future. I don't want to risk anything bad happening, so we can go back one minute after you left or any time after that. It may cause some problems if you appeared at the same age, while the rest of your family have aged. Your mother and brother would understand, but not Jonathan, Rhoda, and Daniel. So think about it. I would like to marry you, but I don't know where! Either way, one of our families would not be present. I could get Bill to send my parents, but what about my brother and his wife? They know nothing of my traveling in time. What do you think?"

"Jerrold, my love! I would enjoy going back and visiting, but I also cannot decide where I want to be married. Of course, I would want my entire family present, but I understand you would like yours present, also! It is truly perplexing!"

"I think I may have a solution! First, though, you have to get used to calling me Jerry because it's my real name! I called myself Jerrold in Salem because Matthew said he had never heard anyone called Jerry! My name is Jerry Kent Tanner, and it will be on our marriage certificate wherever we're married."

"I am so sorry, Jerrold, I mean Jerry! I will learn. You said you may have a solution to our dilemma. Tell me about it!"

Explaining how some couples who had families spread between two major cities sometimes had one wedding but two receptions. In their case, since their families were separated by time, instead of just distance, why couldn't they be married in both places and in both times? Agreeing it was a good idea, Rebecca began to make plans for the two ceremonies with a bemused Jerry loving her animated enthusiasm. So their plans went. After they were married in the present, their absence could be explained by saying they were on their honeymoon in New England. No one had to know "when" they had traveled! When it came to their marriage in Salem, it would be easy to explain they were returning to Jerry's school, and everyone would assume it to be in Virginia. It was a beginning, and so they continued to talk it over as they ate their picnic lunch. After their picnic, they returned home and told Jerry's parents about their decision.

This news triggered Helen to go into full marriage planner mode. In speaking with Betty Jarvis, Betty said Hal would be honored to give the bride away. Since he brought Rebecca into this time, he felt responsible. In further discussion, Bill Blanchard, an old bachelor, wanted to share the bride's expenses with the Jarvises, and he and Hal would walk her down the aisle together. Always one to conserve, Helen had a simple but elegant wedding dress made, with no zippers, so it could be used in both times. Since Rebecca was essentially a member of the Puritan church, though her family had not been staunch supporters, she agreed to have the Bishop of Jerry's church perform their marriage in the present time and assumed their marriage in Salem would be officiated by Reverend Witherspoon. It took three weeks from the day of the picnic to the day of the wedding. Though Helen was glad she had no more children, she was grateful for the experience of planning a wedding as though she had a daughter, since she always thought she would never have the pleasure.

Nearly all the members of the wedding party were privy to the story of Rebecca's origin. The sole exceptions being Jerry's brother David and sister-in-law, Roberta. When they were first introduced to Rebecca, each had been startled. The couple had never known Jerry to be serious about a girl and had rarely seen him date anyone. So to be introduced to a very pretty young woman, who he said was his fiancé, was totally earthshaking. Although both tried to get her alone to draw out her attraction to Jerry, she was watched over by both of Jerry and David's parents and never allowed much probing. They just saw her as a quiet and unassuming woman who seemed to adore Jerry. As surprising as it seemed, they finally gave up and decided they had misjudged Jerry's charm and appeal. Roberta was enlisted as the matron of honor, and David became Jerry's best man.

By their wedding day, Jerry and Rebecca had already assembled a bundle of what they were taking on their honeymoon. Since it was into the past, they had to choose carefully. Jerry had the colonial money Hal had from his trip, and they used the same clothing Jerry had used before. Rebecca had the small number of clothes she had brought with her. By using plain cloth, Rebecca, Helen, and Betty had hand-sewn a few dresses and slips, so they would be authentic for the seventeenth century or at least appear to be. Fortunately, Rebecca had been sewing most of her own clothes for several years and was familiar with laying out the correct styles. Although Helen and Betty had sewn for years also, they were used to using their sewing machines, so this was an enriching experience for them both. Because it was short notice and since they wanted a minimum of fanfare, the wedding was a simple affair with only thirty some-odd guests invited. Most were extended family, while the rest were friends and neighbors. Many were still surprised to see Jerry marrying such a beautiful girl since they had always thought he would choose a mousey type. After all, he seemed so shy around women. And, as expected, the various gifts they received could never be taken to Salem.

The actual ceremony took place at noon, and the wedding dinner for the family was at two in the afternoon. Six o'clock in the evening was the reception, and they expected a light turnout. Surprisingly, at least fifty of Jerry's high school and college classmates came to the reception. When word had spread that Jerry Tanner was getting married, enquiring minds wanted to see what kind of girl married a geek! They were totally taken aback by her grace and beauty. A number of the young women were heard to ask each other why they hadn't noticed how attractive he was before now. Finally, the reception wound down and Jerry found his "friends" had not overlooked the tradition of decorating his car. He was a little put off, but his father said he would take care of cleaning it while they were gone. Rebecca was confused by the whole thing, and the tradition had to be explained to her. It still made no sense to her pragmatic mind. She said something about "hooligans" and disrespect. David stayed to help clean up, allowing his parents to see them off on their honeymoon.

Upon their arrival at the lab, Jerry, Rebecca, his parents, and the

Jarvises were surprised with the changes Bill Blanchard had made to the portal. He had added a covering and an antechamber, explaining how it was not right to see people off in their birthday suits. He thought about removing Jerry's beacon from his thigh, but thought perhaps he should leave it there, just in case the mouthpiece beacons became lost or damaged. Redundancy was a good thing! In fact, he added two extra mouthpieces to their packet, which was quite large compared to the previous jumps. The couple endured remarks about how your burden was doubled when you took on a wife and such teasing. As others were engaged in wishing the new bride well, Bill pulled Jerry off to the side.

"Uh, Jerry, uh, I know you're married now, but I need to caution you about one of my worries."

"Okay, Bill. What is it?"

"I have no idea what affect time travel will have on a fetus."

"What's that got to do with… Oh! I forgot!" Jerry said, blushing furiously.

"Well, just as a precaution, try not to get her pregnant on the honeymoon, sport!"

"I'll try not to, Bill, but I didn't think about any protection, and they don't have those things in the seventeenth century!"

"Well, maybe not in Salem, but I know enough about history to know they had something of the sort they called French Letters but never mind. I got you a box of protection, just as a precaution. Just keep them out of sight, but you will have to explain them to your wife."

"Okay. Thanks, Bill."

"Uh, Jerry, would you do me a favor?"

"Sure, Bill! Anything I can."

"I kind of got interested in Rebecca's mother or at least the pictures Hal brought back. Would you take this picture and show it to her? If she doesn't find me too ugly, I'm thinking I should train you and Hal to operate STUDLY, so I might try out my contraption. I may decide to make a call on a certain widow you know. You probably think I'm an old fool, don't you?"

"Of course not! Bill, Rebecca's mother is a real nice woman, and I would be honored to get you two together! I'll take the picture with me and introduce Mistress Lloyd to you and talk you up."

"Just don't lay it on too thick. I may not be able to live up to her expectations!"

Then it was time for the newlyweds to "jump" into their honeymoon. To be more precise, they would jump into another round of courtship and wedding planning in Salem. The consummation of their marriage would be postponed until their second wedding. It was tormenting to both, but they wanted to continue the masquerade a little longer by observing propriety.

"I hope you two can manage all the baggage you've got! I may have to enlarge my portal. If I had, I would have found some old handcart or wheelbarrow or something to help you carry your luggage! People may find it strange to see you lugging all that stuff through the woods!"

"Thanks, Bill, but we'll manage, even if I have to stash some of it in the bushes and come back for it later. Thank you all for everything, and we love you all!"

"Yes! Thank you so much!" added Rebecca.

Rebecca went into Bill's office and changed out of her clothing, donning a robe. Jerry gave her privacy, though he was entitled to be there. He followed suit and soon, both young people were in robes, waiting their turn in the portal. Bill had sent their luggage on ahead as they changed clothes. Knowing they would not be gone long from the present time, the goodbyes were not tearful. It was just as it would be when newlyweds were seen off on their honeymoon with the full expectation of a speedy return. When Professor Blanchard determined it was time, the young couple moved toward the portal. Jerry would go first, so he would be there to greet his wife's arrival and be available in case something was amiss. For the Tanner parents and Betty Jarvis, this was a new experience—seeing people off to travel time. Because of the covering the professor had put around the portal, the time traveler was shielded from the neck down. So when Jerry was transported, everyone saw his head blink out as he left the portal for seventeenth century Salem. As soon as Jerry left the portal, Rebecca hurried inside so she could quickly rejoin her new husband. When she, too, blinked out, there seemed to be a collective exhalation from the three "newbies." Bill took up the two robes and hung them on pegs outside the portal and looked at the two couples with him.

"Well, that's our show for tonight, folks! I hope you enjoyed what we presented this evening."

Everyone laughed, and the tension in the air evaporated.

"How will we know when they get back?" asked Helen Tanner.

"When they activate the beacon, I usually try to retrieve them as soon as possible. Of course, we've always done this operation in one night, so I stay until they return. So far, the longest Jerry or Hal stayed in the past was two weeks, and that has equated to a few hours, local time. This time, we don't know for sure how long since they'll have to do the courting thing and arrange for the wedding. I've no idea what the customs were back then. I plan on staying here tonight and for a couple days, if necessary. I have a bed in my office and a refrigerator and cupboard, which I keep stocked up. I'll call each of you when I get a signal to retrieve. I don't like to keep them waiting on the other end, as they may be running from a witch hunt!"

Bill smiled, but his humor was rather dark, so there were no smiles returned.

"You folks should go home and continue with whatever you normally do. I'll keep you informed if our travelers return to the coop."

"Bill, Hal tells me you're interested in Rebecca's widowed mother!" Betty Jarvis asked.

Bill blushed and began to bluster. The Tanners perked up their ears. Hal smiled.

"Hal told me when he returned from his jump how attractive he thought she was, and I had to make him promise he wouldn't go time traveling again, the philandering sot! So, how did you learn about her?"

"Hal brought pictures back, most of them about the architecture and candid shots of people at work and play, but he took pictures of all the Lloyd family. Some of those were of Margaret Lloyd, and I thought her a handsome woman."

"Hmmm. Pictures he didn't share with me. I'd like to see the pictures of Rebecca's family, wouldn't you, Helen and Stewart?"

All agreed it would be nice to see the pictures of seventeenth century Salem and the people. Bill went over to his lab computer and brought it up to show the file Hal had taken on his sojourn. Hal looked a little uncomfortable. Some of the pictures were a bit skewed because he had been taking them surreptitiously, but they were clear and showed a great deal of detail. Though the Tanners and Betty were patient through the other pictures, they were most interested to see pictures of the family they had heard so much about. Presently, the family pictures began. Everyone agreed Matthew and Hope were a handsome couple, and the younger Lloyds looked obviously related. Then came the posed portraits of Margaret. Hal saw the scowl on Betty's face, but he also saw the secret smile which told him she was going to tease him about this every chance she got. It gave him a warm, loving feeling for his dear wife.

When the slideshow was completed, all had to agree with Hal and Bill. Margaret Lloyd was attractive. Bill received encouragement from the other two couples.

"I sent a picture of myself with Jerry and asked him to act as my advocate. It all seems so odd!"

"What does?"

"My entire life, I've never gone out of my way to meet and develop relationships with women. I felt my work was enough. I wouldn't have considered a relationship with a woman as far away as the next town, but here I am, contemplating a relationship with someone not only on the other side of the country, but across more than three centuries of time! I suppose I'm being an old fool. I have no idea if she will even be interested in me."

Betty interjected, "You are an old fool, Bill! I've tried to fix you up with some of my friends for years. You are handsome and successful. You just refused to look outside of this damned physics lab! Now, just shut up and let Jerry and the rest of us fix you up with Rebecca's mother. Will you bring her here or are you going to her?"

"I don't know yet, but I think it will be me going to her time. I want her to feel comfortable in the setting she is in and not have to deal with the culture shock. I don't think I'll have as hard a time acclimating. I may not be there long, anyway!"

"Now, there is a novel approach! A man who wants the woman to be comfortable. Not many men are so considerate. I knew you had it in you, you old romantic slob!" Betty smiled her remarks to Bill Blanchard.

With parting words of encouragement, Stewart Tanner and Helen walked out of the building with the Jarvises, leaving Professor Blanchard to stand the vigil alone. Each man had thought to offer to keep him company but felt it important to be with their wives, lest they feel abandoned. The young couple could return before the night was out or it may take a day or two. It all depended on what they decided to do when they arrived in Rebecca's time.

25

When Rebecca stumbled into the woods outside of Middleton, Massachusetts Colony, her new husband almost literally waited with open arms. Knowing she would be coming soon, he had opened the luggage to retrieve the clothing which they planned to wear upon arrival. Just as he pulled his trousers upon his loins, his bride came rushing toward him. Catching her in his arms kept her from sprawling naked on the humus of the forest. Holding her for a moment, he reassured her, as he caressed her. Then feeling arousal overcoming him, he disengaged his arms from Rebecca and urged her to don the clothing he was soon handing her. It was daylight, and he saw her lush body displayed before him for the first time. At last, he saw her in the same state she had seen him in twice before. He felt a sense of satisfaction as his mind recorded the fact her physical beauty went beyond just her face. Reminding himself of propriety despite being lawfully wedded to this beautiful woman, he turned his attention to getting both of them clothed and on the road to the Lloyd family's home. Becoming familiar with this portion of the woods, he felt the luggage could be managed in one trip if both burdened themselves. The packaging had been planned for ease of carrying, so there were shoulder straps and handles available to facilitate transportation.

When they had finished dressing and apportioned the luggage between the two of them, they began their trek. Knowing the area even better, Rebecca struck off in the direction which would take them to her home. Being accustomed to carrying burdens, she seemed in no distress for her load. Jerry was impressed with the hardiness of his young wife. Within ten minutes, they had come to the road, and they could see both Lloyd homes in the distance. Jerry wondered how long Rebecca had been gone, subjectively speaking. If the time period was too short, it would require a plausible explanation, since she may not have had enough time to reach Virginia and return to Middleton. In the distance, they saw someone come out of the family home, look in their direction, then disappear back into the house. Within a minute, the house disgorged the entire family— Mistress Lloyd, Jonathan, Daniel, and Rhoda! Jonathan and Daniel ran toward them, and as they came up to the couple, began relieving them of some of their burden. This allowed them to move more quickly, and soon Rebecca was sobbing and embracing her mother and younger sister. Jerry shook the hands of the boys, and Rhoda gave him a quick embrace. As he looked at Rebecca's mother, she looked at him with the silent question in her eyes, "How have you been treating my daughter?"

Telling her younger children to carry the luggage into the house, she hung back with Rebecca and Jerry. Sensing her questioning glances at them, Rebecca showed her mother her rings. Mistress Lloyd's countenance became immediately suffused with joy, and she again embraced her daughter, then also embraced Jerry for the first time. Her beaming face said a silent "thank you" to Jerry, for being a gentleman and looking after her daughter's virtue. Once her mother had seen the rings, Rebecca made sure her mother saw her removing the wedding band. With a questioning look in her eyes, she could not put a voice to it before Rebecca explained how they were lawfully wedded in Jerry's world but wanted to pose as only betrothed, so they could also be married in Salem, so the family could be present. Mistress Lloyd, always the astute woman, immediately voiced understanding. Rebecca handed her wedding ring to Jerry for safekeeping. As Rebecca again put her hand out to show her mother the engagement ring, Rhoda came dashing out of the house and, with typical young girl squeals, demanded to see the ring also. Engaging the two boys in conversation since they were not interested in looking at rings, Jerry regaled them with sketchy details of their journey from Virginia. This was something he had spent some of his free time concocting, as he and Rebecca planned their weddings and lived in Jerry's time. Soon, Jonathan was sent to Matthew's with the news of Jerry and Rebecca's arrival, and the others went into the house. Rebecca wandered about the house, just looking at and touching familiar things, mentally comparing them to things she saw in Jerry's time. Managing to get his mother-in-law to the side, he asked her how long Rebecca had been absent. With an initial look of puzzlement, she suddenly realized why the question had been asked. She told him Rebecca had been gone for almost six months. This helped Jerry to confirm the calibration of Bill's device, as he had calculated and tried to target Rebecca's absence for approximately six months. The front door opened, and Matthew and Hope entered with excited looks on their faces.

As the two men shook hands and embraced, the women did likewise, then it was time to change partners, and the process was repeated. The two young men genuinely liked each other, and with each marrying within the other's family, the bond was strengthened. Where Matthew and Jerry were true peers, Rebecca saw Hope as an older sister and confidante. What immediately drew Jerry and Rebecca's attention was the fact Hope was very gravid and seemed almost ready to burst. With concern, Rebecca bid Hope to be seated. Smiling with appreciation for their concern, she told them she was just fine. So Rebecca began dragging Hope to her former bedroom but realized it was now Rhoda's room, and what she wanted to discuss with her sister-in-law was not for Rhoda's ears. She just told Hope they would talk later. Hope understood and simply nodded.

"So how was your trip from, uh, Virginia? I trust you did not encounter anymore natives!"

"We did well, and the travel was not too taxing on Rebecca. Master Jarvis sends his regards to you and your family. He told us of Hope's expectancy, but the sight of her, uh, condition is still a surprise! He says he was treated royally and was very impressed and complimentary of your mother."

Mistress Lloyd blushed and turned away to hide her embarrassment and pleasure that a man would appreciate her looks, even if he were married! Everyone smiled at their matriarch's discomfiture.

To recover, she seemed to suddenly remember she needed to begin supper preparations. Asking if Rebecca and Hope would assist her and Rhoda, this left the "men" to talk among themselves. Matthew and Jerry knew they would have to wait to talk about matters also, so they just made idle conversation. Jerry expounded on his fictional travelogue, giving Matthew a wink. Matthew went along, inserting a question here and there, causing Jerry to spin his yarn further than he had intended. Seeing the mischievous look in Matthew's eyes, he grinned at his friend. The two younger boys were agog with the tale of adventure, as narrated by Jerry. None too soon, they were called to the evening meal. Rebecca was tasked to keep up with Jerry's tall tales by questions Rhoda put to her during the meal. Finally, their mother shushed the young girl, telling her to leave off her interrogation.

After the supper was eaten and cleared, Matthew requested if Jerry and Rebecca would walk back to Matthew's home, so the two couples could visit more. Of course, this brought protests from the younger Lloyds until Margaret took charge and told the two couples to run along. Rebecca would return to sleep with Rhoda or her mother, and Jerry would sleep at Matthew's. Propriety was being observed, as far as the unknowing observer was concerned! Amid groans from Jonathan, Rhoda, and Daniel, the four older people left. It was a short walk and they traveled it quickly, so as to reach relative privacy in order to catch up the news.

As soon as the door closed, Rebecca threw herself into Jerry's arms, and they kissed ardently. Matthew was alarmed and was tempted to break up the embrace and bussing, but his wife put her hand on his arm to restrain him. Finally, the time-traveling couple composed themselves.

"I apologize, Matthew and Hope. We act wantonly! I must tell you both Rebecca and I are lawfully married, and our affection is proper in the eyes of God, though a bit shameless in front of you!" Saying the last with admonishing looks at Rebecca.

With unbridled enthusiasm, the Lloyds congratulated the Tanners. Rebecca demanded her wedding ring back, so she could show it and her engagement ring to Hope and then Matthew. It was much more elegant than the simple band Hope wore, but she displayed no envy. Eyes sparkling their emotions, the women fell upon the other's breast and embraced once more. Jerry explained to Matthew and Hope their plan to pose as a betrothed couple and then having Reverend Witherspoon marry them, just as he had Matthew and Hope. Rebecca had been at their wedding, but Jerry had missed it. Matthew questioned whether it was necessary for them to be married twice, but Jerry told him it was for Rebecca, so she could have her family and a few friends present.

"I understand your desire to be married here in Salem, but I fear Reverend Witherspoon may not be a good choice. He was barely civil to Hope and I the last time we encountered him. I think he was unduly critical of the congregation during the witchcraft hysteria. Now that it has died down, the magistrates and clergy are not viewed in the best light. Since the hangings and imprisonments, they are being blamed, though the clearheaded thinkers know the congregations are just as much at fault as those in power at the time. The influence of Cotton Mather is felt everywhere. It is only a matter of time before Reverend Witherspoon will leave the area, I feel, and it will be a good thing for all. And his son, Roger, who inquired after Rebecca a number of times, though I have no idea why! He hardly knew her and only saw her at church services and our wedding. We told him she had traveled to Virginia to become betrothed to you, Jerrold!

He seemed very upset and stormed away. Perhaps it best if you just announce how your marriage took place in Virginia. We can still have a celebration. In this way, you two will not have to continue this deception and can use our other bedroom."

"Uh, Matthew, we left right after the wedding and have not been alone, so, uh, we haven't, uh been together, as uh, man and wife." Jerry blushed at this revelation.

Matthew and Hope both grinned at the nervous couple.

"Perhaps we can let you use our home, and we can spend the night at mother's house?"

"Oh, we couldn't put you out of your house! We thought we could just continue our voluntary separation until the wedding, then… Well, we had not thought that far ahead. Suddenly, I feel very nervous!"

"Do not be nervous! You are lawfully wed, and life is too short to deny yourselves the joys of matrimony. I heartily endorse it, my friend and sister. Now, maybe you can compete with Hope and I to see who has the most children. We will just announce tomorrow it was kept as a surprise. Then, in the next few days, we can plan a celebration. So this is your wedding night, is it not?"

"Uh, yes, it is."

"Then you must have privacy! Hope and I will visit mother and sleep in the great room. We will explain to mother, and if the others are still awake, we will break the news to them, also. Come, my wife! Let Jerry and Rebecca become better acquainted. Use our bed, as it is more comfortable than the floor."

"Thank you, brother! I am nervous also but have waited so long for this time to finally be able to show Jerry how much I love him and not have to hide my true feelings!"

"Ah, impetuous youth!" Matthew remarked with a smirk.

Hope hit his arm, smiling herself, and blushing, remembering their relationship when they were newlyweds. Moving with surprising grace, given her well-advanced pregnancy, Hope took up her nightgown and her husband's hand.

"Good night and congratulations to you both. We will see you tomorrow. We will save you some breakfast!"

Finding themselves alone at last and being husband and wife, they felt a sense of freedom. Jerry was already aroused at the realization he would be with Rebecca, and it was proper. Rebecca was surprisingly direct. She took Jerry's hand and pulled him into the bedroom, where she began pulling at his clothes. When she had him naked, she took her own clothes off. As each gazed at the other, their passion began building.

"I always thought you were beautiful before, but now I realize your entire body is beautiful. I love you, Rebecca, with all my heart!"

"I have always thought you were handsome all over. I love you, too, Jerry. Please, hold me and kiss me before I burn up! I feel like I am sitting inside the hearth."

Moving toward each other, the newlyweds embraced and began their mating dance, expressing their joy and love in ways they had long suppressed. The farthest thing from Jerry's mind at this time was Bill Blanchard's admonition. Not only didn't he remember, but the "protection" was in his luggage at his mother-in-law's home. Despite his passion, Jerry proved a considerate lover and their wedding night was one of exploration and pleasure, and not of pain and discomfort. Having a healthy libido, Rebecca orchestrated frequent encores throughout the night, and morning found them exhausted but happy and momentarily sated. They had brought no other clothing, so they decided a quick dip in the stream, using blankets to get them there and back was the first order of business.

After drying themselves, they donned yesterday's clothes and walked hand in hand, albeit a little stiff, to Margaret's home. Upon entering the front door, they found the rest of the family in arrested motion. With smiles on their faces, the family applauded the couple, as Jerry and Rebecca both blushed to the roots of their hair. Jerry just smiled, but Rebecca quickly went to her mother and sister-in-law and gave them a hug and a short. "It was wonderful!"

"Uh, is there any breakfast left?" Jerry asked.

"You must keep up your strength, my brother!" Matthew teased.

There was much chatter and showing of affection between family members. Food was dished up for the newly married couple, and a party atmosphere ensued. After eating his fill, Jerry remembered everything Bill had talked about before they jumped. Feeling a pang of guilt and anxiety, Jerry hoped he had not caused Rebecca to conceive on their first night together. He went and dug out Bill's picture and approached his new mother-in-law. She felt it important to give him an embrace and officially welcomed him to the family. He showed her the picture of Professor Blanchard. Taking the picture near a window for better light, she gazed at it and then looked to Jerry with a question in her eyes. He quietly told her about the picture and the man.

"That is Professor Bill Blanchard. He invented the time machine, which has allowed me to meet you all and to take my beloved Rebecca to wife. I owe so very much to this man, but that is not the point. Do you remember when Hal Jarvis was here, and he took pictures of you in this very room?"

"Yes, I remember."

"When he returned to our time, he showed them to Professor Blanchard, because he thought you attractive. Bill Blanchard thought so too. He has talked about little else than how beautiful you are. He is about your age but has never married. He had always been a devoted teacher and scientist. He asked me to show you his picture, so you might allow him to visit you."

"You mean he wants to travel all that way through time and distance to see an old widow? Hmmph! Are there no marriageable women in your time?"

"Hal Jarvis, myself, even Hal's wife and my parents agree with the professor! You are a handsome woman! Would you allow him to visit you? He is very proper. I can vouch for him."

"I never really thought about taking up with a man again. Since my husband died, I just presumed it was my lot in life to endure it alone. I must tell you, though, after Hal's visit, and now seeing this picture, I suppose there are some handsome men in the future, present company included."

"Thank you, Mistress Lloyd. May I call you Mother Lloyd?"

"I would be honored, Jerrold, my new son! I cannot express how pleased I am seeing the change in Rebecca. I have no memory of her being happier than you have made her. Thank you, Jerrold. As to your professor, I can only say let him come, and we shall see. I don't want to leave my family, especially with future grandchildren in the offing."

"I understand. And know this, Rebecca has made me extremely happy, also. Professor Blanchard will not be able to visit you until Hal or myself is there to operate his apparatus. I would not be surprised, though if he doesn't come ahead, without knowing what I have arranged with you. He may just show up one day and come looking for you."

"So I should be prepared for his arrival at any time? It will put a strain on me, trying to look my best at all hours!"

They laughed together, and the others wondered what they were talking about.

"Professor Blanchard is pragmatic, and I doubt he expects you to be radiant at all hours of the day. Just be yourself."

26

Wanting to go to Salem, Jerry and Rebecca were aware Hope's impending delivery would not allow her to travel, and Matthew felt his place was near his wife. So Jonathan, now fifteen, was enlisted to drive the carriage to Salem. Trying to show his maturity, the young man displayed his skill at handling the horses. Stopping first at the Meacham home, Jerry and Rebecca gave them news of Hope's condition. Jonathan was introduced to Hope's siblings and found himself accepted as the relative he had become through marriage. Living on the outskirts, the Lloyd family had little opportunity to socialize, so Jonathan opted to spend the time at the Meacham's rather than follow Rebecca and Jerry on their rounds. Of course, the sister of Hope, Lydia, was closest in age to Jonathan.

Excited to show off her new husband, Rebecca made a visit to a few of her friends. During one such visit, she was told about the impending departure of Reverend Witherspoon and his son from Salem. They had fallen so out of favor with the congregation he was giving his sermons to a nearly empty meeting house. The reverend was embittered, and Roger Witherspoon was surly, constantly in trouble with the magistrate for his bullying of the young men in town. Rumors were circulating about the reverend accepting a new position with a church on the outskirts of Boston. As fortune would have it, the newlywed couple would get to bid Roger adieu!

While on the streets of town, Jerry and Rebecca saw Roger in the distance. She asked Jerry to cross over to the other side of the street to avoid a confrontation, but Jerry gently refused. Suddenly, they were face to face with Roger Witherspoon. Although he was broader than Jerry, their height was equal. Jerry looked him straight in the eye and greeted him.

"Hello, Master Witherspoon. I hope you fare well."

It took Roger a moment to recognize Jerry, but when he did and saw who he was with, he sneered and said, "So the boy from Virginia is spreading himself around. First, with the widow Bonner, then Hope and Lydia Meacham, and now with a little country tart!" Jerry didn't know where it came from, but he instinctively clenched his fist and brought it up and hit Roger square on the point of his unprotected chin. Jerry had never really fought anyone before, but the blow, by pure luck, landed so perfectly it snapped Roger's head back and his body followed his head. The town bully landed flat on his back, momentarily stunned.

"No one talks disparagingly of my wife, you…stupid oaf!"

Though the blow had been unexpected, Roger recovered quickly and scrambled to his feet, enraged and wanting to strike at this upstart. Jerry had pushed Rebecca behind him and was braced for whatever Roger brought to him. Although not a fighter, Jerry had spent long hours lifting and carrying furniture, so he was physically fit. Roger, though built naturally broad and strong, had spent too many hours idling about. Roger threw a blow toward Jerry, but it seemed to go over Jerry's left shoulder. Reaching to grab both wrist and upper arm, Jerry used Roger's momentum and threw the heavier man to the ground with an earthshaking impact. Knowing he could expect an eventual beating from this bully, Jerry wanted to inflict as much damage as he could before he took a drubbing. But as he stepped back, moving Rebecca out of range of their tormentor, his view of Roger was suddenly cut off as two men stepped in and stood ready to wield the cudgels they carried in their hands. These two were constables hired by the town to maintain peace. Knowing Roger by reputation, they stood ready to ward off further attack.

Regaining his feet, Roger Witherspoon glared at the two peace officers, then looking past them, he cast a malevolent eye at Jerry. Being keyed up by the adrenaline in his blood, Jerry was not going to let this man cow him. Staring Roger in the eye, he didn't let his stare waiver.

"I pray you keep a civil tongue in your head when addressing me and my wife, Master Witherspoon."

A number of onlookers willingly gave the constables their statement as to what had transpired. Roger was given the choice of posting a peace bond with the constables or being taken to the magistrate directly. Opting for the bond, he paid up and meekly left the street. One of the men who had witnessed the whole encounter advised Jerry to remain on guard. Jerry thanked him and said he would not be in town long but would keep his eyes open. Taking Rebecca's hand, he headed toward the Meacham home. Following her husband, Rebecca Tanner looked on Jerry with undisguised adoration.

Upon their return to the Jeremiah Meacham home, Jerry was reticent to mention the confrontation, but his wife had no such compunctions and gushed her story to anyone in the family who cared to listen. Being hailed a hero made Jerry feel uncomfortable, so he suggested they start back to Middleton. It was not easy to get Jonathan on the road because of Lydia. When the couple had arrived earlier, Lydia was overjoyed to see Jerry again but was saddened to hear Rebecca had snared him. Being young, however, she soon transferred her attentions to Jonathan, who was her own age. This was no surprise to Jerry, as he knew their future, from his second jump, but he teased Lydia about being fickle. Both she and Jonathan blushed, but on the return trip, Jonathan babbled the whole time about Lydia, much to the amusement of Jerry and Rebecca. When they returned to the Lloyd household, Jerry had to endure retelling of his fight with Roger. Matthew and Hope were both impressed and even Margaret lauded his actions, though he was quick to downplay the episode, telling them how he was very fortunate to escape injury or worse.

With the immediate family and her closest friends aware of her newly married status, Rebecca was beside herself with joy. It seemed so long ago since she had first seen Jerry, as he came into their home in borrowed clothes. Since then (subjective for her, over a year; for her family, nearly two years), she had been infatuated, desolated, subjected to extreme culture shock, reunited, courted, married, and now fully a woman, ready to take her place beside her mother and sister-in-law. She vividly recalled her feelings of desperation when she believed she would die a spinster, then when she "wanted" to die because she believed she had lost the love of her young life. Her spirit soared as she also recalled the joys of reunion, courtship, marriage, and lastly the consummation of her marriage. Although they had not specifically discussed it, she wanted to have children as soon as possible, like most women in her time. Thinking she should talk it over with Jerry soon, she felt the best time would be at bedtime.

While the newlyweds were in Salem, life went on in the Lloyd homes. Margaret was sympathetic to Hope's condition and wanted to be near her, so she arranged it so she would stay in Matthew's spare room. She gave her room to Jerry and Rebecca, though the young couple protested. When she expressed her reasons for temporarily moving in with Mathew, they relented. Two nights married and each night in a different bed. Rebecca naturally assumed charge of the family home as eldest woman present. Her siblings, knowing what may be occurring next door, did not squabble. After breakfast, the younger ones were put to their chores while Jerry and his wife went to visit Matthew. On their way there, they saw a solitary figure walking down the road. Immediately recognizing the person as Bill Blanchard, Jerry ran to meet him.

"Bill, you old coot, I figured you'd do something crazy like this! Hal's minding the store, I assume?"

"Yes, and I'm not sure I like what I have wrought! My landing was a bit rough, and now my clothes are mussed!"

"You look fine to me! We don't look showroom fresh here in Old Mass! Besides, Margaret is afraid you'll catch her in disarray anyway!"

"I'm sure she's lovely at all times."

"Save your sweet talk for her, Professor."

Jerry came up to Matthew's home and met Rebecca coming out of the house. He noticed an anxious look on her face.

"What's wrong?"

"Jerry! It's Hope. She is having problems with the birthing!"

"Let's see what's up," Bill Blanchard said, taking charge.

Going into the house, Jerry introduced Bill to Matthew and then to Margaret, who looked embarrassed by her disheveled appearance. She began excusing herself, but Bill told her she looked fine and had reason to not be in top form. She relaxed and went back to be with Hope. Bill followed her in and surveyed the situation. Hope was having very painful contractions. As part of his education, Bill had taken some premed classes and knew the rudiments of childbirth. After a quick exam, he went out to the front room.

"Jerry, you told me she had four children when you jumped forty years from now?"

"Yes. She had four healthy children."

"My friend, I'm about to contradict everything I have ever said. I know now what you meant about witnessing something in history and not being able to keep from helping. Can you hold things together here? I'm going to take Hope back to our time and get Hal to call his brother-in-law for a house call at the lab."

As Bill had assumed, Matthew would not let her go alone, and Margaret wanted to be with her, too, for support. It was a good thing he had brought extra beacon mouthpieces, as had Jerry.

"Jerry, have you gotten your wife pregnant yet?"

"We've only been here for two nights! How would I know?"

"Never mind! I'm about to do an experiment to see what affect time travel has on a fetus! If I don't do something, I'm afraid mother and child will die, and that's not what happened, as far as we know, so I'm making sure history is corrected. I'm just another meddling fool! I wish I could call Hal and get him started getting Bennett to the lab! Can't! So I'm going ahead. No time to worry about nudity. I'm going to signal Hal to retrieve me, then when I get there, I'll have him call the doctor, and I'll be at the controls to get the other three "tourists" through the portal. You activate their beacons at about two-minute intervals. Send Hope first, and I'll have a lab table set up and waiting for her. Then send her husband and mother-in-law in that order. Understand?"

"Yes! Got it! We better get started for the woods!"

"No! We only used the woods so people wouldn't see us arrive and leave. Everyone here knows what's up, so we jump from here! Hope, right from her bed. The others wherever they are."

"Okay!"

Activating his mouthpiece and plunging it into his mouth, he quickly disrobed, much to the embarrassment of Margaret and Rebecca. It took less than thirty seconds before he blinked out. Jerry began mentally counting down as he directed Matthew and his mother to remove Hope's nightgown. As soon as she was nude, he activated the beacon and gently placed it into her mouth. Things were moving too fast for Matthew, but he had faith in his family and friends, so he held it together and did not panic. Margaret was calm, and as soon as Jerry placed the mouthpiece in Matthew's mouth, she calmly disrobed in front of her daughter and son-in-law. Counting down, he put the activated mouthpiece in her mouth, trying not to stare at her handsome middle-aged body. Rebecca quickly bussed her mother's cheek and told her she would pray for them all. Margaret blinked out, leaving Jerry and Rebecca alone in the house.

As Bill Blanchard popped into the portal, he came charging out of it—a bit unsteadily but moving—and bellowing instructions at the same time. His sudden arrival and yelling scared poor Hal witless. He half expected to see dragons or some other variety of creature chasing after his faculty mate. Giving Hal credit, he responded the second time Bill gave instructions. Stepping away from the control panel for STUDLY, he went to the phone on Bill's desk and dialed Dr. Shumway's home number. Making the conversation succinct, he hung up and told Bill his brother-in-law was on the way. As Bill assumed charge of the portal controls, he quickly brought Hal up to speed. In response, he told Bill he should notify Betty and the Tanners, so they could come and add support. This was a family matter despite the fact they had not met yet! While the calls went out, Bill moved a lab table closer to the portal and brought some cushions and a blanket from his office sofa. Hearing the beacon alarm, he warned Hal of the impending arrival of Hope. Hal grabbed two robes off the hooks and tossed one to Bill, who seemed unaware he had been dashing around nude.

Hope entered the portal lying on the floor. Hal quickly helped her out of the confines of the time machine and draping the other robe over her body, assisted her to lie on the table. Disoriented from the trip and still in pain from the contractions, Hope was oblivious to her surroundings, but Hal's presence reassured her. It took just a couple moments, and her husband stumbled into the portal. Being young and agile, he did not fall, and as he got his bearings, he was at Hope's side adding comfort. Taking time to shake hands with Hal, he thanked him for his assistance, then they both concentrated on Hope. Bill took the opportunity between arrivals to get some clothing out of his office and offered Matthew something to cover himself. As soon as the clothing was placed near the portal, Bill went back to the controls and calmly retrieved Margaret Lloyd.

As Matthew's mother blinked into the portal, Bill gave her his undivided attention. Before she even regained her equilibrium, he was assisting her to exit the chamber and handing her clothing to cover herself. Looking up at him, she blushed.

"Sir, I regret the circumstances you find me in. I had hoped to be properly clothed with my hair in order. I fear you catch me at a disadvantage."

"Mistress Lloyd, as I suspected, you are lovely in whatever state you happen to be in. It is a pleasure to make your acquaintance, and I assure you I am not at my best either!"

Then, Margaret was at the side of her daughter-in-law, adding what comfort she could. Hal went to the doorway so he could direct Bennett when he came into sight. It took only ten minutes before the doctor arrived, carrying his bag, with his wife, who had been a nurse, in tow. A quick exam of his new patient and he knew he had his work cut out for him.

"Baby is breech, and I suspect he may have the cord tangled around him. His heart rate is up but strong, so I don't think the cord is around his neck. I wish I had an ultrasound, but then I'd need a technician. I'm going to try manipulating her abdomen and see if I can coax the little tyke around. It's going to be dicey because I could tangle the cord even more."

To his wife, he gave instructions of what he needed. Then he asked the others to give him room to work, allowing only Matthew to remain beside his wife, holding her hand. As he began his task,

Betty Jarvis arrived followed closely by Jerry's parents. Bill brought them up to speed on what was happening, then he introduced them to Margaret Lloyd. Owing to the dramatic circumstances they were in, the women bonded almost immediately, each relating stories of their own experiences in childbirth. Stewart Tanner quietly conversed with Hal, with Bill telling the other men what little he had seen when he arrived in Massachusetts. Time seemed to drag, all eyes darting frequently at what was happening with Hope. Dr. Ben Shumway was working without an anesthesiologist, but he made his patient as comfortable as possible, giving her local anesthesia. His manipulations had turned the baby, and it dropped well into the birth canal. Hoping he had untangled the umbilical; he waited for his young patient to dilate fully and have her contractions speed up. While he waited, his wife watching over the expectant mother, he went to the men. Of course, this brought the women over, too.

"Well, I think everything is going to be okay. Only time will tell. Hal, is this young woman from the same place Rebecca was from?"

Hal gave an affirmative nod.

"They seem to be a hardy lot there. Half of the women I have delivered would have screamed their heads off with the pain." Noticing Margaret for the first time, he asked, "Are you this young woman's mother?"

"Mother-in-law. Her husband is my son!"

"Congratulations. I'm Dr. Shumway."

"I'm Margaret Lloyd, my son is Matthew, and my daughter-in- law is Hope. I'm also Rebecca's mother."

"I can see the resemblance. Your daughter is also quite a young lady. I'm beginning to think I was born about three centuries too early!"

"I'm sure you are a much better doctor than we have in our time. I saw you do many things I have never heard of, nor seen."

"Thank you, Margaret. I feel privileged to know you all." Then to Bill and Hal, "I imagine you did okay moving these adults through time, but how are you going to get the baby back? Or is the little one staying here?"

"I don't believe so, Doctor, unless the parents and grandmother stay, also!" this from Margaret.

Bill broke in to the conversation.

"I've been thinking on that. After the baby is born, and we make sure mother and baby are healthy, we can send Margaret and Matthew ahead, then send the baby through. The baby doesn't need a beacon. None of the, uh, colonials would since it is only required for locking on the wearer for retrieval. When we go back in time, we will just take a variety of different sized mouthpieces. Lastly, Hope will go. I want to return also, since I didn't get a chance to see much! I suggest we wait a day or two before trying any jumps. I'm sure Jerry and Rebecca are on pins and needles, but we can jump just a few minutes after departing, then they will not be in suspense too long."

Dr. Shumway said, "I'm sure it all made sense to some of you, but it's all mumbo-jumbo to me. I'll take care of things medical and leave the science fiction to the rest of you. I also need you to try and explain a few things to my wife when we get a chance because I kind of left her in the dark. She knows something is out of place since we just came to a physics lab to deliver a baby rather than have the mother rushed to the emergency room."

"Ben, the contractions are very close, and she's dilated almost ten. Now, I think you need to be over here with me. I'm a little out of practice."

"Be right there! Well, it looks like showtime. Grandma, you can come over, too, but the rest should stay here!"

After the drama of the last hour or so of subjective time, the delivery was almost mundane. Of course, being Hope's first baby, it was scary for her, but to Margaret and the Shumways, it was fairly routine. Matthew was stalwart throughout the delivery, but after the birth of his first son and while the mother and baby were being cleaned up, he nearly fainted. Bill Blanchard rushed over to ease him to the floor. Hal went into Bill's office and brought out an assortment of canned beverages, not realizing each one would be new and strange to the colonials. He decided to give Margaret and Matthew cans of apple juice. Ben recommended Hope have only water. All the locals were amused watching the expressions of the colonials as they learned to drink from a can and enjoyed pasteurized juice and filtered water. Everyone else took a can of soda for refreshment.

After the mother and her new baby were cleaned up, Ben's wife (and Hal's sister), Julie took a break. While she was seated, sipping a cola, Bill and Hal began explaining the strange situation in which she was now a participant. Being pragmatic, she accepted Hope and her family being here, but they may as well have driven from the center of the earth. Given the fact she had only seen them in contemporary clothing and in the lab setting, there was no frame of reference for her to see them as anything other than perhaps people from across town. Even contemporary hairstyles were diverse enough to include theirs. If they hadn't spoken English, she would suspect they were illegal immigrants trying to get free medical care. Being unable to wrap her mind around these three…no…four people being from three hundred years in the past, her confusion made her blindly accept them as "just people," and they needed her help. She would not allow her mind to dwell on anything else.

Although the questions were probably on everyone's mind, Stewart Tanner was the first to voice them.

"I suppose we should decide where our guests are going to sleep tonight. We also need to shop for some necessities for mother and son. Bill, do we have a means of weighing and measuring our newborn for statistical purposes. Doctor, what kind of paperwork do you need? And, Matthew, do you and Hope have a name for your son?"

Everyone started moving about and answering Stewart's questions. Bill had a wide variety of scales and other measuring instruments. Ben and Julie conferred on the legalities and medical ethics involved. Hope and Matthew had been looking their son over, doing the normal inventory of new parents. Margaret was nearby, with Helen and Betty, admiring her first grandchild. Bill had come up with large towels to wrap the baby in, but Hope had to remain in the robe she had been draped in upon her arrival.

"Hope and I have decided to name our son Jerrold Robert Lloyd! My father's name was Robert."

Congratulations were extended to the new parents, and everyone repeated the name, looking at the infant in Hope's arms. Ben and Julie asked to use Bill's computer. After about fifteen minutes, they printed out a document which appeared to be parchment, and the font looked like it had been written three hundred years ago. Composing the contents, it sounded like a legal document which could be from the same era, but they gave the vital statistics for the baby, adding the weight and length Bill had measured. Before printing the page, they asked Matthew what the date was when they had left his home. Adding that as a birth date, they felt the time was irrelevant. Taking the page out of the printer, Bennett signed as attending physician and Julie as midwife. The presentation of the birth certificate was observed as a solemn occasion, and afterwards, everyone quietly cheered, so they didn't awaken the baby.

By the time the baby was an hour old, everyone agreed the guests, including Margaret would stay at the Tanner home. Again, the deciding factor was Helen was at home, where everyone else had to work. While Stewart and Bill Blanchard took Margaret, Matthew, Hope, and the baby to the Tanner home, Hal went with Helen and Betty to the local superstore to get what they felt the family needed. Ben and Julie were thanked profusely by not only the new parents and grandmother but also by all the others. Dr. Shumway had early morning surgery, so he and Julie left, wishing all good luck. As the rest of the party left the lab, they steeled themselves for the culture shock the colonials would experience in the next day or two, starting with the automobile ride about to begin. Because of the dramatic events of the last hour or so, Margaret and Matthew had not commented on all the modern things they saw in the lab. The lights were most obvious, but everything which ran on electricity and the myriad other things to be seen in a physics lab. Even mundane things like the linoleum on the floor was beyond anything they had seen. For Hope, the administration of anesthesia had been accepted because she had never experienced full childbirth before. Of course, everything was clean and even the clothing and blankets were finely woven, but she was preoccupied with giving birth to her first child, so she could care less what her surroundings were. She would find many things to be amazed about in the next couple days.

As Helen got into the Jarvis's car, Stewart was assisting Hope and the baby into the back seat of his four-door mid-sized car. In awe of this never-before-seen machine, Matthew got in and sat beside her. There was plenty of room in the front seat for Margaret, but Bill Blanchard asked if she would ride with him in his own car. With a shy, blushing expression, the new grandmother agreed. A short trip later, they parked in the Tanner driveway, and the group went in through the front door. To the colonials, the house seemed ostentatious, but Stewart assured them it was an average house. Again, the lights were the first thing they noticed, but after they became adjusted to them, they could only stare at everything twenty-first-century people pretty much took for granted—carpeting, electrical appliances, running water, et al. Stewart hoped his wife would not be too long. He had no idea when a newborn felt its first call of nature, but they only had a small hand towel pressed into service as a diaper. Hope also had sanitary needs normal for a recent, postpartum mother, which had been temporarily handled by a trip to a lady's restroom in the physics building.

Bill and Margaret had talked on the way to the Tanners and continued to do so for ten or so additional minutes before going inside. Finding no one downstairs, they waited in the living room until Stewart called them upstairs. Following his voice, then found him in Jerry's room. Margaret immediately saw the picture of Rebecca on the bulletin board.

"Mrs. Lloyd, would you mind sleeping here in Jerry's room? I'm going to let Matthew and Hope sleep in the guest room. I told Helen to see if she could pick up a small bassinet, a type of cradle, for the baby, and it can be placed beside the bed so Hope can be close by."

"Master Tanner, this will be just fine. It is much better than even my own bed. I am just overwhelmed with all these new things." Showing Margaret the en suite bathroom, she was again speechless when he demonstrated the faucet and toilet. Leaving Bill to continue her education, he went to see how Hope was adjusting. He found her with the baby on the bed but was afraid to lay beside it because she thought the linen was too fine for her to soil. Assuring her it was quite washable, no matter what, she let Matthew draw the covers back to reveal crisp, clean sheets. Again, he showed them how to manipulate the amenities of the en suite bathroom, then told them to relax while he went to check on the return of the shoppers. When he got downstairs, he was soon joined by Bill.

"Margaret was exhausted, so I put her to bed, promising her I would see her tomorrow. I have a late morning class, and my TA can manage the lab, but I need to go in early and clean up all traces of our little party. I'll see you as early tomorrow as I can get away. I hope you don't mind me monopolizing Margaret's time. I know she will want to spend most of the time with Hope and the new babe, but I asked her to spend some time with me also."

"That's fine, Bill. Do you need any help cleaning up?"

"No. I've got it covered! Thanks, anyway!"

"Uh, before you go, Bill, let me ask you something."

"All right! Shoot!"

"Everything I've heard about your philosophy made me think you believed no one should meddle with history. But you're in the past for less than an hour, and you're doing all sorts of things which could alter history! How do you account for it?"

Looking a bit chagrined, Professor Blanchard replied, "Kind of crazy, isn't it? Jerry and I had long discussions before we began our experiments. I was staunch in my belief no one should act as a god, changing history, just because they thought it made history better. Jerry's opinion was, if you can help out an individual by saving their life or making it better, isn't it what life is all about? What I had were ideals about ethics and moral issues. Jerry was just concerned about helping people. When I got to Matthew's and saw the pain and suffering Hope was experiencing, my ideals went out the window. I felt I *had* to help! So if people who travel in time and inadvertently change history in order to help people are called meddling fools, then I'm one also!"

"Bill, I'm not censuring your actions. I would do the very same thing, given the same circumstances. I'm grateful to you for taking action. Hope and the baby may have died if you had not acted. Young Jerrold Lloyd may not be my grandchild, but he is family. Thank you!"

"You're welcome, Stewart. Now, I need to go home and get some sleep!"

As Bill was leaving, the shoppers returned with their arms loaded down. Taking the packages upstairs to supply mother and son, Hal and Stewart assembled the portable crib they had purchased. Taking it upstairs, they watched as Hope lay her freshly diapered and clothed son into the crib. Helen loaned Hope and Margaret a nightgown.

Stewart loaned Mathew a pair of his pajamas, which he rarely wore himself. Telling the colonials to sleep as late as they wanted, Jerry's parents bid Hal and Betty good night and locked up before retiring. Morning brought a new sense of culture shock to the colonials.

Margaret had not slept much, preferring to watch over Hope and young Jerrold. Matthew had no trouble sleeping through the night, and when morning came, he relieved his mother to get rest. Hope showed signs of fatigue, but her maternal instincts gave her strength to care for her new charge. Breast feeding came natural to both mother and son, so the baby was content. Helen brought up a breakfast tray with food for all three adults, but Margaret was asleep. Eggs and ham were familiar, and the toast was not too foreign. Despite the orange juice and hash browns being strange, they were consumed with relish. Matthew helped Helen take the tray downstairs, and he was enthralled with the kitchen. Later, Margaret and Hope both saw the cooking area and marveled at how bright and clean everything appeared. Because they were guests, Helen did the cooking, but she sensed in both colonial women the urge to try their hand at preparing a meal in such modern surroundings. While she cooked, one or the other woman was usually watching every move.

Convenience in cooking was not the only thing to become a hit with the Tanner's guests. Such mundane things as diapering a baby were in sharp contrast to anything the Lloyd family had ever seen. Disposable diapers were a godsend. Showering with almost unlimited hot water was a favorite for Matthew. Refrigeration was high on their list of "wonderful" things. Wonder abounded for the Lloyds, but many things were beyond their comprehension.

In addition to the culture shock, Margaret received Bill Blanchard on a regular basis. Enjoying long talks and walks about the neighborhood, a friendship developed quickly, and Margaret was amazed she could have feelings for a man other than her late husband. For Bill's part, he wondered why no woman, before Margaret Lloyd, ever captured his interest. Knowing their stay would be short, Margaret was reluctant to become too involved, but when the professor asked if he could return to Salem with her and continue seeing her, she began to wonder where it would lead. Unknown to Margaret, Bill Blanchard was seriously taking inventory of his life, trying to decide what he wanted for the remainder.

Young Jerrold showed no signs of distress from his ordeal and traveling through time in his mother's womb. Being a hearty eater, he bonded quickly with his mother and seemed to enjoy his father's presence. Hope, being of hardy stock, recovered almost immediately from the rigors of childbirth. After two visits from Ben Shumway, he said they could probably travel. Wanting to get back home as soon as possible and not understanding the flexibility of traveling into the past, they told their hosts and Bill Blanchard they were ready to return. The professor, knowing their return was inevitable, had prepared a number of packets for sending to Salem. They were mostly for his use but also included items for the Lloyd family and more specifically for Margaret. These packets were cached away in his office.

What does a person from the twenty-first century give a mother and baby returning to the seventeenth century? Most things would cause a stir if seen by someone of that era. Bundles of disposable diapers were out of the question. Most clothing items would have the same consequence. Handmade articles, such as quilts and blankets, may be in order but not very personal. Wracking their brains for the answer, the Tanners and Jarvises could not think of a special gift. Out of desperation, Helen asked Margaret what she thought would be appropriate and needful. Ever the gracious matriarch, she replied, "But you have given them so much already! And myself also. We have a healthy baby boy, a healthy mother, and you've given us something very few people ever receive—a glimpse into the future with such positive aspects we could never feel despair for our children, grandchildren, and our posterity through generations! We have no idea of specifics for the Lloyds, but to see Hope's family's descendants prospering is inspiring. Perhaps a few small things to help insure their continued health. I have no idea what, but maybe the doctor could make recommendations."

"I'll call and have Hal ask him. Thank you, Margaret. How are you and Bill doing?"

Blushing slightly, Margaret replied, "I fear we are getting on too well. He desires to return with me and continue to see me, which in my time means courtship. I am no foolish girl and have little patience for propriety at my age. Either he quickly asks me to make our relationship permanent, or he returns to his own time. I realize my attitude puts sore demands on him. He is a professional scholar here. What is there for him in my time? I fear I am a poor substitute for his career."

"Margaret, he's had his career here, but he's never had a wife. Perhaps he's ready to devote himself to you and give up what has been his mistress for all these years!"

"Perhaps. We shall see."

As send-offs go, the departure of the Lloyd family was sparsely attended but by design. The Tanners, Jarvises, and Shumways were present. Despite the caution against sending gifts which were out of time, a number of baby outfits were given to Hope. Dr. and Mrs. Shumway gave a packet containing a variety of freeze-dried antibiotics (the kind sent to third-world countries), with written directions on when and how to use them. Wooden splints and cotton bandages were also given. These could easily be explained away, where metal, plastic, and synthetic fabric could not. Bill told them he had half a dozen tubes of antibacterial ointment in his bundles, which he was sending in advance of the family. A tearful farewell ensued, as chances were, they would never see each other again. Professor Blanchard sent Matthew through first, so he could receive the others and make sure the arrival point was safe. Next went Hope, then baby Jerrold. When it was Margaret's turn, she gave Bill a buss on the cheek and told him she would see him in a minute. When the colonists had gone, Bill turned the controls over to Hal, telling him he would probably signal for retrieval in about four hours local time. This gave Hal a chance to go home if he desired and then return. Bill told him if he did not get retrieved when he signaled, he would try again within an hour and continue to do so until Hal brought him back. Stepping into the portal, he tossed his robe out, then nodded to everyone. Less than a minute later, he blinked out.

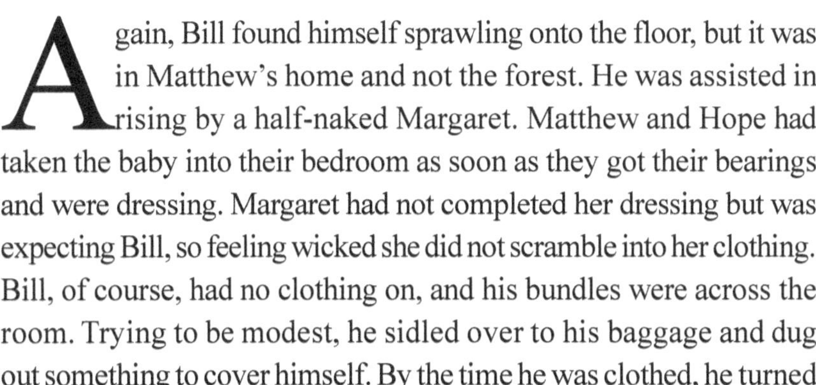

Again, Bill found himself sprawling onto the floor, but it was in Matthew's home and not the forest. He was assisted in rising by a half-naked Margaret. Matthew and Hope had taken the baby into their bedroom as soon as they got their bearings and were dressing. Margaret had not completed her dressing but was expecting Bill, so feeling wicked she did not scramble into her clothing. Bill, of course, had no clothing on, and his bundles were across the room. Trying to be modest, he sidled over to his baggage and dug out something to cover himself. By the time he was clothed, he turned to see Margaret, now fully clothed, watching him.

"You are a healthy and robust man, Bill Blanchard! You should find yourself a young wife and father children! I fear I am past child- bearing age, though it may still be possible."

"As much as I've considered producing offspring, I must confess one of the reasons I'm pursuing you is because I felt you could not bear more children, as I still fear changing history. Does that put you off from me?"

"No. I gave up all thought of having more children after Daniel was born. Robert, my husband, was crippled shortly after Daniel came to us, and he probably couldn't sire again."

"So you would have had more children if you could?"

"Women here sometimes have as many as a dozen children. Hope's mother had nearly that number."

"So many mouths to feed! How do they manage?"

"Hard work mostly! Some die young, but live hard lives. And as the older children mature, they help with the chores and the rearing of the younger children. Are there no large families in your time?"

"Yes. There are some religions which encourage as large a family as you can afford. As you know, Hal has six children. His wife came from a family of ten."

"Interesting. Well… I wonder what time it is? It is dark out, but is it the same evening or some other?"

"I set the time machine for the same night, so it should be right, but I'm not sure how late it is."

"Allow me to look at the moon and stars, and I can tell you within an hour or so. Is this something you cannot do?"

"I'm afraid we're dependent on time pieces which tell us the time of day or night. If it were daylight, I could set up a crude sundial and reset my time piece to approximately near the correct time."

"I feel superior to you for the very first time, but I beg your pardon for being prideful. Come with me, and I will show you."

Going out the front door, Margaret walked away from the house about fifty yards. Looking into the night sky, she noted the location of the moon and then the big dipper. Pausing for a few seconds she did a mental calculation and spoke.

"I think it is a little past midnight but not much later. Let us walk to my home and rouse Jerrold and Rebecca to tell them the news!"

Taking Bill's arm, they walked the short distance to her home. Before entering, she turned to Bill and put her arms around his middle, looking up into his face. Bill took the hint and leaned down to kiss her lips. Not being an expert, he still knew enough to make it a gentle kiss. Pulling back, he gazed into the eyes of the first woman he believed he was in love with. Reaching for another kiss, the forty-something couple embraced as the kiss became more ardent. Finally pulling back, they were both nearly breathless with emotion.

"Let us go inside and awaken the family. It will be better and safer," she said, smiling at Bill.

Upon entering her bedchamber, Margaret could see by moonlight her daughter and husband asleep in her bed. Going to her daughter's side of the bed, she gently shook her shoulder. Awakening quickly and seeing no alarm on her mother's face, she asked how things had gone. Whispering to her daughter a quick synopsis, she had to repeat it for Jerry when he awoke amid the whispering. As the young couple got out of bed and drew on clothes over their night things, they followed Mistress Lloyd out into the great room, where they saw Bill waiting. Going to Bill, Jerry gave him a warm greeting.

"How long?"

"We were home for three days. They stayed with your parents, and Hal's brother-in-law took good care of Hope and your namesake."

"My what?"

"Matthew and Hope named their first son Jerrold Robert Lloyd!"

"Oh. Yeah, I remember from my second jump. That's an honor! How are they? Can we see them now or wait until morning?"

"I think it best to wait, but Margaret may have other ideas."

While Bill had been talking to Jerry, Margaret and Rebecca had gone to the boys and Rhoda and gave them the news. The younger ones did not get out of bed and would visit their new nephew in the morning. For the sake of propriety, Bill walked Margaret back to Matthew's and then returned to sleep in Margaret's great room.

When Bill awoke in the morning, the house was busy, but they had taken pains to be as quiet as possible. He wanted his coffee but had to settle for tea. Breakfast was different also, but: "When in Rome…" He also missed his shower hammering wakefulness into him but refused to go to the stream as Jerry had suggested. When chores were done, overseen by Rebecca, the family walked to Matthew's home. Margaret, having seen to Hope and the baby, was now making breakfast for the adults. By the time the entire family had seen Hope and young Jerrold, Bill had cornered Matthew and asked his permission to court his mother. Smiling broadly, Matthew had said he could do it if he thought he could handle her. Bill told him he would do his best.

For the next two weeks, Bill and Margaret spent many hours together, usually with one of her children as chaperone. Occasionally, they managed to be alone for a short interval, and they began to fear the passion which built between the two of them. It had constantly been on his mind, but Bill Blanchard, long-time bachelor, PhD in physics, decided he wanted something entirely different out of life than he had heretofore experienced. At a family dinner, one night, with the entire allied Lloyd/Tanner family together, he asked for permission to speak.

"Jerry and Rebecca, you've known me longest, but Matthew, Hope, and Margaret have known me in extreme circumstances. I know Jonathan, Rhoda, and Daniel hardly know me at all. So with that said, I would like to ask permission, first of Margaret, but also of Matthew, and the rest of the family, for permission to marry Mistress Margaret Lloyd! I know she will not consider leaving you, so I propose I live here with her…and you. I pledge to honor and respect your mother, and I promise you, Margaret, to be as good a husband as I can learn how to be! I don't know how to farm, but I can do a great many things and could even become a teacher if the need is there. I have brought some things with me to see me through, but depending on whether I am accepted or not, I may have to return to arrange my affairs."

Bill was very careful to couch his phrasing so generically, because of the younger ones not knowing precisely where he, Jerry, and even Hal had come from. Though it may be necessary for them to be included in the "family" secret, he wasn't going to be the one to broach the subject first! Looking around at the family, he saw smiles and nods, but he saw something else on Jerry's face—a question! Before anyone else spoke, Margaret stepped forward, and with tears in her eyes, said, "Master Blanchard, you honor me, and I am flattered! Let us converse on this subject in private if you please. As for the rest of you, my dear ones, you had no say in my first marriage, so I see no reason why you should have anything to say about this, though I appreciate Master Blanchard asking so politely. Besides, I did not give my approval of Rebecca's marriage, though I was not surprised in it. When Master Jarvis took her to Jerrold's home, I felt it the right thing to do, and I fully approve it after the fact! Now, since this is an adult subject, I ask you, Jonathan, and your younger brother and sister to remain here, while the rest adjourn to Matthew's home to discuss it among ourselves, then for Master Blanchard and myself to discuss it further."

"But, Mother, I'm fifteen and doing a man's work. Should I not be included in this?"

"Jonathan, it is true you are doing a man's work, but you are not married, nor betrothed, nor even close to courting yet. I know, however, you may have plans to do so soon. For now, let us talk without you. I promise I will tell you of any decisions which may affect you."

"As you wish, Mother!"

After the adults had gone to Matthew's home and were assembled in his small living room, Margaret opened the conversation.

"Bill, I am not surprised you asked me to marry you. I fear, however, it is a rash decision on your part. What of your career at the university? You have a home and perhaps extended family and undoubtedly friends who would question your sudden disappearance."

"I've been thinking about all that and…"

Jerry interjected, "And what are you going to do about the time machine?"

"As I was saying, I've been thinking about all that! My parents are gone. I have one sister, but we haven't spoken in nearly twenty years. It's not because we had a falling out. It's just because we never had anything in common, so we feel no kinship. I made her my beneficiary, only because I felt my estate should go to a family member, but she doesn't know it and would be totally surprised to find out! Sure, I have friends! But the only close ones—the ones I socialize with occasionally—are Hal and Betty Jarvis. I have acquaintances! People I know and say hello to when I pass them on campus or in town. I have spent a solitary life, immersed in my teaching and research. I have given of my time freely, and I don't regret the sacrifices I've made, especially since it has brought me here, to Margaret!

"Jerry, I had a feeling about you when you came to my class.I knew you were different than all my other students. I liked you almost right off. The time we spent together, running all the time travel experiments was just plain enjoyable. You never once complained about all the monotonous things I asked you to do. We made great progress and pretty much perfected STUDLY. I'm grateful for your efforts and for our friendship. I'm envious of Stewart for having such a son. If I'm allowed to marry Margaret, you'd be my son-in-law, and that would 'almost' make me even with your dad. I'm not forgetting about the time machine. I'm not totally sure how I'm going to pull it off, but I plan on either making a duplicate and leaving you in charge of it, or there may be an accidental explosion in my lab, which will totally destroy all my equipment, and it will be difficult to determine if my machine was destroyed or is missing. Either way, I want to be able to keep connected, though it's use will be judicious. I would move it all here, but there are no provisions for the electrical generation needs in this time.

"I guess the bottom line is this, I want to live with Margaret, knowing it means leaving all I have in my time. I don't want to strand you here, Jerry, because you still have your life ahead of you, but it is also your choice to live where and when you and Rebecca choose. I still don't condone running around in time, 'tweaking' history to please some bureaucrat or do-gooder, so I don't want to turn an operational machine over to the government. It either gets safeguarded or it gets destroyed! There may be crises in our life here, which could be better solved by jumping back to our time, but I'd rather learn to solve them the old-fashioned way. My machine may have saved

Hope's and young Jerrold's life. Maybe not! I stand by my decision to use the machine."

"Look, Bill, I can't imagine my life being the same as it was before I came to this time. There've been so many insights for me. I met my predecessors. I met my beautiful wife and her great family. I will be forever grateful for your research and invention. At the same time, I understand your reluctance to turn it over to the government. I have this image in my mind of people charging out of the future, invading my family's life, 'taking' things from me. It scares the daylights out of me! Rebecca and I haven't decided where we want to make our life. Each time period has many things we love. I think you deserve someone in your life who makes you happy. So I'm with you however you decide to play it."

There were a number of comments from the others present. Though they were not directly involved with the time machine, they had all benefitted from it in one way or another. Discussing STUDLY had dampened some of the enthusiasm of some other issues. It took a few minutes to get back to things. Finally, it was Matthew who got them back on track.

"Well, Mother! I, for one, am in favor of Bill's suit for marriage. What do you think?"

Margaret felt a little uncomfortable being confronted in this manner, but she knew she was among her most loved family, so she answered, "Matthew, my good son, you have put the question to me directly, whereas Master Blanchard was more circumspect. I owe you both an answer. Bill, as I said before, I am honored and flattered. I voiced my concerns and you answered very well. As most of my loved ones are present, let me tell you I am pleased to accept your offer of marriage and pray I do nothing to cause you any regret by taking a backward colonial to wife. Would you marry me here or in your time? I understand, just as Rebecca did, the dilemma this causes. There are people for both of us, who we would like to be present, if not for the wedding, at least for a reception. This is cause for more discussion, but it should be between just you and I. Matthew, you have my decision. You are the man of the house, so it is for you to give me away, if you are able."

"Bill Blanchard, I accept your proposal of marriage."

"Margaret, you make me extremely happy, and I'll do all in my power to make you happy for as long as we live."

Sleeping arrangements had to be rearranged, so Jerry and Rebecca went back to Matthew's home, where Rebecca would assist Hope with her baby. Margaret returned to her own bed, and for propriety's sake, Bill slept in Matthew's living room until the wedding. It was sometimes difficult to discuss things without giving away the truth to the younger Lloyds.

Plans were made to have a simple ceremony in Salem to be attended by the family and a few friends of Margaret and her family. Unbeknownst to everyone but Bill, when he was at home, he'd arranged for another simple ceremony to be held in his time also. His intentions were to resign his teaching position, effective at the end of the semester, which was a couple weeks away, then to just drop out of sight. Only the Jarvises would know where he was living. It was a good plan, and Bill had discussed with Hal and with Jerry, separately, how he was going to disable the time portal in his lab and recreate a fully operational duplicate at a remote site to be overseen by Hal and Jerry.

While Bill and Margaret were planning their future together, Jerry and Rebecca were investigating some aspects of their future also. Taking the carriage to Salem, driven once more by Jonathan, they took a side trip to the town of Peabody, almost due east of Middleton. In Peabody, they visited the home of Rebecca's uncle and aunt on her father's side. Making the visit short, she inquired about her cousin, Rebecca. She was told she was living nearby with her new husband, a fisherman from Virginia…named Samuel Withers! Jerrold had been taken aback, but he had asked if the family knew of any Tanners in the area. He was told they did not.

On the drive into Salem from Peabody, Jerry explained to Rebecca the dilemma he had been facing before Hal brought her to him. He thought it was already foreordained for him to come back to Middleton, marry Rebecca, and ensure his family's forefathers existed in the area. Rebecca was upset at first, thinking he had married her out of obligation to his family rather than the love he professed. Finally, he convinced her he really loved her no matter what time they lived in, as long as they were together. The trip was shorter than normal due to Jonathan's eagerness to see Lydia again. Everyone in the Meacham household were excited to hear about Hope's baby boy. Jerry wished he could have shown them pictures of young Jerrold, but they told the family Hope and Matthew would come to visit as soon as they felt the baby was ready to travel. The younger Jeremiah was aware of the attraction of Lydia and Jonathan, and asked Jerry if Jonathan was an honorable young man. In vouching for Jonathan, Jerry took it upon himself to arrange an understanding between himself and his ancestor concerning future courting rights for Jonathan once he turned sixteen. Calling the young couple into his study, Jeremiah asked Jonathan and Lydia if they would be amenable to such an agreement. Both exhibited shyness but eventually were excited and agreeable.

When they returned to Middleton and Jonathan told his mother and older brother about Lydia and the agreement, they were initially miffed Jerry had presumed to take this action. However, on hearing of what he had learned on his future visit, forty years hence, they relented. Of course, it opened up the subject for Margaret to grill him about what he knew about her future. Reluctantly, and with the support of Bill Blanchard, he revealed her reported death from influenza but was quick to add how Rebecca had died, too, but now she wouldn't. He also pointed out the fact she had never remarried in that particular future line of events, but now it was changing. This logic mollified her and prevented her from descending into a depressed state. Because of Bill and Margaret's mutual attraction, the wedding was held the next week.

With Reverend Witherspoon now absent from their local congregation, it was arranged with a clergyman in Peabody to marry the couple. Borrowing a carriage from neighbors, the entire family was able to make the trip. The actual ceremony was short, so the family decided to stop off in Salem on their return trip so Hope could show her baby off to her family. An impromptu reception was held while they were there, and it was late in the day before they arrived back in Middleton. Matthew offered to let the newlyweds use his home for their wedding night, but the offer was declined, saying they were mature adults, not impetuous young people. In spite of Margaret and Bill's protestations, Matthew had his younger three siblings spend the night at his home, sleeping in his living room.

On the morrow, family life began anew for the Lloyd children, with their mother now Mrs. Blanchard. Liking their new stepfather, things transitioned smoothly, and Bill began casting about for a likely vocation for himself in order to support the family. Finding he liked working with Matthew in the wheelwright shop, he considered doing it full time, but the major drawback was the traveling back and forth. Bill also inquired into the local educational system.

Being the Massachusetts Colony, education was heavily influenced by the Puritan religion, which felt children should be taught to read the Bible so they could learn how to control their baser instincts and thus expiate the sin they were born with. This education was usually given as part of their religious instruction. As non-Puritan settlers became more numerous, it was expected their children should also learn to read, write, and calculate. The Massachusetts Act of 1642 was the driving force behind education. The act required towns of fifty or more families to hire a teacher, who would be paid out of private or public funds. Teachers were required to do more than teach. Cleaning the school, filling in for the local clergy when required, and ringing the church bell were among their collateral duties. Attendance was sporadic, owing to seasonal requirement for the children to help in the fields. Some children were schooled at home, if the parents had education, and some of the wealthier families could afford to hire a tutor. Considering his and Jerry's educational background, either one of them could possibly be a tutor or start a school, but there was no guarantee the income would support a family.

Before he settled into family life in colonial America, Bill had to finalize things in his own era. This included carrying out his goal of disabling STUDLY in the lab. Asking Jerry to travel back and help him, they both assured Jerry's wife they would return shortly. Rebecca was busy helping Hope, so she was occupied. On his last trip to the future, Bill had rigged up a remote signaling device at Hal's home, so he didn't have to hang around the lab. Of course, this meant there was a time lapse between signaling with the beacon and being retrieved. Hoping it would not be a long wait, it turned out it was not. Deciding to jump from the privacy of Matthew's second bedroom, Bill was first, and then Jerry, giving his wife another kiss, then being whisked away to the future!

By the time Jerry had arrived and dressed, the others were ready to shut down the system and go home. Hal offered Jerry a place to stay, so he didn't show up unexpected at his parent's home. Since it wasn't too late, Jerry just phoned home to let them know he was on his way, then hitched a ride with Hal. His parents were up waiting for him. It seemed odd that he had been gone, subjectively for almost a month, but it had only been a couple days for his parents. Remarking how he looked older and more honed down, his mother said she'd fatten him up while he was home. Stewart Tanner was more interested in how things were going in Salem and the environs. Jerry told his father about the "other" Rebecca and how she had not married a Tanner. Jerry's father saw the return of worry on his son's face.

"Well, we're still here, so I guess things will work out. Where have you decided to settle down?"

"We're not sure, Dad; Rebecca has been busy helping Hope with little Jerrold. Oh, and by the way, Bill and Margaret are married now!"

"That's nice, son. I wish them all the happiness in the world."

Helen excused herself to retire, leaving her husband and son to continue their conversation. Telling his father about Bill's decision to live in Salem with Margaret and her family, he also mentioned how Bill wanted to disable his time machine, so the government didn't come in and start fooling around with history. The elder Tanner was concerned with how it would affect their ability to see Jerry and his family from time to time. Explaining how Professor Blanchard wanted to make a duplicate machine in a remote, unknown location, he reassured his father all would be well. He explained how the timing had to be right, so they could obtain the parts and be able to transport them without arousing suspicion in either the government oversight committee members or the faculty of the university. Stewart offered any assistance he could give. Parting with a hug between father and son, they both went to bed.

Dinner was a relaxed, pleasant affair, and since everyone knew the score, there were no restrictions on what they discussed. Helen and Betty talked about the many differences between homemaking now, as contrasted with how Margaret had told them about running a household in colonial America. Among the men, they discussed the building of a second STUDLY. Now most of the trial-and-error research and experimentation were out of the way, Bill felt he could build his second machine at a fraction of the cost of the original. It would be hard to cannibalize any key parts because each major assembly was auditable. Given the chance to do it again, there were major changes he would be able to incorporate to make it smaller, more reliable, and have a more "finished" appearance. Bill told them he had copious notes he had kept separate from his "official" lab notes. These could be used, in his absence, by anyone savvy enough to understand his math. Stewart told them he had acreage in Nevada which had not been developed and was so remote he had no plans to do so. Offering to let Bill utilize some of it, he reported the utilities were not far from his property line. The men felt like true conspirators, unconsciously looking around to see if anyone was lurking in the shadows.

With all his hopping around in time, Jerry had missed a number of class sessions. Being torn between his allegiances, he decided to push forward with a last-ditch effort to salvage his grades. Of course, his mind was on Rebecca, wondering how she was doing and if she was well. Finding it took a lot of effort to concentrate on his studies, he ended up taking shortcuts in his term papers and resigned himself to earning a C grade for the classes. The one exception, of course, was physics, and he knew Bill would give him an A, which he felt he had earned despite doing very little course work. In his spare time, Jerry was assembling a shopping list of material for Bill.

Using funds supplied by Bill and Stewart, Jerry was able to purchase nearly everything "off the shelf" at various retail outlets and some from wholesalers using his father's account. All this equipment was being stored in his and Hal Jarvis's garages, just to make it more difficult to tie it to Bill. On the first weekend after their latest return, Jerry, his dad, and Bill made a trip to Nevada with most of the equipment. Stewart had put up a storage shed on his property years ago, just so they didn't have to transport things back and forth each time they visited. The shed contained mostly camping gear and hand tools such as shovels, rakes, and a well-stocked toolbox. During their discussions, they also decided to purchase a large, prefabricated building to be delivered to the property.

Finding the building had been delivered, they situated it where they wanted by using a tow chain to move it around on its skids. Although the building had a hasp for a padlock, they added a heavyduty bolt-type lock on the door to add to its security. In the years the smaller shed had been on the property, there had been no break-ins, but the outside had collected some graffiti. It was just too remote to attract many visitors. By the time they had transferred the equipment from the truck to the building, it was late in the day, so they covered the windows with tarps to hide the contents from prying eyes. After making sure all was secure, they began their return trip home.

Monday morning found Bill and Jerry in the lab. Bill knew what steps he would take to disable the time machine and had rigged it so he could execute the "scuttling" of his invention on short notice. His plan was to send Jerry back to gather Rebecca and bid the family adieu, then bring them back to the lab. Assuming his resignation had been accepted and his lab inventoried, he would clear his office of personal items, then quickly have Jerry send him back to Salem. After he was gone, Jerry would carry out his instructions to turn STUDLY into a room full of useless hardware. It would then fall to Jerry to go to the desert and begin building the second generation of the Blanchard time machine. When it was complete, Jerry would carry out a short series of trial runs, and then he would send a "care package" to Bill, which would signal a successful first stage. Then Bill would activate the beacon to send back something recognizable from Salem. This would complete the maiden voyage of the new machine, and Jerry would assume duties as the new conductor for time travelers, unless Bill wanted to return and take over once more.

On the last week of the semester, Jerry had completed all his required papers and was winding down. Professor Bill Blanchard had personally handed his resignation to his department head his first week back. His story was, after a long and successful career in academia, foregoing a personal life in favor of dedicating himself to educating future generations, it was now time to find personal fulfillment by taking a wife and devoting himself to her and their life together. Planning to travel for an indeterminate time, they would decide where to settle down afterwards. Now, he would complete his last week grading term assignments and submitting grades to the department, then he would vacate his position and his home, which was ostensibly sold. Leaving little to chance, Bill had signed a "quit claim" deed and left the house to Jerry and Rebecca. Bill was ready.

Wednesday morning, as Professor Blanchard was boxing up the last of his personal books and papers, his department head came into the lab. He was followed by half a dozen men who had the mark of bureaucrats or bean counters upon them.

"Professor Blanchard! These gentlemen are from the Defense Department. They've informed me funding for your research program has been cut off by the new administration in Washington. They are here to inventory, collect, and transport all papers and hardware associated with your grant. It seems the Department of

Defense's decision to cut funding comes at a propitious time since your successor would have to start at square one in continuing your work. I trust you will give these gentlemen your full cooperation."

"Uh, yes! Of course! Welcome to my lab or what 'was' my lab."

As men go, this group were a bunch of officious, pedantic boors. Their condescending manner was abrasive to Bill, and he wanted so badly to tell them where to get off! However, considering the government had funded all his research and development, and this had led him and Jerry to finding wives, he decided to be tolerant of their attitude. The first thing they wanted to do was inventory his lab. They had a large computer readout, which he assumed was compiled from all the invoices he had generated while building up the lab. He had to make sure they were not counting university owned assets since he had carefully and conscientiously labeled everything as government property, as it was acquired at government expense. One of his fears was they would begin dismantling the machine to gain access to internal assets. Once this began, he would never get a chance to leave. To prepare for such a contingency, he called Jerry.

In a matter of minutes, Jerry arrived at the lab. Ignoring what they assumed was just another student since they had come and gone all morning, they continued to look in every nook and cranny in the lab, attempting to account for every single nut, bolt, and screw on their list. Bill pulled his traveling companion into his office.

"Is there anything you need just in case? As I told you on the phone, it may be necessary to disable my baby sooner than expected, and I don't know what damage these goons will inflict on STUDLY! I hoped they'd do this after I left. I suspect there's someone watching, who reported I was leaving."

"I could think of a hundred things I'd like to take, but I'm not sure how long I'll be there before you come and send me and Rebecca back. I left a letter to my parents in my desk, so if it looks like I'll be gone a while, tell them to read it! I hope they don't destroy your machine, Professor, but if they do and you manage to build number two, I'll be waiting. I don't know what to say about Margaret! I'm sure she will understand you may be delayed. When you jump, try to do it soon enough to not miss out on any physical relationship with Margaret."

"Jerry, I'm very glad you're taking this seriously and not taking for granted. All will be well. I fear these auditors will screw something up. Murphy's law has always been very real to me, and the government seems to thrive on its consequences. I'm sure if Margaret were here, she would tell me to do what I had to do, and she'd see me when she sees me. Now, I'm pretty sure, being civil servants, they will take lunch at precisely noon. That will be the time for you to leave. If there is anything you still need, now is the time to get it!"

"Okay, Bill! I'll be back at noon."

Realizing all their plans could be thrown out the window, Jerry decided to call his dad at work. Quickly telling his father about the sudden change in plans, the elder Tanner told Jerry to meet him at home. When he arrived, his mother was already aware of what was happening, and though she seemed calm, he knew she was worried. When his father arrived, he took his son into his study. From his desk, he took a small bundle out and unwrapped it. Inside was a stack of currency which turned out to be duplicates of one of the bills Hal had brought back from Salem.

"I told Bill I would never forge currency, but the more I thought about it, the more I believed a small amount would not be harmful to their economy, and it may come in handy in times of need. I only created a few of the smallest denomination bill Hal brought back. Use them wisely. I don't think they could be detected as counterfeit, but be careful. I don't want my son to go penniless, especially with a new family. I love you, son. I'm proud of you, and I know you will do great things no matter what era you end up living in. I hope you return and get to finish your education, but if you don't, you are still better educated than maybe ninety percent of the men in Salem or even the whole Massachusetts Colony. Of course, much of your knowledge is of things which have been revealed since that time."

Embracing his son and handing him the bundle of currency, they went into Jerry's room to make sure there was nothing he still needed to pack. Going downstairs, it was apparent Jerry's mother had been crying. He hugged her and told her he loved her, then told them about the letter in case he did not return quickly. Leaving his car in the garage, he had left all other tokens of his century in his room. Offering to take him to the university, Stewart Tanner tried to keep his own emotions in check. Just before Jerry got out of the car, his father gripped his hand tightly and bussed him on the cheek in an uncharacteristic display of affection.

"I hope to see you soon, son! My prayers go with you. May God protect you and Rebecca!"

"Thanks, Dad, for everything! If we can, Rebecca and I will come back. If we don't, I'll find some way to let you know, even if it takes three hundred years to find it!"

Leaving his father's car at the curb, Jerry carried his small bundle into the physics building. It was just before noon. Walking down the hallway, he passed the government men on their way out of the lab. Chuckling to himself, Jerry was amused at the predictability of government drones. Hurrying in to the lab, Jerry saw Bill was already at the controls of his invention.

"Thanks for being punctual, Jerry. I don't know how far they'll go for lunch. I gave them directions to some places across town, but one of them had knowledge of places closer. I see you're ready for travel. I've taken the opportunity to send you with some of the items I thought may be useful for Margaret and myself. If I don't show up soon, feel free to make use of them. I can always bring more. I'd better get you on your way, so I can disable my baby before the bean counters return.

"Jerry, my boy, we've had some great adventures, and you know how I felt about meddling in history, but I find myself being a damned fool after all! With your knowledge of what happens to the

Lloyd family, if you can do anything to change history, for their sake, please do so! Good luck, Jerry. I'll come if I can!"

The two men embraced, and Jerry gathered the bundles he and Bill had assembled and placed them inside the portal. Soon after he placed them inside, Bill energized STUDLY, and the packets disappeared. Jerry removed the brief clothing he had worn to the lab. Winking at his professor and friend, he stepped inside the time machine and calmly looked around the lab, as though committing everything to memory. At the precise time Professor Blanchard had calculated for Jerry to arrive just after his bundles, he energized his invention for what could be the last time.

chapter

30

Somewhere in time, Jerry's emotions let go, and as he popped into the latter seventeenth century, he found his cheeks wet with tears, and he was sobbing. His next realization was standing inside Matthew's living room, his bundles at his feet. No one was in the room, so he opened his packet and found clothing to don. Afterward, getting his emotions in check, he went in search of his wife and the rest of the family. Finding Matthew first, working in the fields between the two Lloyd homes, he went quickly to his friend. Seeing the look on Jerry's face, Matthew mentally prepared himself for the worst news.

Quickly telling his friend what had transpired in his time, he reassured him Bill was doing all he could to return to his new wife in Salem. Both men were realistic enough to accept what the worst-case scenario would entail. Only Margaret, Hope, and Rebecca would be told the entire truth. Jonathan, Rhoda, and Daniel would be told their mother's new husband had been delayed on a business trip. Sometime in the future, if Bill did not arrive, they would be told more, though maybe not the whole truth. It was six months before everyone but Jerry lost hope and moved on with their life, mourning the loss of their new stepfather. Having some idea what building the new machine would take, in terms of time and cost, he held out hope but finally admitted to himself they could take years to build it, but still arrive in Salem at any time, presumably shortly after Jerry's last arrival. Finally, the entire Lloyd-Tanner family worked together to make a living and raise their quickly growing family.

Enduring the entire week of constant questions and requests from the government auditors on Friday, agents for the FBI entered his office with a warrant. The Federal government was charging him with fraud for allegedly using federal funds to purchase lab equipment for the university. Not being able to prove he'd taken any money for personal use, they still froze all his assets until their investigation was complete. Living off his salary, which was traceable income, he had to cash each check and pay for things with cash. Legal fees became exorbitant, and he had to get permission from Uncle Sam to remortgage his house to pay them. To add more restrictions, he was not allowed to travel outside the city unless on official university business. His once high-tech lab was dismantled, and though he had written proof of purchase, using university funds, much of the lab equipment was temporarily confiscated while the investigation was in progress. STUDLY ceased to exist, as it was broken into its component parts, and all stored in a government warehouse. At last, after nearly two years, the investigation was over! No evidence of wrongdoing was uncovered. The government did not apologize, nor offer to compensate him for legal fees. Though he had continued teaching through all the fiasco, he was unable to conduct lab experiments, so had to farm his students out to other professors for the practical applications. One bright side to it all, if one could be found, was the whistleblower, an assistant professor, lost out on what he perceived was going to be a windfall. Since there was no fine levied on the university, there could be no reward, so he got no "blood money." Of course, it was against the law to fire the assistant professor in retaliation, the university simply denied his request for tenure.

For Bill Blanchard, the stress and worry had taken its toll. He was still glad the ordeal was over. Now, he felt he had to try and make up for lost time. As soon as possible after the judgment, he made plans to go to Nevada and begin the task of building version two of his invention. His friends would go with him to bring additional supplies and help with some of the labor.

Bill and Hal were in the front seat of the Blanchard sedan, and Betty Jarvis was in the back. It was almost like old times for the three old friends. Following behind the group of three was a truck driven by Stewart Tanner, with his wife acting as navigator. The truck was laden with all manner of equipment, including more food and a larger refrigerator. All five friends had planned a week away from their jobs and family. It was early afternoon and a clear, sunny day in June. The highway was clear and dry. Hal had just finished telling a joke to the group. After throwing his head back in laughter, Bill lowered his head in time to see a semi-tractor trailer drift across the middle line. In reflex, he stiffened and clutched harder at the wheel. A scream tore from his throat as the semi hit the sedan head on. Bill had not had time to avoid the collision. The Tanners watched in horror as the car ahead of them seemed to disintegrate as it was "eaten up" by the front of the semi. Stewart was far enough back to be able to avoid becoming involved in the accident. Helen immediately took her cell phone out and dialed 911. The dispatcher wanted to know where they were, and they frantically looked around to find the highway mile marker.

As soon as Stewart could bring the truck to a stop on the side of the road, he was out the door and running toward the wreck. Before he was closer than thirty feet, he knew no one could have survived a collision like this. Seeing the hood and motor pushed up into the passenger compartment, he looked into the sightless eyes of Bill and

Hal, both of their faces covered in blood. Seat belts had been worn, but all they managed to do was keep the front seat occupants from catapulting through the shattered windshield. In the back seat, he saw Betty, also strapped in, but she still looked like she had been thrown around like a rag doll. Betty Jarvis was covered in blood, but she was moaning and moving slightly. Quickly stealing a glance at the semi cab, he saw the horrified look on the driver's face. Shock was setting in, and he would need treatment, but it was not as urgent as trying to help Betty.

Thirty minutes later, sirens could be heard approaching the crash site. A few other cars had stopped to help. One man was directing traffic around the accident, using flares from his trunk. Another couple had helped the semi driver down from his cab and were treating him for shock by laying him down on a tarp laid out on the pavement. The first vehicle to stop was an old pickup truck, and the driver, dressed in well-worn farming clothes identified himself as a Vietnam vet, who had been a medic some thirty-five years previous. Helping Stewart try to comfort Betty and stop any major blood flow, they would not take the chance of moving her, just in case there was internal bleeding or broken bones. Someone else had brought tarps to drape over the other two after the former medic had checked thoroughly for any sign of pulses.

Following the ambulance back to the nearest hospital, Helen and Stewart waited to see what the diagnosis was for Betty. Finding her purse, they had looked on her cell phone for their children's phone numbers. Stewart asked the police and ambulance attendants if he should notify the family. Of course, they had told them to go ahead. Police officers get tired telling families of the deaths of loved ones. Stewart called each of Hal and Betty's children and gave them the information, and by that time, the prognosis for their mother. Betty suffered two broken legs, below the knee, a ruptured spleen, and multiple contusions. She was expected to recover. Both Bill and Hal sustained severe head and upper torso trauma, which caused almost instantaneous death. They had not suffered.

Now, besides the long and slow recovery of Betty Jarvis and mourning the loss of two friends they had become very close with, both Tanner parents were in a deep additional agony. Throughout Bill Blanchard's ordeal, both Stewart and Helen had been staunch supporters, along with Hal and Betty. The thought of what could be accomplished when the debacle of the government investigation was at an end had buoyed them up. Once they began working on their goal for building STUDLY number two, their hopes had soared! Bill had the expertise, and with help from Stewart and Hal, they could once more see their son, Jerry, and their new daughter-in- law. Because they never lost hope, they never felt like reading Jerry's letter.

Returning home from Hal Jarvis's funeral, they sat stoically in their living room. The funeral for Bill Blanchard had taken place three days previous, which Betty had been unable to attend. With special permission from her physician, she had been allowed to attend her husband's memorial. Looking up into the eyes of his long-ago bride, the elder Tanner asked, "Do you feel it's time to read what Jerry left for us? Are you strong enough or shall we wait a while longer?"

"It couldn't get much worse. We may as well read it!"

"All right, dear. Let me go get it."

Slowly climbing the stairs to the upper floor, Helen could follow his movement by the sound of his steps. When she could hear his steps returning, she gave out a deep sigh and mentally steeled herself. Once again entering the living room, Stewart took his seat across from his wife. He had paused in Jerry's room long enough to use the letter opener on the letter. Looking at the front of the white envelope, he showed the handwritten characters.

"Dad and Mom. I love you! Thanks for everything."

Reaching into the opening, Jerry's father removed the typewritten pages, which had been tri-folded like a business letter. Opening the folds, he peered at the words and began to read:

Dear Dad and Mom,

If you are reading this, then something has happened to me and it's okay. I chose to take this path with my life. I know we had planned on me finishing my degree and going on to some career which would make you proud of me. Since I don't know exactly what is happening in your life, I don't know how to address it. What I do know about my life is I am happy with my choice to marry Rebecca. She is a wonderful woman, and I love her very much. For some reason, I am not coming back, at least not very soon, so I will be with Rebecca in her time, and she, Matthew, and Hope will help me adjust to living without all the things I've grown up with and taken for granted. That includes you, Mom and Dad! I know I've not taken every opportunity I could to tell you how much I love you and how thankful I am to have you for parents. I love David, too, and Roberta, of course.

Now, since for some reason, I'm still in Salem, or maybe even dead, let me tell you what I planned. Since there is no area code for sixteen ninety-something Salem, I can't tell you all that's happening. If I spend much time here, I assume Rebecca and I will have children. I plan to name our first boy Stewart and our first girl Helen! I'm doing this for a reason, Dad! Remember how I got the idea I was "meant" to be in Salem, and I was the one to start the Tanner lineage way back in colonial times? I don't know if it's true or not. I agonized over it for weeks, remember? I never looked at our family group sheets for the Tanners. I just studied the Meacham line. If you look at the genealogy and see Jerrold and Rebecca Tanner had a boy named Stewart and a girl named Helen, then you can be pretty certain I "did' start at least "our" branch of the Tanner line. My big fear is, I'll be here and my family line will die out with me or my children, and that will be the end for Rebecca and I.

I love you and hope you live a long life. Give David my best and try to come up with a good story for why I'm no longer around. Pray for me, and I'll pray for you, too!

Jerry Kent Tanner (aka Jerrold Kent Tanner, Esq, I hope!)

PS: I'll try to send you something through time, the old-fashioned way!

Comparative silence stretched out for long minutes, the only sound, a woman softly weeping. Stewart arose and went to join his wife on the sofa. Once seated, he pulled her into an embrace to impart comfort and hopefully gain comfort in return for his weeping soul. It took weeks for Helen to cease mourning for their youngest child. It had been difficult to explain to David Tanner why his younger brother was no longer present. It would have been easy if they had a body to show and to bury. Finally, Stewart sat his son down in his study and attempted to make his son believe the truth. It seemed an impossible task, but eventually, with the help of the family records, the elder Tanner got his oldest son to see how things happened. The entire town knew of Professor Blanchard's legal problems and the violent death suffered by professors Blanchard and Jarvis. It was nearly a deal breaker to make David believe Rebecca had been from the past, but his limited exposure to her had made him suspect she was not totally here in this time. Stewart did not want to try to convince Roberta Tanner of the truth. Neither did her husband.

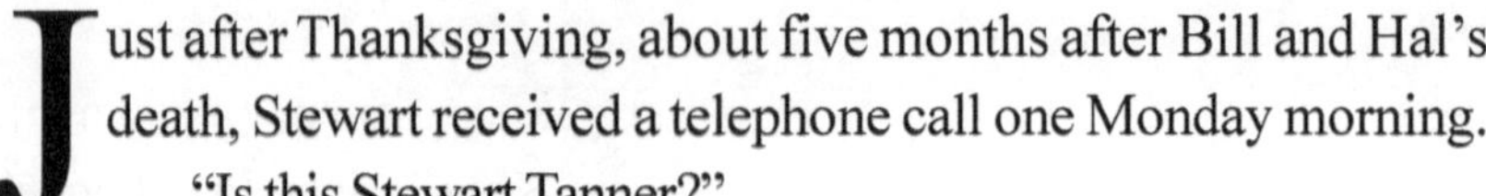

Just after Thanksgiving, about five months after Bill and Hal's death, Stewart received a telephone call one Monday morning.

"Is this Stewart Tanner?"

"Yes. How may I help you?"

"Is your wife named Helen?"

"I must ask the nature of your inquiry before I can answer, sir!"

"This is going to sound strange to you, Mister Tanner, but I've been asked to locate all Stewart Tanners with wives named Helen, who live in California. You'd think it would be easy, but there happen to be forty-seven Stewart Tanners in California, and so far, I've found three with wives named Helen, if that is your wife's name! Is it?"

"Yes! What are you selling?"

"Oh, nothing, I assure you! Do you know anything about genealogy?"

"Yes. I have quite a bit compiled on my extended family."

"Any Taylors or Meachams by chance?"

"Both. Why do you ask?"

"Something very odd has come about, and the legal firm I work for has been tasked with locating some people."

"Okay. I'm listening."

"Mr. Tanner, could I visit you at home? I would prefer a face-to- face interview. Would it be acceptable to you?"

"I suppose it would be all right. When could I expect you?"

"I'm on the East Coast, but I can fly out tomorrow and meet with you in the evening, if it is convenient."

"This must be important to fly clear across the country."

"It is important to my firm and their clients. My name is Fred Wagner, Mr. Tanner. I will call you when I get in and settled in my hotel. This should take about an hour, and if everything works out, we may have you visit with one of the partners of the firm. All expenses will be paid for your trip. Your wife is also invited to accompany you."

"Is this a time-share sales pitch?"

"Certainly not, sir! This is a bona fide legal matter."

"Am I in legal trouble?"

"Not at all! I'm not at liberty to discuss the matter further, though some things may be revealed tomorrow evening."

"Okay! See you tomorrow, Mr. Wagner!"

Though the phone call nagged at his mind, Stewart did not let it interfere with his other projects. Discussing it briefly with Helen, there was such a vague "something" about it, they decided the only thing they could do was wait for the meeting with Mr. Wagner. As promised, Fred Wagner called the Tanner home as soon as he was settled into his hotel room. He was invited to visit the Tanners at home at 7:00 p.m. on Tuesday evening. Being punctual was a matter of pride for Fred, so he was ringing the doorbell at precisely 7:00 p.m. Opening the front door, Stewart invited his visitor into the living room where Helen sat. Refreshments were offered and politely refused.

"I'm sure you've wondered what this was all about, so I'll get right to the point! My legal firm represents the interests of some of the wealthier residents of Salem, Massachusetts, and the surrounding area. Our clients are also found all over Boston. We've been engaged to also represent municipalities in the same area. This matter concerns the City of Salem itself. Salem has a long and mostly proud history. Unfortunately, it is also associated with some darker events in American history, namely the witchcraft trials."

"Yes, I'm familiar with the history of Salem, as both myself and my wife had ancestors living in and around Salem at the time."

"I'm glad you've brought your ancestry into the conversation. It saves me having to lay out all the historical context. Do you know who your ancestors were in Salem during the last of the seventeenth century?"

"I could get my genealogy and show you, but I know there were Tanners, notably Jerrold Tanner, and on my wife's side were Jeremiah Meacham, both elder and younger. Both families allied themselves with the Lloyds of nearby Middleton if I recall."

Stewart felt slightly smug about being able to rattle off names from long past history, but for him, of course, it was much more recent. He felt the pain of loss once again.

"My! You certainly know your family history! There may be a requirement to see some of your documentation before we're finished if it is convenient."

"Certainly!"

"Do you know what a time capsule is?"

"Yes. I believe it to be a box or other container either buried or sometimes put into the cornerstone of some building. It has things placed in it, such as current newspapers, letters from civic leaders, topical trinkets, and other documents the people who are planning it feel would be important or interesting to people at the time the capsule is opened."

"Very matter-of-fact and succinct! Yes, that is how we view them in this time, but there are many different types and made up for many different reasons. Do you know when the first time capsule was used?"

"I have no idea, but isn't it a pretty modern thing?"

"Let me tell you up front how little I knew of time capsules six months ago. Since then, I've spent a large amount of time researching the subject. The term 'time capsule' is fairly recent, being attributed to a man named George E. Pendray. There is even an international group trying to identify all time capsules and their locations. The International Time-Capsule Society estimates there are between ten thousand to fifteen thousand time capsules worldwide. It is estimated more than eighty percent of all time capsules are lost and will not be opened on their intended date. It seems like a huge number, and these are classed as 'intentional' time capsules. Ancient ruins, like Pompeii, are considered 'unintentional' time capsules but still reflect the academic ideal of what one should be like. Glimpses into the lifestyles and lives of an ancient civilization are a dream come true.

Detractors complain modern, intentional time capsules are usually frivolous and most likely contain nothing useful for future generations to study. Personally, I find collections of old newspapers and magazines fascinating! I'm sorry to go on and on!"

"It's quite all right! I'm finding it fascinating! How about you, dear?"

"Oh, yes! Please continue."

"To sum up what I began to say, the oldest known, intentional time capsule, which has been opened, was an 1834 time capsule discovered in 2009 under a statue of Miguel de Cervantes in Madrid. It contained a guide and a three-volume 1819 edition of *Don Quixote*."

"Amazing!"

"Quite! Now, getting back to what I've come for. As part of a local celebration in Salem, in 1992, to observe the three-hundredth anniversary of the witchcraft trials, archived documents were sifted through by town clerks for any interesting facts, hopefully as far back as the late sixteen nineties. Some of the old stuff is pretty delicate, so they had to be careful. One of the ledgers which had minutes of city council meetings was a rare find. It dated to 1706. A bit newer than they were looking for, but the minutes had a wealth of information about a city project. This project called Presents for Posterity was essentially an early form of time capsule. A couple members of the town council introduced the idea and promoted it. You may be familiar with the names, Matthew Lloyd and Jerrold Tanner."

Helen almost burst into tears at the mention of those names, and even Stewart was moved greatly. Reaching deep down for control of their emotions, the Tanners gave stellar performances.

"I know those names, Fred, and I'm proud of their community spirit. So did they successfully create and store a time capsule or did it become one of the many lost?"

"They were successful beyond belief, and it was well documented as to where to find the PFP, as we call it. You know, Presents for Posterity, PFP!"

"Yes. We see. But what does this have to do with us? Surely, we're not the only descendants of those two men. In fact, we're not directly descended from the Lloyd's."

"When the minutes were deciphered (they really had different handwriting back then, all spiderweb-like!), they learned not only the location of the cache, but instructions for it to be opened exactly three hundred years after it was deposited, which means this year! An amazing amount of anticipation and speculation went on for the last thirteen years, but the modern-day town council kept it pretty quiet, and the story was whispered around town, but the press did not promote the news, which shows an amazing amount of restraint. Finally, plans were made to recover the time capsule and have a big public 'reveal.' This occurred two months ago. It was quite a show! Looked like the circus came to town. City, county, and state historians were in attendance. Feeling they had jurisdiction over the contents of the cache, they were ready to swoop down and take possession.

Salem has a pretty astute and cagey mayor. His name is Lloyd, by the way! He says he doesn't know if he's related. He retained my firm to represent the city and to have an airtight lock on who would get possession of the capsule. It seems the present mayor was not the only cagey one. The city council back in 1706 leased a small plot of real estate on private property. This lease gave the city an easement in perpetuity! To hold this plot, the city commissioned a statue of the original owner and used the base of the statue as a storage vault for the PFP. A lot of time capsules are destroyed by ground water if built below ground. I don't know how they figured it, but the PFP was safe from such destruction either by luck or by shrewd planning. This property is the oldest residence in Salem…"

"The House of Seven Gables."

"Yes! How did you know?"

"I don't just research names and dates. I also research the places."

"Officially, it is known as the Turner-Ingersoll Mansion, but everyone just calls it the House of Seven Gables. The statue the city erected was of Captain Turner, the original owner. The place is a museum now and on the National Historical Register, but the city has always maintained the lease payments to whoever owned the house. The original lease payment was equivalent to about ten dollars a year, and the lease stipulated the price would never increase. Am I boring you?"

"No, no! Go on, please!"

"At any rate, the plot belonged to the city, as does the statue and its base. All the historians were fit to be tied! My firm defended the city against no less than five suits and won each one. When it was time to open up the base, no one knew what to expect. Finding an interior compartment which held a stone box was a surprise. The stone box contained the artifacts. Each seam in the box had been sealed with wax and with pitch in and out. There was no sign of water intrusion. It was bone dry! Telling you about the fascinating collection of artifacts would probably bore you, but everyone was blown away with the insights into early eighteenth-century colonial life. Now comes the culmination of my visit. Among the many letters contained in the capsule was an envelope addressed simply: 'Stewart and Helen Tanner, California! For their eyes only.' I know California existed that far back, but I didn't think anyone in Massachusetts was aware of it! And how did they know there would be anyone with your names in three hundred years. If everything in the vault had not been validated and scientifically dated, I would suspect someone broke into the vault and planted the letter. Still, it's the responsibility of my firm to deliver the letter, and you're the only ones to qualify."

"Do you have the letter with you?"

"No. It's still an artifact. Although it's addressed to… I guess you, it legally belongs to the city until delivered. My firm will pay for you two to go to Salem and be presented with the letter. If at all possible, we would like to retain the letter, but since it ethically will belong to you, you have the right to refuse to give it to the city. I just wonder what some forebear, three hundred years ago, thought to write in a letter to someone they would never know?"

"I couldn't tell you right now, but I may be able to do so after we read the letter."

"When would it be convenient for you to travel?"

"I think day after tomorrow would be convenient."

"I'll have our secretary book round-trip tickets and a couple nights at a hotel. No use making it a rush trip. You may want to see some of the local sites where your ancestors lived. I'll contact you tomorrow with the details."

Thanking Fred Wagner, both Stewart and Helen saw him to the door. After the door was closed and they were sure he was out of hearing range, Helen fell into her husband's arms, sobbing inconsolably.

Late into the evening, they talked, discussing the turn of events and expressing curiosity as to what the letter may contain. Having no one else to confide in, except for perhaps Betty Jarvis, they had to be content. Helen did make a point of calling Betty the next day and telling her the news. Making Helen promise to tell her about what the letter said, Betty wished her a safe and enjoyable trip.

33

On Thursday morning, Stewart and Helen drove to the airport to board a plane for Boston, where they had a rental car waiting for them, with directions to Salem and the law firm where Fred Wagner worked. With parking available adjacent to the office, Stewart parked, then guided his wife through the front door of the office where they were asked to take a seat in the waiting room. Someone would be out presently.

Less than ten minutes later, a well-dressed man in his thirties came into the reception area.

"Mr. and Mrs. Tanner! How pleased I am to meet you! My name is Oscar Holman, one of the senior partners in the firm. I hope your trip was comfortable."

Walking up to them and shaking hands with both, he asked them to follow him to his office. Attorneys seem to have fabulous offices, and this was no exception. Deep-pile carpeting on the floor, expensive hardwood desk, and padded office chair. Two office walls were lined with bookshelves, and a third had a window and small wet bar. Directing them to comfortable chairs, drinks were offered, and declined. Settling himself in his own chair, Mr. Holman shifted papers on his desk, seeming to search for an opening gambit of conversation.

"This case has been unusual from the beginning. Most of our cases involving local governments are routinely labor disputes, property issues, or maybe injuries on public property. To defend a city to uphold an agreement this old has been a challenge but most fulfilling in the long run. I'm proud to be part of the issue. As to why you're here, I have to say it would be easier to defend such a matter if the letter addressed, ostensibly to you, had been posted after the establishment of our nation, and the beginning of the US Post Office. Then it would be a federal matter, and no one could take possession of the letter unless it was addressed to them, by name, as we believe this was intended for… you! I don't know what I'm saying! I'm totally out of my depth in this matter. You have the correct names, but how on earth could the letter 'really' be meant for you? It's mind-boggling to me how someone in seventeen-oh-six would know someone named Stewart and Helen Tanner would be living in California and be related directly to them?"

"Do you have the letter here, Mr. Holman? A lot of questions may be answered if my wife and I are able to open and read the letter. It may be of no importance or it could be historic in content."

"Yes, of course! I agree."

Keying his intercom, Oscar Holman asked for his partner, Steven Oldburg, to get the "Tanner Letter" from the vault and bring it to the office. Ten minutes later, a large, bald-headed man entered. In his hands was a flat Styrofoam container. Placing the container on his partner's desk, he stepped back expectantly. Carefully removing the lid from the box, he allowed the Tanners to look upon the contents.

"May I?" Stewart asked, though he didn't expect to be denied.

"Yes. We expect it to be delicate but don't know for sure."

Lifting the missive from the container, Stewart examined it. More a small parcel than a letter, the outer covering seemed to be a sort of oilcloth. Bound with twine which had deteriorated to the point it took just a tug to break and remove it. Edges sealed with a waxy substance; the Tanner patriarch gingerly unwrapped the "envelope." Inside the oilcloth was another envelope, which appeared to be a heavy paper or parchment. This envelope was sealed with a wax seal having an imprint resembling an animal skin stretched out.

Stewart chuckled at the symbolism—a tanned hide… Tanner. He quickly explained his thoughts to the others. Carefully trying to remove the seal intact to save as a keepsake, he placed the seal inside the Styrofoam container. Continuing to unwrap the letter, all eyes were on the object in his hands. Had he decided to go no further, he surmised there would be outcries of frustration. The second envelope proved to be part of the missive itself, which was a common practice. Additional pages were inside and comprised some six pages of scrip Stewart recognized as his son's penmanship.

"Could my wife and I have a moment, please? I will share anything I feel is important and allow you a cursory examination."

"As you wish, Mr. and Mrs. Tanner. Steve and I will be just outside."

As the two men left the room, Helen moved her chair closer to her husband's, and they began reading:

Dear Dad and Mom,

It's been almost fifteen years since my last return to Salem. I assume by now Professor Blanchard has failed to rebuild his machine. I don't have a clue about what is happening to everyone there. I hope Bill has been able to carry on, without Margaret, and be comparatively happy, and also Hal and Betty Jarvis. Most of all, I pray you two are well. Give David and Roberta my best, and I hope by now David has given you grandkids you can play with. I so wish you could see the wonderful children Rebecca has blessed me with. She is such a good mother to our six children: four boys and two girls. By order of birth, there is Stewart, Helen, Robert, Margaret, William, and Harold. We are proud of them all. They are healthy and intelligent. You would be proud of them, as is their grandmother, Margaret, who has resigned herself to another widowhood. Matthew and Hope have four children, as I already knew they would. Matthew has been very active politically and has pulled me in as an ally. One of the reasons you may be reading this letter is because I decided to put my two cents in and suggested this cache. Like I told you, I would try to communicate with you the old-fashioned way. This is it! The only way I could be somewhat certain you would get this was to make it part of a larger project, so it would not be forgotten through the years. Hopefully, this is being read only by you two!

Margaret browbeat me into telling her about her children's future, and Daniel did not go to sea! We gave him so much responsibility around here, he feels a part of the farming industry Matthew has developed. Unfortunately, part of Matthew's cash crops is tobacco! Sorry! I'm just peripherally involved in the farming. I teach school and they are talking about starting a local college, though most want to leave that to Boston or some other town. I wish there were a university I could attend, but there isn't yet, and I'm pretty busy anyway. Matthew and his siblings mourned the loss of their new stepfather, and they were told he probably died of disease or accident while on his business trip. The rest of us wish the best for Bill in your time.

Tell Bill and Hal I miss their classes, and let Bill know I'm not angry with him for leaving me here. It's been a struggle at times, but I have the knowledge of what will come in the future, so my attitude is positive. I've also been taught self-reliance by some pretty wonderful parents! I may not be around for the revolution, but I'll probably stay involved locally to try and move things along.

Dad, as far as I can tell, I'm the only "Jerrold Tanner from Virginia" in these parts, so I'm pretty sure I was destined to come here. I may not be your forefather, but I think, throughout this whole adventure, I've followed the admonition from Malachi 4:6. I don't know if you will hear anything more from me, personally, but I want you both to know I love you, and I'm thankful to be your son. The following pages are family group sheets for us here in Salem. I pray you have long, happy lives!

All our love,
Jerry and Rebecca (1708, Salem,
Massachusetts Colony)

Helen was openly sobbing, and Stewart was sniffling. Taking a cursory glance at the other pages, he saw a number of names and dates arranged by family, and each in their son's distinctive handwriting. Folding the letter, he placed it on top of the oilcloth in the Styrofoam container. Getting up and going to the door, he bid the attorneys to reenter the office. Looking at the Tanners, Mr. Holman and Mr. Oldburg saw their emotional state and remained respectfully quiet.

"I'm not sure I want you to read the entire letter, but you can see what the majority of the information entails."

Removing the top sheet, he handed the others to the attorneys, who reverently handled the heavy paper with care. After perusing the genealogical information, Oscar Holman asked, "I take it you don't want to share the contents of the first page? Is it so personal? I can't imagine it being so, but I must respect your wishes."

"Mr. Holman, I know you're curious about this letter, considering the circumstances surrounding it and us. How binding is the 'attorney-client' privileged communication?"

"It is one of our most sacred tenets of the legal profession. Why do you ask?"

"If I retained you or your firm, would anything I revealed to you be held in strictest confidence?"

"Most assuredly!"

"I will pay you a retainer at the going rate, and everything I reveal will go no further than this office. Is this the understanding you are willing to agree to?"

"We cannot cover up a crime, so if one has occurred, I must decline representation."

"No crime has been committed!"

"Very well, let me get my secretary to draw up the papers. If I accept a token payment, I can give you my word I will invoke the privilege before the paperwork is prepared and signed."

Stewart took his wallet out and removed a hundred dollars from it. Handing the bills to Oscar Holman, the two men shook hands on the deal. Out of formality, Steven Oldburg also shook hands. Both attorneys then waited expectantly. Stewart handed the first page to them and let them read it. Each one repeatedly glanced at the Tanners with questions in their eyes. When they had finished reading the first page, they handed it back to Stewart, who refolded the entire packet and stored it in the foam container. Nervously licking his lips, Oscar looked directly into Stewarts eyes.

"Uh, am I reading the letter correctly? Do you expect me to believe you two are the parents of the author of this letter? Preposterous! What type of hoax are you trying to pull?"

"No hoax. Gentlemen, I consider an attorney to be intellectually beyond pedestrian mentality. Let me tell you a story. It's all true, but you may not believe it."

Starting with a quick overview of their family life, Stewart revealed the relationship between their youngest son Jerry and his physics professor. The story took nearly an hour, as some points were questioned by the two lawyers in their best courtroom manner. At the completion of his narrative, he watched the stunned expression of the faces of misters Holman and Oldburg. Silence reigned for another few minutes before Oscar cleared his throat and tried to assume a professional air.

"Quite a story, and you say it's true? You're not old enough to be suffering from Alzheimer's or dementia. I should give you your money back! No one would believe it if I told them!"

"I prefer to keep this on a professional basis, Mr. Holman. Before I leave today, I want the papers signed and in my pocket."

"It will be as you wish, Mr. Tanner! I'm still amazed! How long has he been gone in 'real time'?"

"Subjectively speaking, he left almost three years ago."

"If I wanted, I could verify all this! I mean his transcript is available, and the record of his professors?"

"You weary me with your doubting nature, Mr. Holman! But yes! Everything about my son and his professors are a matter of public record. Please don't insult me by going to the trouble of verifying the facts."

"What am I supposed to do?

"You were curious about the letter! I let you read it, and I gave you the background concerning it! Other than appeasing your interest, I expect you to do nothing, except protect me and my wife from people who feel it's their right to access documents such as this! I will add the vital statistics information to my family records, but I will not publish any of the letter. It was written to us to reassure us our son was well. It is personal, and as such, no one else needs to know anything. Do you have a problem with it?"

"None! Your confidentiality is assured!"

"Thank you! Now, I believe my wife and I would like to take a look around Salem since we are here. Perhaps you could have someone give us directions to a few places?"

"Yes. Since you know Fred, I'll have him show you around."

34

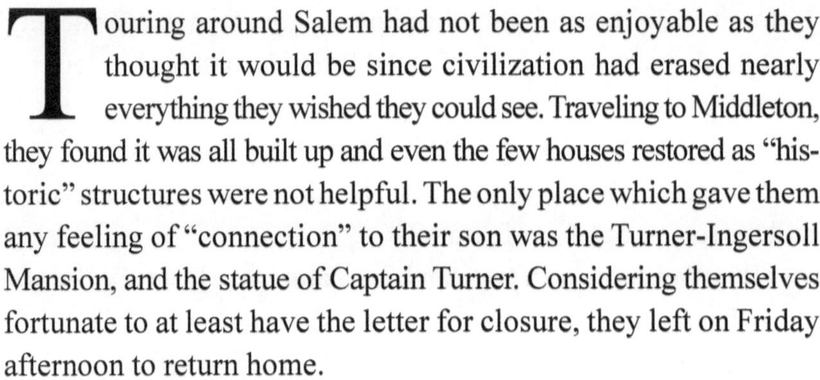

Touring around Salem had not been as enjoyable as they thought it would be since civilization had erased nearly everything they wished they could see. Traveling to Middleton, they found it was all built up and even the few houses restored as "historic" structures were not helpful. The only place which gave them any feeling of "connection" to their son was the Turner-Ingersoll Mansion, and the statue of Captain Turner. Considering themselves fortunate to at least have the letter for closure, they left on Friday afternoon to return home.

Sharing the letter with Betty Jarvis and their son David, they put the original in a safe deposit box and kept a photocopy Stewart made at his own company in their home records. Not a day went by without them speaking of Jerry, just as it had always been. Finding it impossible to think of Jerry as "dead," they considered him "away" on a business trip. As proud as they were of David and the eventual grandchildren he produced, they were justifiably proud of their other son, and though they had no contact, they loved him nevertheless. Friends who inquired after their children, they gave out bulletins. Having the birthdates of Jerry and Rebecca's children, they observed each grandchild's birthday and tried to imagine how they had grown up and became productive members of society. Fortunately, they were able to shower their love on David and Roberta's children. They were seen as doting grandparents, and only their son perhaps perceived they were giving each of his children a little more love than they deserved in recompense for the grandchildren they never saw.

Stewart lived a full life well into his eighties. Helen was beside him as he spent his last night on earth. She heard his last prayer. In it, he thanked the Lord for all his blessings and added a note to his son Jerry.

"Jerry, I hope I've been a credit to you as my forefather. I pray I've been as good a son as you always were. I hope to see you in the eternities! I love you…my son, my father!"

About the Author

This novel is not the author's first effort but rather his first to be published. Being a retired US Navy chief petty officer, William Mecham has traveled extensively. By doing so, he has gathered interesting insights and many stories. He has written several short stories and numerous poems, still unpublished. After his naval career, he was employed in the aerospace industry, where he expanded his life's experiences and subsequently retired. His interest in writing and genealogy has been lifelong, and he is a self-described romantic. Having eclectic interests and an active imagination, he is continually working on various writing projects, with hopes of creating continued publishing opportunities.